Cover Design By: Marisa Shor, Cover Me, Darling
Editing By: Jenny Carlsrud Sims, Editing 4 Indies
Proofreading By: Nichole Strauss, Perfectly Publishable
Interior Design and Formatting By: Christine Borgford, Perfectly Publishable

DEDICATION

This book is dedicated to the victims of sexual abuse and human trafficking. You are true survivors, inspirations and fighters.

"What lies behind you and what lies in front of you, pales in comparison to what lies inside of you."
~ Ralph Waldo Emerson

KAYNE

PROLOGUE

I LIKE YOU COLLARED, BABY. I like you naked. I like you mine.

ELLIE

I HURRY OUT OF THE subway.

Of all days for me to be late, I choose this one.

My phone rings, and I know exactly who it is. My boss, Mark. My anal retentive, no nonsense, perfectionist boss—whom I adore.

He drives me nuts, but he is the most supportive man I have ever met, so I'm giving him a pass this morning. I know why he's wound tight. His biggest client is coming in for a meeting and everything needs to be just right. Which is part of the reason I'm late in the first place. I couldn't decide what to wear! Every time Kayne Roberts walks into the building my pulse races, my heart rate spikes, and my knees go weak. He's a walking god in an Armani suit.

"Hello?" I answer as I turn the corner, picking up the pace.

"Where are you?" Mark snaps.

"I'll be in the office in five minutes."

"Three minutes. Roberts will be here any second. The conference room needs to be prepped and coffee needs to be made."

I sigh. "I prepped last night, and the coffee is on a timer." Okay, so maybe I knew I was going to be late.

"You're magic glitter in high heels," he says then hangs up. Did I mention Mark is flaming gay? Makes him that much more fun to work for.

There's a pedestrian traffic jam right outside of my building's entrance. Of course. I push through the mass, battling my way to the double doors I have in sight. I emerge from the throng, but not before my heel gets caught in a crack in the sidewalk, and I fly face first onto my hands and knees. Shit. Everyone saw that. I allow myself to feel humiliated for just a second, and then proceed to pick myself up.

"Okay down there?" A smooth, masculine voice vibrates through my limbs. I look up to find Kayne Roberts himself holding his hand out to help me. I'm stuck. Kneeling at his feet as my brain forgets how to command my body.

He frowns. "Ellie, are you hurt badly? Do you need me to carry you inside?"

Carry me? *Yes please!*

"No." I finally find my wits. "I'm okay."

Kayne plucks me up, and I'm caught staring into his beautiful crystal blue eyes. Well, one beautiful crystal blue eye. His right eye has a large patch of brown that looks like a lightning bolt is striking his pupil.

It makes them even more of a spectacle to stare at.

He smiles down at me and then drops his gaze a little lower, smirking wickedly. I look down immediately to find the top button of my shirt popped open and my cleavage fully exposed.

I want to crawl into a hole and die of embarrassment, mortification, and shame.

"Nice," Kayne quips.

I grab my shirt and yank it closed.

"Thank you." It's the only thing I can think to say and makes my embarrassment burn brighter, right on the apples of my cheeks. I right myself as Kayne opens the door for me, and we walk to the elevator together. Him haughty, me abashed.

As we ride to the tenth floor in silence, I pull my black pencil skirt up and check my knees. Kayne watches with entertained eyes as I expose more leg. I feel claustrophobic under his gaze. My right one is scraped and stings slightly, but I don't notice the pain. All I can think about is that old expression *you should be careful what you wish for*. Because ever since he strolled into this company, I have lusted after him. Wishing that just once he would notice me. Well, today he did. And all I want to do is die.

Mark is waiting by the elevators when we arrive. I swear if he could stick his whole head up Kayne's ass instead of just his nose, he would. I guess I can't blame him. Kayne is his number one client. Expo is an import/export company and Mark's baby. He hired me straight out of high school and I have worked my way up from novice secretary to irreplaceable personal assistant during that four year time. My family couldn't afford to send me to college, and I didn't want to rack up one hundred thousand dollars worth of debt by going to the top-ten school of my dreams. So, I decided to forgo college until I could save up enough to attend. Mark has been overly generous with my paychecks and bonuses ever since he found out I had half a brain. Coming from the poor family I did, I learned quickly that I am the master of my own destiny. If I want something out of life, the only person who can afford it to me, is me. My upbringing wasn't all bad though. Contrary to the bottom line of their bank account, my family had a wealth of love to give.

Mark is wearing his power suit—a dark grey jacket and matching pants with a bright purple shirt and printed tie. Despite the way Mark dresses, he is brilliant, and I have learned an abundance since he took me under his wing.

"Kayne." He and Mark shake after we walk out of the elevator.

"Mark."

"Everything is set up. Ellie, please escort Mr. Roberts to the conference room. And tend to whatever he needs."

I suddenly flush. Whatever he needs? My mind races with erotic images. I'll tend to *anything* he needs.

"Yes, Mark," I answer dutifully.

Kayne gazes down at me with vigilant eyes. His glare heats my skin. It's as hot as the sun.

I walk Kayne to the conference room with him trailing slightly behind me, and if I didn't know any better, I'd swear he's stealing glimpses of my ass. It turns me on and makes me uncomfortable all at the same time. I guess that's what I get for wearing the tightest pencil skirt I own.

"Do you need to clean your knee?" Kayne asks.

"It will be fine. I'll take care of it after you're settled."

He nods.

Kayne relaxes himself in one of the large leather office chairs adjacent to where Mark usually sits.

"Coffee?" I ask.

"Yes, please." He smoothes his tie. "Milk—"

"No sugar." I finish his sentence.

"You remembered." He smiles brightly, and I almost dissolve.

"It's my job not to forget." Jesus, is that even my voice? It sounds husky, thick with desire. *Can I be any more desperate?*

"Rare quality. Attentiveness," he muses.

"I guess." I shrug, backpedaling toward the door. "I'll be right back."

I flee the room, seriously needing to pull my shit together.

By the time I return with Kayne's coffee, a tea for Mark, and the tray of baked goods Mark always requests, the meeting is already under way. I hand Kayne his coffee first. He winks at me and our fingers brush during the exchange. The contact feels like an electrical current.

I shakily place Mark's tea in front of him as he reads through the agenda, and then set the silver platter of muffins, scones, and miniature cupcakes in the middle of the table. After that, I leave the room, stealing a glance at Kayne right before I exit.

I clean my knee, then spend the rest of the morning spying into the conference room, swooning over the very desirable and even more unattainable Mr. Roberts.

"I see your boyfriend's back." Susie, one of Mark's logisticians, bumps my hip.

"I don't know what you're talking about," I say with a huge smile. Everyone in the office knows how bad I have it for Kayne.

"Yeah right." She laughs with her throaty voice. "You're standing there with your tongue unraveled."

"Am I that obvious?" I scrunch my face.

"You're like a white dot on a wall of red."

"Is the red because I heat up every time I see him?" I ask chewing my lip and twirling the end of my light brown hair compulsively.

"Not just you, honey. The building."

"I'm a desperate loser." I drop my face into my hands.

"Don't beat yourself up about it. That man is walking sex with a side of pheromones. No one blames you." She stirs her coffee with the thin orange plastic stick.

"He'll never notice me." I sigh as I eye him through the glass. He's engrossed in whatever Mark's talking about. I'm engrossed by his body, his face, his hands and his hair.

I finally look back at Susie. She's smiling, chewing on her coffee stirrer. "You want him to notice you? Give him something to look at. You'll never know if he's interested if you don't put yourself out there."

"He's Mark's most important client. I wouldn't want to mess anything up for him by mixing business with pleasure."

Susie shrugs. "A risk comes with every reward."

She throws her stirrer in the trash. "See if he's going to the party tonight. If not, invite him," she advises before she saunters away.

Ask *him* out?

I glance up to find the meeting coming to an end. Everyone is slowly but surely clearing out of the conference room. Except Kayne. He's still sitting, jotting notes.

"Ellie. Can you clean up in there? I'm heading to lunch," Mark calls.

"Yes, Mark," I once again dutifully respond, and Kayne looks up.

His stare makes the insides of my thighs heat up. *Get a grip!*

I head into the conference room, steeling my nerves.

"How was the meeting?" I ask Kayne sweetly as I begin to collect the information folders left behind.

"Excellent. Mark is a genius at logistics. He found an alternate flight route out of Mexico that will save a few hundred thousand over the next year. I'm pleased."

Kayne utilizes Expo to import limes and his own personal brand of tequila out of Mexico. He's making a fortune right now on that little green fruit. Because of weather conditions and poor crops, the price per bushel of limes has quadrupled. Mark sees dollar signs every time we have margaritas after work.

"That's good." I smile. "No lunch for you?" I ask casually.

"I have another meeting in an hour. I'll be having lunch then. Mark said I could utilize the conference room to do some work to kill time."

"I see," I say as I pick up the last folder.

"What about you?" He tracks my movements with his majestic blue eyes. They remind me of a wild jungle cat.

"My lunch is sitting right in front of you. I'll be dining on miniature cupcakes."

"Healthy," he mocks.

"I know, but they're little. So ... less calories?" I shrug playfully.

"I guess that's one way to spin it." He smiles, pulling the silver tray toward him. "Which flavor is your favorite?" Kayne looks up at me like *I'm* a confection sweet enough to eat. I swallow hard.

"It's a toss-up between the red velvet and lemon drop."

"Well, I'm a red velvet man myself." He picks up the lone red velvet cupcake on the plate. "Would you mind sharing your lunch with me, Ellie?"

"Of course not. It's only polite to share." I fiddle with the collar of my dress shirt.

Kayne pulls the wrapper off of the dyed cake, and then splits it in two. "Sit."

I take a seat next to him, still clutching the file folders in my arms.

He offers me one half of the cupcake, and I take it with trembling fingers.

"Do I make you nervous, Ellie?" he asks as he lightly licks the cream cheese frosting.

"No." I try to play it cool. "Just too much coffee."

"I see." He stares at me intensely as he laps the top of the cupcake clean. I think I just came watching his tongue work the icing. "Aren't you going to eat?" he asks enticingly, right before he stuffs the naked cupcake into his mouth. I just sit there frozen, trying not to squish the dessert still in my hand.

This man could write a handbook on seduction. Chapter one: Cupcakes.

Kayne looks at me expectantly. Without even thinking, I shove my half into my mouth. Not seductively at all. I'd be the first one to buy that handbook. Kayne smirks, his eyes alight. Then he brushes a crumb off my bottom lip. I nearly pass out.

"Did you decide what school you're going to attend in the fall?" he asks as he lounges back in his chair. I can't believe it. We had that conversation over three months ago, the last time he was here.

"You remembered?" I can't stop the smile from spreading across my face.

"I'm in the business of not forgetting." He skims his tie slowly between his thumb and index finger. Lucky tie.

"It's between the University of Miami, NC State, and Hawaii," I tell him.

"Inclined to warm weather."

I pout my lip. "I've never been away from the East Coast. I wanted a change. I plan to visit Europe next summer."

"Ambitious."

His responses are so simple, so controlled, yet so inveigling it feels like I'm falling into a trance.

"I want more than a two-bedroom apartment shared by four people," I divulge meekly.

"I admire your aspirations. Do you know what you're going to study?"

"Logistics."

"Thinking about starting your own import/export? I'd hire you." His gaze is heavy, probing almost. Is it suddenly hot in here?

"Well, thank you for the vote of confidence. But I'm not sure what I want to do yet. I just know it's an open field. And something I've come to learn."

"Do what you know?"

"Something like that."

Kayne nods, glancing at his watch. "Crap, Ellie, I have to go."

"I understand." We both stand up, our chests landing an inch apart. I stop breathing.

Kayne stares down at me with those mesmerizing eyes. "Thank you for sharing your lunch with me."

"Anytime," I breathe. Inhaling the clean scent of his expensive cologne. The smell is heady.

"Kayne?"

"Mmmm hmmm, Ellie?" He leans a little closer.

"Are you going to Mark's party tonight?" I ask, a little lightheaded from his scent and his proximity.

A smile plays on his lips. "I was invited."

"And are you going?"

"Will you be there?" he counters.

"It depends."

"On what?"

"If I'll be spending the evening alone or not." I stare straight up at him, trying not to waver.

"Are you asking me out, Ellie?"

Am I?

"Maybe." I bite my lip.

"Then maybe I'll be there."

Did he just accept?

With that, Kayne picks up his phone from the table and drops it into his pocket. I just watch him like a dumbstruck fool.

"Until tonight," he says, then steps away from me and starts for the door. "Oh, and Ellie." He stops short right next to me so we are shoulder to shoulder. "The next time you want to get my attention. Bend over. Your tits are nice, but I'm more of an ass man."

He then leaves.

With me nailed to the floor.

AYNE

I SHOULD HAVE SAID NO.

I should've just blown Ellie off then apologized for it the next time I saw her. Blaming it on a business issue that needed my immediate attention. But I didn't. Because right now I'm standing at the bar in the middle of a trendy downtown restaurant waiting for Ellie the way a dog would wait for a bone.

I'll give it to Mark. He knows where to throw a party. You had to walk through a pawn shop to get into the place. The first floor is a lounge. The second is where dinner is served. The diners can look down over the railing at the patrons mingling on the white leather couches shrouded in florescent light. Like a legal peep show.

Only in fucking Manhattan.

I've already said hello to Mark and some other employees of his. I was introduced to some of his other clients as well. Very kissy kissy, shaky shaky business shit. It goes with the territory. Now I'm sucking down bourbon like a drain in a distillery, regretting that I'm here. I regret even more that I told Ellie she has nice tits. Good going. Then, just to add fuel to the fire, I told her I was an ass man. If she only knew how true that was. It's exactly why I shouldn't be here. Ellie is too sweet. Too playful. I would never want to take those traits away from her. She reminds me of a frisky kitten tangled in a strand of yarn. She has no idea how tangled she'll be if she gets involved with me.

I slug some more bourbon. If she's not here by the time I finish this drink, I'm out. I suck down the last drops of alcohol in the glass and get ready to jet.

That's when I spot her. I stop dead in my tracks as she walks toward me. She's wearing a scrap of material I think she's trying to pass off as a dress. It's all skintight, long-sleeved, and super short.

"Hi." She greets me with a bright smile. "Are you leaving?"

I jingle the keys in my hand. I should say yes. I should bolt out of this room and never look back. But instead I say, "I was beginning to think you stood me up."

"Never. I'm a woman. We're always fashionably late." She bats her eyelashes flirtatiously.

Not if you were my woman.

"Buy you a drink?" I ask as I greedily ingest every sexy inch of her in that skintight dress.

"Yes please, a vodka and tonic with lemon."

"Lemon?" I curl my lip.

"Yes." She giggles.

"Most people drink it with a lime."

Ellie shrugs. "I'm not most people."

You certainly are not.

I order our drinks just as Mark appears from the masses. "There she is. My magic glitter in high heels." He holds out his arms like she's a Broadway diva who just gave the performance of her life.

He's definitely a little trashed. It's only when Ellie turns to kiss Mark hello do I notice the back of her dress; a huge oval cut-out is exposing her bare skin. Holy shit. It's provocative as hell, and I nearly choke.

"So glad you could make it, Kayne." He shakes my hand and tells me again—for the third time. "Take care of my little Ellie here. She's leaving us soon, and I won't be able to find my ass without her."

"Aww," Ellie coos. "That is the sweetest thing you've ever said to me."

"Hold on to your knickers, kid. If you're even wearing any under that dress. It barely covers your bottom," he muses.

And I love it.

Mark pauses, looking between us with his bloodshot eyes. "What was I saying?"

"Goodbye," I chime in.

He lifts his glass to cheer us and goes on his merry way. I shake my head as he gets lost in the crowd. He is a character. Brilliant, but still a character.

"When do you start school?" I ask Ellie as the bartender serves us our drinks.

"September. I finally made my decision."

"And where are you going?"

"Hawaii. I mailed the deposit check on my way here." She's practically glowing.

"Definitely the school I would have picked," I say, excited for her, yet at the same time I suddenly feel sad. I shake off the odd sentiment. Maybe the bourbon is going to my head. I raise my glass. "To rainbows, surfing, and getting lei'd."

Ellie laughs freely, clinking my glass. "To getting lei'd."
Our eyes linger long after we take a sip of our drinks. I feel
the heated stare radiate through the whole room.

"Do you want to sit?" I finally ask her.

"Sure." She bites on her little red straw enticingly. *Don't
look at me like that Ellie.* I want to tell her. I want to warn her. It
will only get you into trouble. Who am I kidding? Just by me
being here, she's in trouble.

It's putting us both in trouble.

"I like your dress." I lean into her, glancing down at her
barely covered ass. She smells sweet. Like cotton candy. "Did
you wear it to get someone's attention?"

"Yes."

"Whose?"

"Yours." She looks straight into my eyes.

"You've got it," I murmur in her ear. "Undividedly."

Aww, shit. If I'm going to hell, I might as well have some
fun getting there. Presently in the form of a playful little kitten
named Ellie. I take her hand and lead her to the darkest, most
hidden corner of the room. We sit on one of the white leather
couches, and she snuggles into me as the catchy tune of *Sing*
by Ed Sheeran resonates around us. It's the perfect match for
the trendy atmosphere and flirtatious vibe.

Trouble. So much trouble.

Ellie and I talk about this and that. Nothing of utter
importance. I can't remember the last time I had a mundane
conversation. She tells me how much she hates spiders
because one crawled into her shirt when she was child and
scared her half to death. I tell her how I hate cinnamon but
can chew an entire pack of Big Red gum.

By our second drink, my hand is on her knee. By the third, it's on her thigh and we're both having trouble denying the uninhibited attraction kindling between us.

"Kayne?" Ellie sighs as I stroke my thumb right under the hem of her scarcely there dress.

I lean into her, my face an inch away from hers. "Ellie. Do you really want this with me?" I give her one chance for an out. If she consents, I'm taking her back to my penthouse and fucking her till morning.

"Yes." Her voice doesn't waver. Then she spreads her legs a little wider and allows my hand to move farther up her thigh, a whisper away from the sweet spot I have been fantasizing about for over a year.

"There's something you should know about me." I brush my lips against hers.

"What's that?" She returns the affection by sliding her tongue into my mouth. Little lioness.

I like to dominate. I want submission. I'll tie you up and have my way with you until you beg me to stop.

"Kayne?" She breathes my name, and I nearly combust.

"Ellie, I—"

"Amigo?" I'm interrupted by a thick Spanish accent. I glare up at the man standing in front of us, and Ellie shifts uncomfortably away from me. I could decapitate Javier. The homegrown Mexican scumbag—and my house guest for the next I don't know how long—has just ruined a defining moment. I stand menacingly and shake his hand.

"I wasn't expecting you until tomorrow," I say as politely as possible.

"I caught an early flight." He slaps my shoulder. "Too excited to see you."

Ellie watches our exchange. I can't tell if she notices anything is off or not.

"Ellie?" I hold out my hand for her to stand up. "Would you mind getting some water?" I pull out a fifty. She nods with a small smile, acknowledging both of us. She takes the money then slips silently away.

When Ellie is out of earshot, I snap at Javier. "What the fuck are you doing showing your face here?"

"Your driver said you were out for the evening. Sounded like fun." He smiles at me with that wicked grin that I want to wipe right off his face.

"I don't think it's wise to be seen in public together." I speak through clenched teeth.

Javier shrugs. "It's dark in here."

I huff.

"The girl, is she one of yours?" He ogles in the direction of the bar, where Ellie is standing with her back to us, ass on display.

"Not exactly."

"Available then?" He raises his eyebrows.

"For what?" I sneer.

"Something to occupy my time with while I'm here. She looks *entertaining*." His eyes sparkle with something sinister, something that spurs a disturbing memory to flash before me.

It feels like someone just tied a noose around my neck.

"I have plenty of girls to keep your time occupied," I inform him directly.

"Yes, but I want *that* girl. In my room. Tied to my bed, tonight."

Why? So you can rape her repeatedly and beat her within an inch of her life? Like hell.

22

"I'm afraid that can't happen," I respond coolly, while my blood simmers in my veins.

"And why is that?"

I make a drastic decision.

"Because I've already claimed her. She's mine."

I just fucking hung myself.

"I DIDN'T REALIZE YOU WERE in the business of acquiring slaves."

My heart rate spikes. "I wasn't, but spending time with you has given me a new perspective."

Javier's mouth twists. "Glad to be an influence. Too bad you found her first."

"Yeah, well, you know what they say. Finders keepers and all."

"Yes." He looks at me perversely, and I don't like it one bit. His black eyes are hollow. Soulless. I know all too well what he's capable of. "Better keep her close."

Oh, I will.

I pull my keys out of my pocket and slap them into Javier's hand. "Get out of here. My Maserati is parked in the lot on the corner. Hit Mansion on the GPS. It will direct you where to go."

I watch as Ellie approaches. Completely innocent. Completely unaware her whole life is about to change. Tonight.

Javier lifts her hand and brings it to his mouth when she reaches us. "Señorita."

He sounds so suave. So genuine. I want to punch his goddamn lights out for even touching her.

He doesn't say a word to me when he leaves.

I look down regretfully at Ellie. I knew I put her in danger by being here. I just didn't realize how much fucking danger.

"Are you ready to go?" I ask. My heart twists, but my arousal roars to life.

"Yes." She's so sure, so confident. She has no idea who she's leaving with.

"Leave first. I'll have my driver pick you up in the back alley. I think it will look better if we go separately."

She nods, all blushed cheeks and starry eyes. I wonder if she'll look at me that way in the morning. I watch grimly as Ellie walks away. Then I pull out my phone.

"Jett," I snap at my driver, the house caretaker, and my best friend. "Why the fuck would you bring him here?"

"He whipped out a knife and demanded that I take him wherever you were. Bit mistrusting, don't you think?"

"Coming in a day early unannounced? Nah."

In the business we're in, trust is a nonexistent commodity. "Why didn't you let me know he was here before you picked him up?"

"I called and text, shithead."

I pull the phone away from my ear and check it. It's on silent. Stupid fuck. And sure enough there are several missed calls and texts. I groan in frustration.

"We have a situation," I tell Jett as I hurry through the restaurant. "Meet me out front. I sent Javier back in the Maserati."

"Oh, that was smart. I wonder what kind of trouble he can get into with that," Jett patronizes.

"He better not get in any. It's risky enough he's on American soil."

"True. So what's the situation?"

"Ellie."

"Ellie? The girl you've been obsessing over?"

"I haven't been obsessing!" I snap.

"Mmmm hmmmm," Jett responds. "She rejected you? Need some ice cream?"

"No, cocksucker. Javier. He wants her. I made an executive decision."

"Oh no. Kayne, you and executive decisions are never good." He sounds worried.

"Yeah, well, it was either that or let Javier get his sadistic hands on her. And like hell I was going to let that happen." Another disturbing image flashes across my mind. I shudder. "You have any stuff stashed?"

"Yes."

"Good."

Jett pulls up just as I get outside. I hop in the limo. "Go around to the back alley. Where's the stuff?"

"Under the ice bin," he tells me, looking straight ahead. The back of his blond head is all I can see.

I pull out the ice bin, grab one of the little white pills, and dissolve it in a glass of champagne. Ellie is waiting just where I told her to. I wasn't lying when I said I was going to hell.

She slides in when Jett opens the door. I pull her near me, not wasting a moment, and devour her mouth. I need to taste it just one time with her permission. One time, while she still wants me.

She's gripping my shirt by the time I pull away.

"Where are we going?" she asks, a little breathless as I hand her the champagne.

"My place." I clink our glasses, and she takes a sip. "Drink up," I urge. We both finish our champagne in record time. I only poured a quarter of a glass.

Then I pull her onto my lap, straddling her legs over mine. The sexual chemistry circling the car is potent enough to put an elephant on its ass. Speaking of asses, I grab Ellie's and force her against me. She moans as her hips collide with mine. My cock has been swollen since the moment I saw her in that fucking dress, with her long goldish brown hair and sultry green eyes.

"Have you ever fucked in the back of a limo, Ellie?"

She shakes her head.

"Would you let me fuck you right here if I wanted to?"

"Yes." Her eyes are starting to get heavy.

"Right answer. Good girl. Next time though, it's yes, Kayne."

Hell. I am going straight to hell.

"I feel funny." She starts to sway.

"Too much to drink." I steady her as her eyes roll into the back of her head and her body goes limp.

Fuck! Fuck! Fuck!

A moment later she's gone.

Passed out against me.

ELLIE

I WAKE UP WITH THE worst headache I have ever had.

I flutter my eyes open and don't recognize my surroundings. It's cold. I pull my legs up to my chest and realize I still have on the same clothes from last night. Where am I? What happened? The last thing I remember is waiting for Kayne in the alley. I sit up. Why am I in a cage? It looks like a jail cell. What the fuck? I start to panic. I get up and pull on the locked door. "Hello?" my voice echoes. "Hello, is anyone out there?" I yank harder on the door but it won't budge. Don't freak out, don't freak out.

"Morning, Ellie." I hear Kayne's voice from somewhere out of sight.

"Kayne? Kayne! Let me out! Is this some kind of sick joke?"

"It's no joke, Ellie. I'm sorry."

"Sorry for what?" I ask confused and slightly terrified.

He shows himself. Standing in front of the steel bars, he's dressed in black pants and a white button up shirt. His hair is a brown mess on top of his head and his blue eyes are acute. Watchful. Cunning.

"You're mine now, Ellie."

"What the fuck does that mean?"

"It means I have acquired you and you belong to me."

"Like fucking hell. Let me out!"

"I will, Ellie. When you submit."

"Fuck you," I spit.

"Yes, we'll be doing a lot of fucking. Don't you worry about that." He smiles, but the emotion doesn't reach his eyes. "That is what you want, right? To fuck me? Isn't that why you wore that dress and practically threw yourself at me?"

"I didn't throw myself at you. You arrogant asshole!"

"Tomato, tomatoe. Regardless. I know you want me. And I definitely want you." He moves closer to the cell door and I immediately back away. "You're going to do everything I say if you want to get out of that cage."

I stand there staring at him. Angry tears threaten my eyes.

"And what exactly do you want me to do?" I ask spitefully.

"Take your clothes off. All of them."

"Go to hell," I snap.

"You weren't so opposed last night."

"Last night I thought I was with someone sane. Not a psychopath!"

"I won't hold it against you for being a bad judge of character."

I shake my head. "This isn't you."

"It is me. There are so many things you don't know about me, but are going to find out." His voice is so calm, it's eerie.

"Let me out," I demand.

"Strip."

"Never."

"Suit yourself. You'll stay in there until you're ready. I want your submission, Ellie. And I'll get it."

He starts to walk away.

"Kayne!" I throw myself against the bars. "I have a family! I have a life! People will be looking for me! You can't do this!" I scream, sobbing now, yanking on the steel door. What did I get myself into? How did this happen? Is it all my fault? Why kidnap a girl who was willing to give herself freely? I wish I could remember more of last night. When did it all go so terribly wrong?

KAYNE

I'VE WATCHED ELLIE WASTE AWAY for the last three days.

I'm staring at her right now on the security feed in my office. Mansion's ground zero. Nothing happens in this house without Jett or me knowing about it. And that includes every breath Ellie takes.

"How long do you think she's going to hold out?" Jett asks from behind me. There may be seventeen screens on the wall, but he knows exactly which one has my undivided attention.

"I don't think much longer. I could see the desperation in her eyes this morning."

Presently, Ellie is huddled in a ball on the bench in her cell. I know she's cold. There's no heat in the dungeon, and she's only wearing that tiny, sexy-as-sin dress from Mark's party. I also know she's hungry too. I barely feed her.

"What if she doesn't give in?"

"She'll impress me." I laugh. "But I know she will," I respond with inflated certainty. Reading people is what I do. What I've been trained for. And Ellie is crumbling like a cupcake. Prisoner of war tactics: isolation, starvation, sleep deprivation. A slow dismantling of the human psyche.

"Are you sure you're going to be able to do this? She's not like the other girls." Jett uses that probing tone. The one he knows I hate.

"I'll have to, won't I? We've come this far." I rock back in my chair, hitting him square in the nuts.

"You fucker, you did that on purpose," he grunts.

"Prove it." I grin widely, with my eyes glued on Ellie.

ELLIE

I DON'T KNOW HOW LONG I've been in here.

What I do know is that I'm freezing and hungry and have barely slept. Kayne has visited me six times. And each time he has told me the same thing. I belong to him. I'm his property. His pet. He feeds me just enough bread and water to sustain my consciousness, but that's it. And every time I nod off, a loud blaring siren startles me awake. I'm miserable, angry, confused, scared, and worst of all, close to giving in—because being in this dark, damp, isolated cell is making me go mad.

"Morning, Ellie." Kayne greets me the same each time. I have no idea if it's really morning or night. A weekday or a weekend.

I don't respond. I just recoil tighter into my ball on the bench. That's where I sit and attempt to sleep. A wooden bench. No pillow, or cushion or blanket. I'm shivering I'm so cold and covered in goose bumps. My tiny dress gives my body no protection against the elements.

"Are you ready to come out? I know you're cold and hungry and dirty. I'll take you someplace warm. More comfortable. If you agree to come out." For all the times

Kayne has come to taunt me, he has never once stepped foot inside my cell. Never once tried to touch me or hurt me. "It doesn't have to be like this."

I trust him about as far as I can throw him. I'm afraid of the unknown if I step out of this cage, and I'm afraid of the unknown if I stay in it.

"Fine," I say feebly, finally breaking down.

"Good." He smiles victoriously. Like he had some bet going or something. "You know what you have to do."

"Why?" I gripe.

"Because that's the way it is. I know this is all new. But you'll learn. I'm going to teach you to be a good kitten."

I look up at him. *Kitten?*

We stare at each other for what seems like an eternity. "Come on, Ellie. Don't keep me waiting."

"Are you going to hurt me?" I ask apprehensively.

"Not if you don't make me."

"What does that mean?"

"It means if you're obedient and give me what I want, no harm will come to you."

I hesitate for just a beat. Then on shaky legs, I stand. Kayne's mouth curves into salacious smile. He knows he has me. I haven't even removed my clothes yet and he's already licking his lips. *Asshole.* I unbutton the clasp at the nape of my neck, hating this dress for what it represents. I bought it to catch Kayne's attention. I wanted to dress as sexy and alluring as I could with high hopes he'd be attracted to me. Right now all I want is to shred the material into a million pieces. Maybe if I'd worn something different, less appealing, things would have turned out different.

I pull my arms through the sleeves, covering my breasts until the very last second. I can't do it.

"Ellie," Kayne urges firmly.

I take a deep breath, trembling, and then in one swift motion, like removing a Band-Aid, I slide the dress completely off. Kayne inhales, staring at me wondrously as I stand there completely naked.

"No panties, Ellie? You did want me."

"*Did* being the operative word." I try to cover my breasts with one arm and cross my legs. But in any position I am completely bare.

"That will change. By the time I'm done with you, you'll beg to come every time you see me."

He lifts something off the wall and it clinks. Then he opens the door.

"Come, Ellie." It's a command, like how you'd call a dog.

"No," I defy him.

"Fine." He glares irritated. "I'll come to you. But I promise that's the one and only time you'll ever say no. And the one and only time I'll ever acquiesce." It's a threat.

He steps inside the cell and I step back; the room feels like it's shrinking. I bump into the wall with Kayne crowding me. He's holding black leather things attached to chains.

"Perfect. Be a good girl and hold still." He reaches up and secures something around my neck. *A collar!*

"No!" I protest, but it's too late. I hear the click of a lock. It's thick and heavy and digs into my skin.

"Mmmm. Perfect fit." Then he grabs my wrists, even though I try to struggle. His strength is Herculean compared to mine. He cuffs them and binds my hands to the hook on the front of the collar.

I'm completely helpless, totally naked, and close to crying. This is a nightmare.

Just when I think it can't get any worse, he attaches a leash.

"Come, kitten."

The tears start to roll.

"I hate you," I expel, my voice thick with emotion.

"I know. But you'll get over that." He yanks the chain and we start walking. He totes me like a puppy through a hallway of cells. *What is this place?* Then up a dark winding staircase with sconces on the wall. When we emerge, I squint at the bright light. We're in a house. An opulent, spacious mansion.

If my fear and humiliation were on red alert before, they're at DEFCON 1 now. The house is eerily quiet but has a sexual undercurrent running through it that shocks you like electricity. There are nude statues everywhere depicting sexual acts and large portraits of naked women in compromising positions hanging on the walls. Dispersed throughout the large hall are curved gold leaf couches and oversized wingback chairs.

As I walk past one of the chairs, I notice hooks sticking out of the folds. What the fuck? We leave the large banquet hall and enter an open, spacious foyer with a grand staircase that has three tiers, pink and cream colored marble stairs, and an intricate black iron railing. The decor is magnificent; a dream home with a stark European flare. The arched doorways and humongous hand-blown glass chandelier reminds me of an expensive hotel or elegant casino.

I try to cover myself with my elbows as I walk stark naked through the enormous house. It's wrong. It's weird. And I know I'm in so much trouble. Kayne ascends the stairs with me in tow, never looking back. It feels like we are climbing forever, my naked skin hyperaware of every subtle draft. When we make it to the top of the never-ending staircase, Kayne leads me right, down a long hallway scattered with doors. It's dimmer than the rest of the house with a dark purple carpet and smaller chandeliers exactly like the one in the immense foyer. The corridor is mysterious with a sense of seductiveness. As we walk I hear muttered noises becoming louder and louder. My skin prickles. One of the doors is cracked open and I sneak a peek inside. I wish I hadn't. What I see shocks me. A woman chained with her hands above her head is being—I don't even know the right word to use—ravished, assaulted, violated by three men at one time. One is sucking her nipple, another has his head between her legs. The third is having sex with her from behind. My insides spin.

"What is this place?!" I cry, pulling at the restraints.

Kayne jerks me forward by the chain. "Your new home."

A daunting sense of dread takes over.

He finally stops at the last door on the end. He unlocks it with a set of keys and ushers me inside. If it were under any other circumstance, I would be in awe. The room is imperial. It looks like a queen's master suite. There's an enormous bed turned down with shiny gold sheets and a headboard made out of vining white iron and pink tufted satin. Decorative molding covers the walls and high vaulted ceilings, giving the decor a very Parisian feel. A large flat screen hangs directly in front of the bed and the armoire right next to it is impossible to ignore. It's stark white with huge ornately decorated doors.

But as magnificent as the space is, it's the semicircular adjoining room with large bay windows that's giving me palpitations. If this was a normal suite, I'd take it for a sitting room. But trust me when I tell you it's not. In its center is a table with thick leather straps and stirrups. A horror movie version of a gynecologist's exam table. Underneath it are several metal drawers. I stop myself from imagining what could be in them. A crop, a flogger, and a wooden paddle are hanging between each window on the wall. My stomach tightens. He's going to hurt me. I know it. I can feel it.

"This way." Kayne flicks the leash, leading me through another doorway into the bathroom. It's a large space with off-white marble floors, matching counters, and a large stone shower. There's also a clawed soaking tub so big you could swim in it. Kayne opens the glass door of the shower and turns a knob, spurring several shower fixtures to spring to life.

Then he strips down to nothing. "Look at me, Ellie."

I keep my eyes closed and my head turned as much as the collar will allow.

"I said look." He tugs the chain hard. "You need to start learning to obey commands."

That gets my attention. I open my eyes and gape at him. Not because he is gloriously naked in front of me. Because the words obey and command rattle my soul. I want to scream, I want to yell. But my emotions are choking me worse than the collar.

Kayne unhooks my wrists, and then unclasps the uncomfortable leather. I rub my sore skin. He then removes my new neck jewelry.

"In," he orders. But I don't move. I can't move. My head is spinning. He slaps me on the ass and I jump. *"In."*

"You hit me!" My eyes water from the sting.

"I'll do it again if you don't listen to me."

I escape immediately into the shower. Not that it's really an escape because Kayne steps in right behind me. I cower into the corner, trying to get as far away from him as possible. Only a world of wrong can happen now, with both of us naked and him looking at me with carnivorous want in his eyes.

"Turn around, put your hands against the wall." I never thought I would wish to be back in that cell. But cold and hungry is way better than being raped.

"Kayne. Don't," I beg, sounding pathetic. Where is my fight?

It's stinging your ass! Resist him, and he'll beat you!

"Now, Ellie." He grabs my arm and faces me away from him, shoving me against the wall. My palms smack against the light colored stone.

Then he juts my hips out and I fray at the seams. My breathing is heavy and my head is light all at the same time. I brace myself against the wall, trying to put my mind anywhere but here.

"I love your ass, Ellie." He smacks me again and I yelp. That smarts. Then he rubs my throbbing cheek. It feels wrong; him touching me.

The warm water rains down on my prickly skin as Kayne runs his hands up my back and over my shoulders. I shudder. Then I hear the pop of a cap. My insides jolt. I'm worse than a spooked cat.

The smell of eucalyptus fills the shower as Kayne begins to wash me, lathering my breasts, my stomach, my arms, and my backside. I hold my breath. I once would have killed for this man to touch me. Now that he is, all I do is cringe. He works his way between my thighs, and I instinctively squeeze them together.

"That's not going to keep me out. You need to get used to me touching you," he murmurs lasciviously into my ear.

"Why are you doing this?" I ask disgusted.

"I have my reasons."

"Want to share them with me?"

"All you need to know is that I want you, Ellie. I want your obedience, I want your submission, and I want your body." He skims my clit with one of his fingers and I jump.

"What the fuck are you waiting for then? Why are you fucking with my head?" I erupt, fear dragging me under.

Kayne chuckles. "Hot for me baby? Want me to take you right here? Think you can handle it?" He presses his body against mine.

I tremble from the inside out. My fright and rage getting the best of me.

"You're a bastard!"

"Name calling doesn't really do it for me." He smacks me again. *That fucking hurts!* "And I'm not in the business of raping women. That doesn't do it for me either. I want you to hand yourself over willingly. Submit. Until then, we'll just play."

"Play?"

"Mmmm hmmm." He goes back to rubbing my clit. "This is mine." He slips one finger inside me and I gasp, digging my fingernails into the tile.

"Who do you belong to, Ellie?"

"No one!"

"Wrong answer." He withdraws his finger. Half of me wants to scream, half wants to cry. "Stay," he commands. *I'm not a fucking dog!*

Kayne turns off the shower, steps out, and towel dries himself, all while I stand there naked and emotionally exposed. Then he opens a towel to me. "Come."

I scowl at him.

"Come, or I'll spank you again. And this time I won't stop." His eyes narrow.

I take a deep breath, trying to control the tears. This can't be happening. Reluctantly, I step out of the shower and into his waiting arms. He dries me off, not missing one part of my body. He touches it like he has license. Like he owns it.

Once I'm dry, Kayne lifts the collar from the floor.

"No." I instinctively step back, but Kayne catches my wrist.

"Yes." He pulls me forward with a dangerous look.

He fastens the collar around my neck and locks it. It's tight and uncomfortable. The chain that's still attached dangles between my naked breasts. I hate it. I hate the way it feels and what it signifies.

Kayne walks me back into the bedroom. There's a plate of food sitting on the modest-size round table underneath the large wagon wheel window that only has one chair.

"Go eat. I'll be back to put you to bed later."

"Don't I get any clothes?"

"Clothes?" He cocks an eye brow at me.

"Yeah, you know, shirt, pants, socks?" I want to spit. I can't just walk around naked in a collar. *Can I?*

Kayne cuts across the plush shag rug to the dresser on the opposite side of the room. He opens a drawer and pulls something out. Then he walks back to me and kneels. "Here." He holds up a sheer pair of panties.

"That's it?" I look down at him.

"That's it. Get used to being naked baby. That's how I want you twenty-four seven."

Twenty-four seven?

Kayne jerks my panties on, and then goes into the bathroom. A few moments later he emerges fully clothed and heads straight for the door.

"You have twenty minutes to eat, then bed. I'll be back." His tone is flat, almost detached.

The door clicks shut behind him, and I'm alone again, in yet another cell.

In a fit of desperation I attack the door, yanking on the handle with some sliver of hope it might open. Tears run down my cheeks. I'm a captive. Going to be forced to do things with a man I once obsessed over and now hate. I pull at the collar and scream. *This can't be happening!* It just can't. I have a family, I have a future. I have a life waiting for me beyond this room. I pound harder, yell louder. But it's no use. Deep down I know it. I can feel it. I'm his.

When my energy is depleted, I slump down onto the floor. I can't stop the tears from flowing as I lie there defeated. That's when Kayne returns. Has it been twenty minutes already?

He opens the door and it jams against my body. "Ellie, what the fuck?" He steps over me and into the room.

"Not hungry?" He takes notice of the untouched food.

"Fuck you," I spit.

"I hope so." He lifts my limp body off the ground. *Keep dreaming.* I will never give my body or my will over to him. "You're going to need your strength." He places me on the enormous bed that can sleep ten.

"For what?" I ask dejectedly.

"Me."

He picks up the end of the chain attached to the collar and locks it around one of the curves of the iron headboard.

"What the fuck!" I yank and pull.

"This is how you'll sleep. New puppies need to be chained up."

"I'm not a fucking puppy!" I erupt.

41

"No, you're right," Kayne muses. "You're more like a frisky little kitten." He runs one finger down my face the way you would pet a cat. I jerk my head away.

He jerks me back by the collar. Fucking thing. Rage burns a hole through my chest.

"You'll learn, kitten."

"*I hate you.*"

"We've established that. We've also established that you'll get over it." He kisses me quickly on the lips. "Tomorrow we start."

"Start what?" I snarl.

"Obedience training."

KAYNE

I LEAVE ELLIE'S ROOM WITH my emotions in a stir. I stand by the door and listen to her scream bloody murder for the second time tonight. Part of me hates myself for doing this. Part of me knows it's the only way.

Part of me can't wait to tie her up and dominate the fuck out of her. I'll have her begging. You just wait.

The only way to keep her safe is to turn her into the one thing I'm trying to protect her from. The last three days have been hell watching her waste away in that tiny cell. They would have been worse if I had to witness her at the mercy of Javier. I may have collared and chained her to the bed, but her screams would be blood-curdling if she were confined to his room. He'd have no sympathy for her pain or tolerance for her disobedience. He'd starve her, torture her, and leave her for dead. Fuck that. I may run an elaborate whore house, but no one has the right to treat another human being like that. Listen to me, righteous motherfucker. I'm the one who has a captive on the other side of this door.

But no one can know. No one can know I had any other reason for taking Ellie than to make her my slave. Not even

Ellie. It would be too dangerous. Make me too vulnerable. Make her a target.

And I can't let that happen. There's too much at stake.

I leave Ellie to scream herself to sleep. With the lack of food and earlier outburst, I doubt she'll last much longer.

ELLIE

SUNLIGHT BECKONS ME AWAKE.

My mouth is dry and my throat is sore. Where am I? Then I remember. The chain clinks as I move. I'm a prisoner. I pull on the collar and fiddle with the lock. Off. I just want it fucking off.

Suddenly the door opens and I instinctively huddle into a ball, naked and completely defenseless.

"Ah, you're up." A tall, nice looking man with turquoise eyes and a shock of blond hair saunters toward me. I recoil.

"There, there," he coos. Pulling on the chain once he reaches the bed. I resist him. "Aren't you a pretty thing? No wonder Kayne wanted you. Come here."

"No. Who are you?" I fight him.

"Jett." He yanks harder, forcing me closer to him. "I'm your keeper."

"I don't need a keeper. I need to go home!"

Jett grabs my face, ignoring me. He moves it around like he's inspecting me.

"Sweetheart, the only place you're going is into the shower."

"I took a shower last night," I say bitterly, recalling the way Kayne manhandled and spanked me.

"It's time for another. You also need to be groomed."

"Groomed! I'm not an animal!" I try to snap my head back.

Jett looks into my eyes, clutching my face tighter. "Technically you're owned, so you're the equivalent."

Tears threaten.

"Ellie. I will tell you this once. Cooperate with me or I will tie you down and spank you until you do."

"Is that my life now? Beating after beating?"

"It doesn't have to be. But you have to listen and do as Kayne and I say."

"Do I belong to both of you?" The words slice my tongue as they roll out of my mouth.

"No. You're just Kayne's. But I do have the authority to punish you if you don't behave." His pretty eyes flash with something dark. Jett looks like he belongs on a beach with a surfboard. But it's clear he's no laidback surfer.

"So, what's it going to be sweet thing? We can be friends or we can be enemies. It's up to you. Personally, I'd like to be friends. It will make things easier for everyone involved."

I only stare up at him. I can't bring myself to submit. It's not who I am, it's not who I was raised to be. After a few drawn out moments Jett nods, then pulls out a set of keys from his pocket and unlocks the padlock linking the chain to the collar. I just sit until he tells me to move. At this point I don't know what else to do. I don't want to get hurt.

"Bathroom?" he points. I get up and walk into the room. Covering as much of my nakedness as I can.

"Good girl," he says in a condescending tone as he walks behind me. I hate it. Once in the bathroom, he turns on the shower. "We'll groom you first, then breakfast."

"Groom?" I repeat curiously.

"Mmmm hmmm." He pulls out a table from the linen closet and opens it up.

"What's that for?"

"You'll see." He pulls the key ring out from his pocket and unlocks the collar, removing it from my neck. I immediately rub my sore throat. "In you go."

I step into the stall and allow the water to scald my skin. The temperature of my shower is about the only thing I have control over at the moment.

"Wash," Jett instructs. I stick my tongue out at him as I turn for the soap.

"I saw that," he says amused. I guess better amused than pissed off.

I wash my hair and my body slowly, elongating the shower as much as possible. The smell of eucalyptus engulfs my senses, but the calming scent does nothing to unwind the anxiety coiled around me.

"Done," Jett announces. He opens the door and turns the shower off.

"Hey!" I immediately jump and cover myself. He pulls my arms away from chest. "Get over the modesty. And get used to being naked."

"Why?"

"Because that's how Kayne wants you." He wraps me in a towel and dries me off. I feel like I'm losing all self-sufficiency.

"Why me?" I ask forlornly.

"He has his reasons." Jett works to dry my hair.

"I wish someone would share them with me."

"You don't need to worry about his reasons. All you need to do is what you're told."

"What if I can't be submissive? Then what?" I challenge.

"I don't think you want to know."

My lip quivers. "He's going to hurt me, isn't he?" An image of the table in the other room flashes in front of my face.

"Not if you listen."

"What does he want from me?" I demand with my emotions bubbling over.

Jett gives me an *I think you know* look. "Don't be naive, Ellie. It doesn't become you. You know exactly what he wants." *Your obedience, your submission, your body.* "You've been acquired as a sex slave."

"Don't use that word!" I scream with my head in my hands, tears bursting from eyes. The word slave sounds like nails being dragged down a chalkboard. "I can't do this. You have to let me go!" I sob.

"Shhh, Ellie." Jett wraps me in his arms. "You can and you will."

"Why?" I cry into his shoulder.

"Because—" Jett pulls away and looks into my eyes. I see compassion there. "Listen to me Ellie. You need to trust Kayne. I know that might be hard, but he's doing this for a reason."

"How can I trust him?" I ask with my universe in turmoil. "He puts a collar on me and forces me to walk around naked. And soon ..." I wipe my eyes. "Soon ... I don't know what's going to happen."

"The only thing I can tell you is things aren't always as they seem."

I search Jett's eyes. "What does that mean?"

He just shakes his head. "Trust Kayne."

Easy for him to say.

"Enough talk, Ellie. It's time to be strong. Lay on the table."

"What are you going to do?" I sniff.

Jett looks at me with an annoyed expression. "Here's your first lesson in submission. Don't ask questions, don't talk back, and do as you're told."

I frown.

"Now go, or I'll force you down and tie you to it."

His eyes tell me all I need to know: Don't fuck with me.

I lay on the table, naked with my hair still damp and my emotions spiraling out of control.

"Pull your knees up and spread your legs. Put your hands over your head." I do as he says, panting nervously.

"Breathe, Ellie."

"What are you going to do?" I ask again.

"Wax you." He smears warm sticky stuff all over my pubic hair. I flinch. He holds me still with firm hands. "Don't move."

Then he covers the smeared wax with strips of cloth. I breathe heavily, anticipating the pain.

"Have you ever had a Brazilian before?" Jett asks as he rips the first strip off.

"No!" I shriek as scalding pain burns my skin and tears run out of my eyes. God, will I ever stop crying?

Jett rips off strip after agonizing strip, until I am completely bare. Bare physically and bare emotionally. "Aloe," he says showing me a green blob of something on his fingers before he applies it to my sensitive skin. The cool gel eases the pain slightly, but not nearly enough. The way he handles me makes me feel like an object. Like my humanity is being stripped away layer by precious layer.

"Up you go." He takes one of my hands, and I stand, a little wobbly, on my feet.

"Turn around and rest your hands on the table," Jett instructs. "We're not done yet."

Dear God, what now? I reluctantly do as he says. Hating every second of this new life.

"Are you on any birth control?" he asks matter-of-factly.

"No, why?" I look over my shoulder. He's holding a syringe.

"Good." He stabs me in the ass.

"What is that?" I grit my teeth and wince as the needle penetrates my skin. How much more must I endure today?

"Depo-Provera," he informs me, and the realization as to why I need birth control hits home. This is really happening. I'm becoming Kayne's whore. I start to hyperventilate.

"Ellie, calm down." Jett rubs my back. "You need to eat." He takes my arm and leads me back into the bedroom. "Lie down, I'll be right back. Is there anything you're allergic to?"

"No," I cry into the pillow. My ass is sore, my vagina is throbbing, and I feel like a humiliated mess.

I don't know how long Jett is gone. But I'm still suffocating myself with the pillow when he returns.

"Time to eat." He pulls me up and forces me to sit at the small table where a silver dome is waiting for me. Jett lifts it to reveal scrambled eggs and buttered toast.

"Eat it. All of it. It will make you feel better."

I stare at the food with puffy eyes. As much as I don't want to eat, my stomach rumbles loudly, so I pick up the fork and slowly take a bite. It's good, really good, and still warm. I finish everything on the plate while Jett stands over me.

Once satisfied, he covers the dish then lifts the platter off the table.

"I'll be back later to get you ready." *Ready?* "Try to relax. You'll need your strength for Kayne tonight."

I look up at him callously.

"Retain that frame of mind, Ellie. Remember what I told you. Strong."

Then he leaves the room. I hear the lock click and my heart squeezes. I'm supposed to stay cooped up in here all day? I look around, taking in my jail cell. It's a room people like me only dream about—opulent and luxurious, with silk window treatments and expensive furnishings. I stare out the window at the rolling green hills. I'm high in the air with no escape in sight and nothing but trees and grass for miles. I see the future I worked so hard for slipping away. *I'm a slave.* Kayne's slave. Tears roll down my cheeks. But they aren't tears of sadness, they're tears of rage. I'll figure a way out of this mess.

I have to.

Or I'll die trying.

HOURS UPON HOURS ALONE IS a tad bit maddening.

I tried the television, but there was no cable. There was, however, a porno DVD. I shut it off immediately when I heard the moaning and saw a girl being fucked from behind. I tried some books on the shelves, but realized just as quickly it was all erotica. Titles like *Bound by Passion* and *Temptation* were all I could find. It's like he wants me hopped-up on hormones at all times.

My worst mistake was wandering into the adjoining circular room. I'm standing next to a table that reminds me of a torture device. The black cushions look unforgiving. The straps on the sides and on the stirrups are thick leather with silver buckles. They seem implacable. But the things that scare me the most are the whipping tools on the wall; a crop, a flogger, and a wooden paddle with a heart-shape cutout. I shiver with fear just looking at them.

The drawers under the table are full of sex toys. I can't begin to imagine what you do with some of these things. Vibrators of all different shapes and sizes. Small bullet looking things with chains on the end. Belts, handcuffs, and ball gags that remind me of muzzles. I shake just looking at them. When the door clicks, I jump, slamming the drawer shut. I walk quickly back into the bedroom as Jett appears. His aqua eyes are wide as he regards me.

"Exploring?"

I look down timidly. "I was bored."

"I see. Find anything that interests you?"

"No." I wrap my arms around my naked chest begrudgingly.

"There's an old saying. Don't knock it until you try it." Jett pulls my arms away from my body. "No hiding. Your body is beautiful, show it."

"I know an old saying too," I retort. "Easier said than done."

Jett chuckles. "Smartass. Come on, kitten. Time to go back on your leash."

Jett motions to the bed. Then he retrieves the collar and chain from the bathroom. I sort of hoped it was its final resting place.

Jett makes quick work of fastening the thick leather around my neck. The cold steel chain once again brushes between my breasts and dangles down to my knees.

"Stay," he says. Then walks over to the dresser and pulls out a pair of black see-through panties. I have déjà vu as he slides them on me. Underwear seems to be the only article of clothing I'm allowed to wear.

"On the bed, kitten. Kayne will be here soon." My heart rate quickens. I'm not sure I'm ready for this. I climb onto the huge opulent bed covered with rich, plush throw pillows.

"Remember what I told you. Behave. Listen to Kayne and you should be able to walk just fine tomorrow." I pale as he fastens the chain to the elaborate iron and tufted headboard. "See you in the morning, sweet thing."

He closes the door with a light click.

I'm alone again, chained to a bed like a scared puppy about to have her first obedience lesson with her new owner. What could this possibly entail? *Nothing good*, I conclude. I bring my legs up to my chest and curl into a ball, trying to cover up as much of myself as possible. I don't know how long I sit and just stare at the door. The waiting is almost as maddening as the anticipation of what's to come. Then the door clicks and my heart jumps into my throat. Kayne walks in to the room with an air of authority. His face is tight, his eyes are dark, and his presence is oppressive. I stare stoically as he approaches me like he's stalking a wounded animal. I pull my legs tighter to my body.

He's wearing black suit pants and a blood red dress shirt. His collar is open and his shirt sleeves are rolled up to his elbows. I swallow thickly. He's also holding something in his right hand.

"Evening, kitten," he says in an even tone. It's almost chilling. "How was your day?"

I don't respond.

Kayne narrows his eyes. "I asked how your day was, kitten. When I address you directly, you answer. Lesson one."

I stare him down with my defenses up.

"Kitten?" he goads.

"My name is Ellie."

"Your name is whatever I choose to call you. And right now, it's kitten." He grabs me by the collar and pulls me effortlessly across the silken sheets, drawing my face close to his. I pull at his hand as he nearly lifts me off the mattress. "We can do this my way or we can do it yours. I'll be fine with either. The end result will be the same."

I struggle against his grip, my knees barely grazing the smooth fabric underneath me.

With the collar choking me I spit out, "Boring. It was boring."

Kayne releases me, and I drop back down on all fours.

"There. Was that so hard?"

I stare up at him with hatred.

"Save your hostility, kitten. It doesn't intimidate me, and it will only make things worse for you."

He fondles one of my naked breasts. I cower away, but he pulls me closer.

"Time for your first lesson." He grabs my chin and forces me to look at him. "You only speak when you are directly spoken to. And even then it is yes Kayne, please Kayne, more Kayne, can I come Kayne."

I flinch in his grip. "Commands. Kneel. I expect you in this position every time I walk into the room. It doesn't matter where you are or what you're doing. You stop immediately and drop. Sit on your haunches, tuck your feet under your ass, splay your hands on your thighs and bow your head. Let me see."

"No," I snarl.

"No?"

"I will never kneel." My independence roars. I can't do this. I'm not submissive. I'm not a slave.

"Fine." In a flash he grabs me by the collar again and forces me forward. My face is hanging over the side of the bed, my ass is sticking straight up in the air. Then he hits me with the object in his hand. A rolled up newspaper. I cry out when it connects with my bottom. It's concealing a stick of some kind. I can't move in the awkward position as he hits me again. My ass stings painfully as he hits me a third time.

"Please stop!" I scream, and he hits me once more. Then he lifts me back up. Totally dominating my body with the control he has holding the collar.

"Are you ready to submit?" he asks authoritatively.

"Never!" I snap, even though my body is rebelling against my will. "You can beat me all you want. I don't care if you kill me! I'll never be yours!"

Kayne's dark gaze bores into mine. His strange, majestic eyes calculating. He lets go of the collar and I grab at my neck, only feeling the thick leather under my fingertips. He unlocks the chain from the bed. "I would never kill you. But I will break you. I'll give you one last chance to cooperate, Ellie." He winds the chain around his hand. "Kneel."

"Fuck off."

"Fine. We'll do it your way." He drags me off the bed. "Maybe a night with my clients is all you need. I'll string you up, gag you, and blindfold you. Then watch as they have their way with you. Just like you saw the other night."

Images of the naked helpless woman spring unbidden into my mind.

"Kayne, no!" I screech as I fight against him, thrashing my body as he pulls on the chain like I'm a disobedient puppy who doesn't want to go out in the rain.

"I gave you your chance, kitten." He has me almost out the door. I drop to my knees. "No, please," I beg with my forehead pressed against the ground. I would much rather kneel to him than be gangbanged and emotionally destroyed for the rest of my life. Tears stream down my face. I'm pathetic. Naked, on a leash, being commanded by a man who is going to use me as a living sex toy.

"Good girl. Now we're getting somewhere. That position is called drop. Get used to it. You'll be in it a lot. Don't move until I say so." I keep my head down as I hear his footsteps around me. He smacks my ass with the newspaper again and I cry out. The tears streaming harder now.

I whimper on the floor, my butt throbbing and my soul fractured. I stay in this drop position until my knees hurt and my back aches. Fucking prick.

"Very good, kitten. You can get up." I raise my head and look around the room. I find Kayne sitting behind me in the chair at the table. He looks relaxed with his legs spread and large hands resting on his thighs.

"Come," he says, crooking his finger at me. I move to stand.

"Crawl, kitten. Crawl to me."

I pause on all fours. He's being fucking serious.

"I'm waiting." His eyes are cold, hard.

I begin to crawl across the room, over the plush white rug, past the bed, to the chair he's sitting in under the large circular window. The night sky is dotted with stars, and the moon is full and bright behind him. Once I reach him I stare up, still on my hands and knees. He cracks a small smile. I want to spit on him. Then he leans forward and places a finger under my chin, forcing my face up to his.

"That fire in your eyes will dim. I promise you, kitten. I know it's hard. Giving up control. But I want you to understand house rules. Listen carefully, I'll only say this once. I tell you what to do, you say yes, Kayne. You will please me. End of story."

I remain quiet but glare at him callously.

"Kneel," he commands. My stomach rolls, my freedom fraying as I rise to my knees. I sit just the way he described. On my haunches with my hands splayed on my thighs. Right between his legs. An obedient pet. He groans approvingly. "My kitten." He leans forward and fondles both of my breasts. Skimming his thumbs over my nipples until they are straining and hard. I breathe rapidly. I don't want him to touch me, but my body responds involuntarily. The sensations networking straight to my burning core.

"You're so perfect, Ellie." He breathes hard as touches me. It seems my body isn't the only one involuntarily responding. The bulge in his pants is undeniable.

"Another command. On your back. Lay down, bend your knees, spread your legs and place your hands over your head. Do it. Now."

Kayne tracks my every move as I slowly lay on the floor and open my legs wide for him. I want to fight. I want to say no, but my stinging ass and the image of that woman from last night is a constant reminder of what will happen if I resist.

"Now we're getting somewhere."

He stares down at me for a very long time. His gaze feels heavy, and after what feels like forever, he gets up and walks into the semicircular room with the table of torture. My anxiety spikes tenfold as I hear the opening and closing of drawers. I almost get up and dart into the bathroom, but Kayne returns before I can force my limbs to move. He stands above my mostly naked body. Two pairs of handcuffs dangling in one hand.

"You've been a good girl. Time for a treat." His breath is ragged as he drops to his knees. I squirm away, but he grabs my legs and fastens one handcuff to each ankle.

"Give me your hands." I don't move.

"Ellie." He says my name harshly. "Do you want me to turn you over and spank you instead? Pleasure or pain. Your choice. It doesn't matter to me either way. I like giving both."

He reaches over me and grabs my right hand, securing it to the handcuff on my right ankle.

"Kayne, please," I beg, as he repeats the motion with my left side. I'm bound.

Completely helpless.

No matter which way I move, the restraints act like marionette strings biting into my skin. Pulling one of my wrists up, my leg follows. Pull my ankle down, my arm gets yanked.

I'm gasping with fear.

Kayne hovers over me. My senses on overload.

I tremble as I stare up at him. His eyes are fierce, lustful, wanton, and unrepentant. I know exactly what he wants.

Me.

"Tell me you don't want me to touch you," he dares me.

"I don't want you to touch me." The words flow, but there's no fire behind them.

"Are you sure, kitten?" He massages me over the thin fabric of my panties.

"Yes." *No.*

"I think you do." He slides my panties over and I squirm harder in the restraints. My heartbeat palpitating. The metal clinking as I shift. He circles his finger gently over my clit. I close my eyes trying to reject his touch. When he sinks his finger inside me, I gasp.

"You're so fucking wet for me." He slides his finger in and out, every so often spreading the slickness through my folds. My body tightens and aches, but I fight the urges he's bringing forth. I will not come. I will not give this man my pleasure. Kayne works his hand faster, insistent. The sensations build and I clench my fists, fighting the orgasm he's demanding. As if aware I'm resisting, he simultaneously rubs my swollen clit with his thumb while he fingers me relentlessly. I moan uncontrollably.

No! No! No!

Yes! Yes! Yes!

Just before I explode, Kayne removes his hand, and I nearly weep.

"Not yet, kitten. I didn't give you permission." If I wasn't bound, I'd slap him. "I tell you when to come. Understand?" I'm panting beneath him, burning a hole through his head with my stare. He smirks arrogantly at me. Then leans down and whispers, taunting me, "Ask my permission."

"No."

"You'll regret that." There's amusement in his eyes. This is all just a game. With no warning at all, he rips my panties. The thin material tearing right in two. I jerk, the metal cuffs cutting into my skin. He skims his tongue down the inside of one of my thighs, and then licks a slow hot drag over my slit.

"Fuck, you taste so good. Like cupcakes," he pants. His specific description isn't lost on me. A simple cupcake is how all this began.

Kayne swirls his tongue over my heated flesh, nipping and sucking, driving me mad. My body is bowing in ecstasy, my mind trying to reject the pleasure. If I give in, what will that mean?

Kayne stabs his tongue into my entrance, and I moan loudly. Oh God, an orgasm is looming; hot and fast.

"Ask permission." His hot breath skims against my overly sensitive skin. I resist. Fighting him the only way I can. With my will.

He sinks a finger deep inside me and sucks on my clit, bringing me right to the breaking point. My heart is hammering and so is my core.

"Ask permission. The way I told you," he orders.

I'm writhing in my restraints so hard I know I'm going to have marks, but I need to disperse the buildup somehow. I can barely breathe as he dangles me over the edge again and again, yet another form of torture to get me to obey. I feel the slightest caress of my orgasm, and I fracture, unable to withstand the torment anymore. "Please, Kayne, may I come!" I scream out.

He chuckles. *That fucking bastard.*

"Yes, you may, kitten." He attacks me, fingering me swiftly while lavishing my clit. I splinter in every direction, my climax shredding me to pieces. I pull on the handcuffs— the pain as potent as the pleasure—as I writhe and moan. When the quake dissipates, I'm left limp on the floor, breathing raggedly and close to tears. Kayne brushes his face against my inner thigh, smearing my arousal all over my skin.

"Good, kitten," he patronizes, rising to his knees, unbuttoning his shirt slowly. I stare up at him dazed. Inch by inch, he bares his chest, then tosses his shirt on the floor. He's sculpted and lean, a demonic perfection. Several tattoos adorn his body, a compass on his left pec, barbed wire dripping with blood around his arm, and a quote written across his rib cage. 'A certain kind of darkness is needed to see the stars.'

When he starts to unbuckle his belt, I tense. He doesn't say a word as he sheds the rest of his clothes, but the energy in the room is unmistakable. It's thick with sex and lust.

He said he wouldn't rape me. He said he wouldn't rape me. I repeat the mantra trying to stay calm. Once he's as bare as me, Kayne hovers over my bound body, bracing his hands on each side of my head.

"Who owns you, Ellie?" He stares down at me with his majestic eyes.

"You do," I answer reluctantly.

"That's right." He kisses my jaw softly.

"What do I want?"

I swallow hard. "My obedience, my submission, my body." The words barely come out as a whisper.

"Right again." He brings his mouth to mine, skimming his tongue along my lower lip.

"Can I fuck you, Ellie?"

"No, Kayne." I fight back the tears.

"Fine." He kisses me tenderly. Rolling his tongue against mine, allowing me to taste myself on his lips.

His change in demeanor is unexpected. I don't understand it one bit. My defenses stand at attention. Kayne then shifts, grabbing his erection with one hand and moving down to take one of my nipples into his mouth. Swirling his tongue against me, he strokes himself, lightly at first and then more urgently. As his jerks become stronger, so does the pressure of his mouth, nipping and sucking my nipple as he works himself to a climax. There's nothing I can do. There's no place I can go tethered beneath him. He bites my nipple as he comes, sending a shock of pain straight through my body. I strain, helpless as he comes on my stomach. His groans vibrating against my breast. He releases my abused nipple once he's finished. It's red and swollen.

"Mine," he declares victoriously against my lips, like he just marked his territory. Then he kisses me hard and unapologetically, making my head spin.

When he's finished with my mouth, I drop my head to the side, exhausted. My emotions are a shitstorm inside of me. There are too many to even process at the moment. So I just shove them all away.

Kayne admires his handiwork on my abdomen for a few perverted seconds before he unlocks the handcuffs. Once removed, I immediately stretch my arms and legs. They're stiff. He rubs my ankles then my wrists, kissing the inside of each one softly.

"Go clean up, kitten."

I jump to my feet and disappear into the bathroom, desperate to be alone. I grab a hand towel off the rack and run it under some warm water. When I look into the mirror, what I see startles me. There are red rings around my wrists, my hair is a mess, and my cheeks are flushed. With the collar around my neck and ejaculation on my stomach, my lip quivers uncontrollably as I wipe away Kayne's remnants. I discard the towel on the floor then grab another and clean between my legs. I feel so odd—disconnected, alone, abused—light and heavy all at the same time. I don't understand what's happening.

I prolong going back into the bedroom. I wish I could escape, just hurl myself right out the window. I spy the door to my freedom. It's visible from the bathroom. I wonder idly if it's locked. Could I make a run for it before Kayne grabs me? Where would I go if I made it out alive; collared, chained, and completely naked?

"Ellie?" Kayne calls, pulling me out of my reverie. My legs start moving before I can process what I'm doing. I bolt to the door and grab at the handle, jiggling it for dear life. It opens!

"Son of a bitch!" I hear Kayne bark as I escape down the dark hallway, sprinting toward the staircase. Just as I reach the first landing on the stairs I hear Kayne behind me. I keep my eyes on the front door as we both battle downwards, me strenuously trying not to tumble and fall. I jump the last five steps and hit the foyer floor with a thud, managing somehow to remain on my feet and keep oxygen pumping through my lungs. I dart across the cold marble with my heart beating out of control. When I reach the front door, I haul it open, even though the fucking thing weighs a ton. Just as I feel the cool breeze of outside, the door slams closed.

"No!" I scream as Kayne throws me over his shoulder, kicking the air and punching his back.

"You're a fast little thing. I'll give you that." He smacks my naked, vulnerable ass.

"Oww!" My whole body jolts as the hard slap echoes around the opulent foyer.

"You're going to pay for that, kitten." He huffs up the stairs in bare feet and boxer briefs.

"Kayne, no!" I squirm with tears threatening.

The trek back to my cell is a terrifying one. Kayne doesn't say a word as I dangle over his shoulder, fighting for my life.

Once back inside, he marches straight into the circular room with the table of torture.

"Kayne!" I cry.

"You brought this on yourself, kitten." He grabs something off the wall. I nearly go slack from the stress. The only thing keeping my body moving is the spasms of fear.

Kayne tosses me on the bed face down with me begging and pleading, and holds me there by my collar. "Don't do this. You don't have to do this!"

He ignores me as he positions my body; my feet spread on the floor, my chest pressed into the mattress. My behind exposed for the spanking.

"Kayne please! I'll be good!" I implore one last time.

"You're goddamn right you will."

Smack!

He hits my bottom with something hard and the sound rings out through the room. "Ouch!" I yell.

Smack!

"Please! Please!" I beg some more as the object lands straight across my behind.

"You were a bad girl, kitten. You need to be punished. That's how it works around here."

Smack!

Smack!

Smack!

He paddles my ass continuously until I'm choking with tears.

"Please stop!" I fight fruitlessly against him. His grip on my collar impenetrable. My behind on fire.

"What I really want to know, is where do you think you were going to go butt naked and collared?"

Smack!

"Anywhere is better than here! I'd rather be lost in the wilderness!"

"You think so, huh?"

Smack!

"Yes!" I screech.

One more immobilizing hit, then he stops, with me heaving for air. I hear the object fall to the floor.

Kayne yanks at my collar, flipping me over, and then crawls on top of me. My tiny frame nothing more than a weightless rag doll to him. He pins my sore wrists to the mattress with a tight grip, bringing his face an inch from mine. His eyes are wild and scary as hell. My tender butt screaming in agony, pressed against the bed.

"Don't try that shit again," he snaps. "There are monsters way worse than me on the other side of that door. The next time you think about escaping, do it at your own risk."

I stare back at him with choppy breaths, tear-soaked cheeks, and a stinging behind. I have no response. He made his point. I broke the rules; he showed me who's boss.

"You're mine now, Ellie. Just accept it." He lingers over me for a few long beats, our eyes locked, our breathing labored. A zap of something rousing passes between us in that moment. My heart flutters and so does my pussy. Traitorous body.

I hate him. I hate him. I hate him, I remind myself.

"Have you learned your lesson?" he asks still restraining me.

I nod.

"Answer correctly."

My lip quivers. "Yes, Kayne." The words barely leave my mouth.

"Good girl. If I let you up will you behave?"

I nod again, silently. My eyes still locked on his.

Kayne pushes himself off me with a huff.

You're mine now, Ellie. Just accept it.

I'll never accept I belong to him. I belong to no one. Do what you want to this body, hold it captive, beat it, pleasure it. But my mind he can never have. It's the one thing I can still control. The one place he can't penetrate.

"Time for bed." He jerks my leash, forcing me higher on the luxurious bed. I look down and catch a glimpse of what he used to beat me. The wooden paddle with the heart shape cut out. Kayne locks the end of the chain to the white vining iron in the center of the headboard with the padlock. The click pierces through me. It's my reminder I'll never be free.

"Lay down," he orders.

I stretch my body out, placing my head on one of the golden pillows. The satin sheets are a welcoming cold against my heated skin. I'm so tired, completely drained, and totally defeated.

"Listen to me, Ellie, you need to behave," Kayne reiterates. "I'd much rather shower you with pleasure than torture you with pain." He runs his thumb across my bottom lip. "But I'll do what I have to do to make you submit."

He bends and kisses my naked shoulder. The gesture is almost sweet. It makes no sense to me at all. A minute ago he was pummeling my ass. This man is a walking enigma. "Get some sleep."

All I can do is watch as he turns and heads for the door.

"Till tomorrow." He looks back at me with infiltrating blue eyes. Eyes that promise, eyes that threaten. My emotions feel like they're about to capsize.

OWNED

When the door clicks, I let it all loose. The frustration, the sadness, the emptiness, the rage; sobbing inconsolably in the dark, desperate for slumber to take me.

AYNE

I BEAT THE CRAP OUT of the punching bag.

My frustration level has reached max capacity. All I keep picturing are Ellie's sad eyes and abused behind. Over and over, I hear the sounds of the strikes ring out.

Smack!

Smack!

Smack!

Foreign sensations swim through my veins, like a straight shot of adrenalin. A euphoric high and a debilitating low.

"A little late to be training?" I hear Jett's voice behind me.

I slam the bag. "Never a bad time to train."

"What was all the commotion earlier?" He comes to stand where I can see him. The gym is dark except for the small light over the boxing ring and heavy bags.

"Ellie and I had a disagreement." I jab with my left then uppercut with my right.

"*About?*" He drags out the word.

"About whether the wilderness is a dangerous place or not." I kick the bag, and it swings left.

"Excuse me?" Jett raises his eyebrows.

I hit the bag in succession until my biceps hurt. "She tried to run. I punished her." I slam the bag square in the middle.

"Run? Where?"

"The door was unlocked. She made it all the way to the foyer. She's freakin' quick. She had me sprinting." I catch myself smirking. Jett notices too.

"Bit more of a challenge than you expected, huh?"

"Yeah, you can say that." I concentrate on hitting the black bag, trying to avoid all eye contact with Jett.

"She gave you a run for your money? That's why you're in here punching a defenseless heavy bag at three am?"

I glare at Jett. So much for avoiding eye contact. He's fishing. I hate it when he fishes. I wish he would just let me punch out my emotions and be done with it. But no. Jett believes in talking. Getting your feelings off your chest and all that kumbaya crap. He thinks he's my personal fucking shrink and has been analyzing me since the day we met. *Skinny prick.*

"No, I knew she wouldn't get far," I tell him point blankly.

"So what's the issue?"

"No issue. Can't a man just work out in the middle of the night?"

"A man? Yes. You? No."

"Jett!" I holler as I punch. "I don't want to talk about it."

"Do you remember the last time you didn't want to talk about something? A very innocent fishing boat was blown up."

I stop mid punch. "I take no responsibility for that. The pin on the grenade popped by itself."

"Sure it did." He crosses his arms and looks at me like I'm full of shit. Maybe I am, maybe I'm not.

"Besides, better the fishing boat than us. Right?"

"Yes," he agrees.

"Damn straight." I clam up and go back to slamming the bag. Jett just stands there eyeing me.

When I take a moment of reprieve, he strikes.

"So nothing's bothering you?" the calculating motherfucker questions again.

"Yes, something's bothering me. You." I kick the bag, the frustration blistering under my skin. *I don't want to talk!*

"I always bother you, it's what I live for. And I'll pester you all night until you spill. I don't want another explosive catastrophe."

"Jett," I warn, crackling like a live wire. He needs to lay off.

"Kayne!" he shouts shoving the black bag in my face.

My emotions burst. "I punished her okay! I picked up a goddamn paddle and beat her ass!"

Jett pauses, looking at me funny. "And that's bad because?"

"Because I liked it!" I hit the punching bag so hard my knuckles crunch. Fuck!

"Oh?" He studies me. I growl at him as I rip off my boxing gloves. "What has you conflicted? You've punished women before."

"I've punished a *willing* submissive before. Ellie is different," I clarify.

"She's your slave. You treat her as such. She disobeyed. You delivered the consequences. That's how it works. You knew this when you took her. Yes, she's different, but that's the harsh reality."

"I don't want to become the thing I'm fighting against." I toss the gloves on the ground.

"You won't," Jett says simply. I'm glad one of us is convinced. "Warrior mindset, my friend. Ellie got caught in the crossfire and now you have to protect her by any means possible. Don't overthink it. It will only drive you mad. Just remember, your hand may be firm, but Javier's is deadly. And if you like it, so be it." He shrugs. "Our business is stressful. Being with her is a release. Give her some time, she'll come around."

"You sure about that?" I respond skeptically as I unravel the tape from my hand.

"I am. I've been training girls a long time. Her biggest hang-up is perception. The taboo lifestyle. Break down the barriers of belief and she'll be eating out of your hand."

"I'm trying." I drop my head, concentrating on the rivulets of sweat dripping down my chest.

"Keep it up. She's strong, but you're Master."

"What if she ends up hating me in the end?" I look up at him with just my eyes.

"What if she ends up loving you?" he counters.

"I don't for one second believe that will happen," I scoff.

"You never know. People can surprise you. Ellie never saw you coming."

"That's because I'm trained to be invisible."

"Well you're not transparent anymore. Make her believe what she has to for now. It's for her own good."

I groan. "I'm definitely going to hell."

"I'll be right there with ya, brother. Wearing a hat and sunscreen." He slaps me on the shoulder.

"You're a pain in my ass, you know that?"

"Yup. Someone has to be." Jett glances at his watch and grimaces. "Speaking of pains in the ass."

"Javier?"

"Yes," he seethes. "I don't like the way he's treating the girls. Especially Spice. He's way too rough."

"Warrior mindset, my friend," I throw his words back at him.

Jett glares, then slugs me.

ELLIE

THE SUNLIGHT WAKES ME UP.

I'm still in the same position I was lying in when I fell asleep. On my side, hugging the pillow, chained to the bed.

My emotions feel like they've been put in a mixing glass and shaken up. I don't know what to feel, so I choose nothing at all.

I hear the door click, but I don't move. Kayne said I was supposed to kneel every time he came into the room. *Well fuck him*, my subconscious screams. My body, on the other hand, trembles knowing I'll be subjected to punishment if I disobey.

"Morning, sweet thing." I see Jett hovering over me in my peripheral vision.

"Go away," I say petulantly, squeezing the pillow tighter.

"Feeling a little used and abused this morning?"

"Yes!" I yell distraught. I'm not doing a very good job at reining my emotions in. So much for not feeling anything.

"I heard you tried to make a great escape."

"*Tried* being the operative word," I talk into the pillow.

"Didn't go so well, did it?" he mocks.

"Ask my ass, it'll tell you. I hate him."

"Rough night," he muses. I groan in response. I want to punch him in his patronizing mouth.

Jett pulls on my shoulder, rolling me over onto my back. I wince as my tender behind makes contact with the mattress. "It wasn't all bad, was it?" His aqua eyes are wide and sparkling.

I look at him like he's a loon. "He spanked me, hit me with a newspaper, and made me crawl around on all fours. Then he handcuffed me ..." I stop right there.

"Handcuffed you and did what?" Jett probes salaciously.

I stay silent with tears welling in my eyes.

"Made you feel good?" he questions. "Made you come?"

"*Made*. That is exactly the word," I growl.

"And feeling good is a problem because?"

"It's not the fact he made me feel good. It's the fact he treats me less than human. That he forced me!"

"Maybe he's trying to liberate you."

"Maybe that's utter and total horse shit!"

"We can argue the maybes all day. Bottom line, you came and you liked it."

"It's empty," I dispute furiously.

"Sex slave," Jett reiterates. "Power, ownership, pleasure."

I nearly burst into tears.

"Keep your eye on the prize sweetheart. Please him, and he'll please you. It doesn't have to be any more complicated than that."

"It goes against everything I know."

"Then maybe you need to learn a few new things." Jett shrugs.

"And I should let Kayne teach me?" I sneer.

"You said it, I didn't."

I curl my lip at him.

"Come on. Get up. A shower will make you feel better. Then I'm going to pretty you up." He hits my leg good-naturedly.

"Pretty me up?"

"Yes." He pulls the key ring that holds my freedom out of his pocket and unlocks the collar. Once off, I immediately rub my neck. That thing is restrictive as fuck. "This manicure has died and gone to hell." He lifts my hands, pointing out my chipped pink polish.

I begrudgingly roll off the bed. My ass is so sore. I curse Kayne with each step I take—*fucking bastard, asshole, shithead, douchebag*. As Jett turns on the shower, I catch a glimpse of my battered behind in the mirror, and gasp. It's beet red with flesh-colored hearts all over my butt cheeks. "Oh my God."

Jett looks at me through the mirror and smirks. "Kayne spanked you with love."

"I don't think he's capable of love," I bitterly retort.

"Of course he is. Everyone is capable of love."

"He's a monster."

"Maybe, but even beauty loved the beast."

"I'm not living a fairy tale. I'm living an American horror story."

Jett shrugs. "It's whatever kind of literature you make it. If you believe it's a horror story, it is. If you believe it's a dark erotic romance, it is. The choice is yours. The mind is a powerful thing."

I look at him like he's crazy.

"Just trying to help," he states.

"It's not working," I respond flatly.

He rolls his eyes. "No more chitchat. In you go." Jett ushers me into the steaming shower, and as soon as I step under stream, I jump. "It hurts," I whine as the running water hits my abused bottom. It feels like tiny needles stabbing me.

"It's supposed to. It's a reminder of who you belong to and what happens when you disobey. Makes you think twice about running again, huh?"

I stick my tongue out at him. It's the only rebellion I have left.

"Wash, Ellie," Jett instructs curtly.

I do as I'm told. Delicately. Every movement hurts. Once I'm done with the most torturous shower of my life, I dry off carefully. Jett tries to have me sit on the folding table, but that's just not happening. My butt is way too sore. Instead, I stand as he blow dries my hair with a round brush making it smooth. Good thing he's a foot taller than me. After that, he opens a drawer and retrieves two bottles of nail polish. A light peach colored one and a red.

"Which?" he asks.

"You're giving me a choice?"

"Yes. I'm not your owner. I have no interest in dominating you."

I survey the bottles, debating carefully. "Which do you think he'll like?"

Jett cocks an eyebrow at me.

I purse my lips. "I don't want to pick the wrong color and displease him. My ass would like to avoid another beating," I clarify.

Jett shakes the peach color. The bottle jingles. "He won't care. Trust me. He likes anything when it comes to you."

I stare at Jett quizzically. He just smiles and starts removing my chipped polish.

"How long have you known Kayne?" I inquire tactfully as he carefully paints my nails. I don't pretend to believe I have a friend or ally in Jett. But he doesn't come off as threatening as long as I behave. He's shown compassion, and even though I don't trust him completely, it doesn't mean I can't pump him for information.

Jett flicks his eyes up at me. Then starts on a second coat. "A while."

"What's a while?"

"Years."

"How did you meet?" I ask, my gaze jumping between his face and my hand.

"Mutual friends," he says flatly.

"How did you start working *here?*" I don't really even know where here is. I just know Kayne has 'clients' and 'women' who he keeps captive and strings up for their pleasure.

Jett scoffs. "I don't work for him. I work with him. Don't confuse my duties. I may not be the face of the company, but I do my fair share. Actually, I do more."

"What's the 'company' specifically?" It's obviously more than just tequila. "What is this place exactly?"

"The less you know the better." He sidesteps my question.

"Jett, please," I beg with big puppy dog eyes. Hey, if I am going to be compared to a pet, I might as well use the goods. "Tell me something."

He groans under his breath, hesitant to talk. Once he finishes painting my pinky finger with the shimmery peach, he looks up at me with an entertained expression.

"I have a feeling you are going to give Kayne a run for his money in more ways than one." He shoves the brush back into the bottle, and then huffs. "It's a whore house, Ellie. An upscale brothel. We keep women here for pleasure."

"How many women?" My eyes widen.

"A good amount. And I'm responsible for their well-being. All of them."

"Are they all locked up like me?" My voice strains at the image of dozens of women chained to a bed.

Jett looks at me like he's trying to dance around words. "No. They aren't locked up like you."

"They're not? It's just me then?"

Jett nods.

"Why?"

"Because you're special and that's all you need to know."

"Because I'm Kayne's?" I speculate.

"Now you're learning."

I frown. This shit's fucked-up.

Jett rests his hands gently on my shoulders. "I will tell you this one thing about me. I care about each and every one of them. Including you."

KAYNE

I WAIT OUTSIDE ELLIE'S ROOM.

I don't know for how long, because time seems to stand still.

I'm leaning against the wall off to the side, so Jett doesn't notice me immediately when he exits.

"How is she?" I ask as he locks the door. He jumps, snapping his head in my direction.

"Must you lurk?" he scowls.

"Yes. It's what I do. How is she?" I reiterate.

"A little upset, feeling abused, but she'll be okay. This is hard for her. She doesn't understand."

"We agreed that was the best way."

"I still believe it is. But if you're worried, go in and see her."

"You know I can't do that. I have to keep my distance. It's safer for everyone involved."

"I know that too." He puts the key ring holding Ellie's protection and freedom back in his pocket.

"Just make sure ..." I falter, not exactly sure what I'm trying to say. "Make sure—"

"She's taken care of?" Jett answers astutely.

I nod with stern eyes. I haven't been able to think of much else since Ellie was carried into this house. Last night felt like an injection into my veins. I didn't think I could do it—command someone against their will—but it came easier than expected. Fighting her, overcoming her, watching her slow descent into submission. Then tasting my sweet, sweet victory in the end—it changed something in me. And I want more. So much more that I'm counting the seconds until I can go back in that room again.

"It's what I'm here for," he reminds me.

"It's not the only thing you're here for." I punch him in the arm. Don't let his skinny ass fool you. Jett may spend a majority of his time with women, but he can throw down with the best of them. I know, because I fucked with him once. *Once*. The first time I met Jett I couldn't understand what he was doing with a bunch of hooligans like me. He was quiet and reserved and when he looked at you, those aqua eyes felt like they were digging under your skin. At least that's how it felt to me. I didn't like it, and I made it known—I threatened to stab them out. That toothpick motherfucker actually got in my face. He scored a point for formidability. I'm half a foot taller than him, double his weight and muscle mass. But it didn't matter. The minute I lunged at him, he took out my knee, quick as a jackrabbit. Dirty little shit. I ended up on my back with Jett's hand around my throat. For a puny guy, he has a death grip. It was my first lesson in don't judge a book by its cover. I was put on my ass by someone I would normally be able to knock into next week.

It took a little while, but Jett and I finally cleared the air. My ego was bruised and so was my knee, but he never stopped pushing—for some reason he wanted to be friends *with me*. That was a tough concept. I was a loner. Still sort of am I guess. I didn't have the most favorable upbringing; I bounced from foster home to foster home my entire life. Trust is hard to come by when you're verbally and physically abused, starved and locked in closets at seven years old. Most of the time it felt like I was living with a wild pack of wolves. Everyone out for themselves, survival of the fittest. And even though Jett grew up with a loving mother and stable home, his life wasn't much easier. He was a target; a black sheep because of the business his family was involved in. Growing up he fought for his life every day. In and out of hospitals, being treated for concussions and broken bones, after seven guys would gang up on him after school, smashing bottles over his head or breaking two or three of his fingers.

Seven to one? Those are some seriously fucked-up odds.

We had torture in common, and the same torment in our eyes. Except he was the trusting human and I was the untamed animal. He definitely helped shape the man I am today. He taught me about discipline and control. He opened my trust with loyalty, my mind with books, and my body with women. I was a virgin until I was nineteen. No lie. When I said I had trust issues, I wasn't kidding. Especially when it came to women. Having your birth mother promise to come back and save you from the hell you're living in, and then never hear from her again kind of fucks with a little boy's head. So much so it ripples into adulthood.

Jett introduced me to the BDSM lifestyle and was my mentor in all aspects of sexual exploration and dominance. He is not just a business partner or good friend. He's my brother, and the only true family I've ever had.

"Speaking of other things," Jett hints. "Where is our Mexican house guest?"

81

"Slithering around the mansion like the snake he is." I have eyes on him at all times. I know where he goes and whom he's with, making sure he doesn't slither within a mile of Ellie's room. He asks about her every night.

"How's your whore Kayne?"

I ignore him.

"When she's ready I want a taste," he antagonizes me.

Drop fucking dead, *I want to say. Instead, I bite my tongue till it bleeds.*

"What's mine is mine," is my only reply.

"Has he indicated when the meeting with El Rey will take place?" Jett inquires.

"No. He's still feeling us out. He's not stupid." I cross my arms. "We just have to go on like normal and hope he finds everything kosher."

"Well I hope he hurries up, and then slithers right into some oncoming traffic."

"If everything goes as planned, amigo, he will." We bump fists.

ELLIE

MY OBEDIENCE TRAINING HAS CONTINUED the last five nights. It's always the same. Kayne comes to me as soon as the sun goes down.

He feeds me dinner with his fingers while I kneel between his legs. That's why there's only one chair at the table. He quizzes me with commands, making me roll over and sit up repeatedly. He forces me to lay down at his feet to rest. When I don't obey or move quickly enough, he punishes me.

At times he's ruthless. Other times he's tender. Regardless of his mood, the night always ends the same. He ties me up and makes me come, afterwards asking if he can fuck me. When I refuse, he jerks off and marks me. He allows me to clean up then puts me to bed.

This is the vicious circle my life is becoming. Alone all day, misused at night. I'm nothing more than a pet to play with.

I hear the door click, and I immediately jump to my knees. He's training me whether I want to admit it or not. My body reacts in spite of my brain's objections.

"Evening, kitten." He scratches me under my chin. "How was your day?"

"Boring." I've learned the hard way he wants an honest answer to this.

"That's a shame. We'll have to do something to make up for that. Bend over I want to spank you."

"Kayne, why?" I protest, and instantly know I fucked up. Shit.

He shakes his head at me, vastly disappointed. "That was a test kitten, and you failed. Miserably."

"I'm sorry," I immediately respond.

"Me too. But not really," he gloats. He likes hurting me. The other night he chained me to the bed by the collar. Strategically placing it high enough so I was strained on all fours. Then he proceeded to spank me until I cried. Immediately after, he laid down, put his head between my legs and forced me to come. I was a limp nothing by the time he was done.

"Come, kitten. I'm going to teach you a lesson that will stick tonight."

I balloon with fear. I watch, removed, as he unlocks my chain then drags me into the circular room. The one with the table of torture. We've never been in here before. I know tonight is going to be bad.

"Kayne, please," I beg as he positions me between the stirrups of the table. He turns me around, smacks me hard on the ass then fastens each of my wrists in the straps. He's so quick, and they're so tight, the tears form before I even realize what's happening.

"You don't have to do this." I tug, bent over.

"You need to learn to do as I say, without question, without hesitation." He kisses my shoulder softly, sliding my hair over to one side.

"I'll be good. I'll behave," I whimper.

"I know you will once I'm through with you. I'm going to quiz you so you don't mess up again." He squeezes my stinging behind. I think it's been permanently stained red. "Then I'm going to make you come so hard you'll pass out."

My breathing is ragged, but as fearful as I am, the thought of Kayne's mouth on me makes me instantly wet. My body altogether loves him and hates him. The past few days have broken down so many barriers it's becoming harder and harder to refuse him. The things he can make me feel, the pleasure he can dispense, is unequivocal. And he's only just used his fingers and tongue. I can't begin to imagine what he can do with his body. He wants inside me. It's no secret. But he's never forced himself on me, or forced me to touch him. It's bizarre and maddening all at the same time; it's the ultimate mind game. Because he knows the moment I willingly surrender, I'll truly be his. Irrevocably.

Kayne peels the white lacy panties Jett dressed me in down to my thighs.

My head spins.

I can't see behind me, but I hear the crack against his hand from whatever object he's chosen to use.

"Let's review." He walks in front of me holding the crop, his eyes a smoldering blue. My breathing slows. He positions the end of the crop under my chin and lifts my face. "I will ask you a question. You will provide me with the correct answer."

"And you won't hit me?"

"No. You're getting spanked regardless. But as soon as you answer all the questions correctly, the spanking will cease."

I quiver. Seeing the crop in his hand is terrifying. This is so bad.

He vanishes from my sight and the tears spill.

Whack! He hits me without any warning and I cry out. It stings and bites my bare skin all at the same time.

"Who owns you, Ellie?"

"You do," I answer rapidly.

"Scream, kitten, so the whole house hears. I want everyone to know who owns you."

Whack!

"You do!" I scream like he ordered me to.

Whack!

"When I tell you to kneel, what do you say?"

"Yes, Kayne," I yell.

Whack!

"When I tell you to lie down and open your legs, what do you say?"

"Yes, Kayne." I suck in a deep breath.

Whack!

"When I tell you to bend over so I can spank you, what do you say?"

"Yes, Kayne!" I choke out through sobs.

Whack!

"What do I want from you, Ellie?"

"My obedience."

Whack!

"And?"

"My submission," I cry uncontrollably.

Whack!

"And?"

"My body," I wheeze, my legs nearly giving out.

I hear Kayne drop the crop then feel him wrap his arms around me delicately from behind.

"Shhhh, baby." He kisses my hair as I sob. "You did so good."

I tremble in his arms. My face is soaked and I swear my backside is broken and bleeding. My ass feels so raw. I hate him more in this moment than I have ever hated anyone in my entire life.

He holds me securely, raining soft kisses all over my face and neck until my sobs taper off. It doesn't happen quickly. When I'm calm, he reaches over and opens one of the drawers beneath the table. I watch distantly as he pulls out a tiny silver bullet with a chain attached to the flat end.

"I'm going to make you come so hard," he rasps, then brings the plug to my lips. I shiver, half with fear, half with lust. "Open." I open my mouth. "Suck." I close my lips around the cool metal and do as I'm told. When he tugs on the chain, I release it. He then kneels down behind me, spreads my cheeks, and licks my secret little buttonhole. I jerk forward.

"Ellie," Kayne warns, and I know right then not to test him. When I feel the pressure at my back entrance, my head becomes light and my breathing becomes erratic. No one has ever touched me there.

"Relax, Ellie," he coaxes as he takes his time inching the plug into me, my body battling against the foreign sensation. It feels like decades have passed by the time he's done inserting it. The object is small, but it feels like it's filling me completely, the pressure hitting me right in the core every time I move.

"Fuck. Good, kitten." He kisses my sore behind, and then shifts around me on his knees until his hot breath is tickling my sensitive flesh. He has no idea how much I need this. *To escape.*

He lightly licks between my folds and I moan, desperate for the mental break. I spread my legs wider, my panties ripping, crazy for him to get closer and press harder. Kayne groans as he slashes his tongue against me repeatedly. I pant uncontrollably as I ride his face while he fucks me with his mouth. The feeling is unparalleled.

"Please may I come?" I beg. I don't even care what I sound like, I just need the release; I need to get away.

"Say my name." He grips my thighs tightly, stabbing my throbbing entrance with his tongue over and over. Everything inside me builds, my climax urged on by the spine tingling pressure of the plug and Kayne's expert mouth. I can't hold back much longer.

"Kayne, please may I come!" I implore desperately. Writhing against this face.

"Come, baby." He sucks my clit. "Come as many times as you want." His fingers dig into my skin and I let go. My orgasm blasting through me like dynamite. My mind is blank for a few blissful seconds. There's no pain or chains. Nothing confining me. In the midst of my climax, Kayne yanks out the butt plug and another wave of ecstasy thunders through me. I scream, falling forward as my limbs give out. I'm wrecked. This man demands every ounce I have, and then leaves me with nothing.

"Good girl." I feel him wipe his face on the inside of my leg. Once again smearing my arousal on my own skin.

As he moves from underneath me, I hear him unfasten his belt and unzip his fly. I know what comes next.

"Can I fuck you, Ellie?" he asks, his voice rough and unsteady.

"No." *Yes!* I breathe shallowly, bent over the table.

My ass is bruised, my pussy is swollen, my limbs are as heavy as lead, and he's not through with me yet.

I hear him moan behind me, as he strokes himself. Rubbing my back with jerky movements while my face is pressed against the thin pad of the table and my wrists are bound.

"You have no idea how bad I want you. How bad I want to slide my cock inside you and fuck you senseless."

I think I do.

I hear his discomposed groan, and then feel the warm spurts of his climax shoot all over my back.

"Mine," he declares as he comes.

Kayne leans over and grabs the collar around my neck, jerking it so I look at him out of the corner of my eye. "One day soon, kitten," he licks my face. "I'm going to come in your hot little mouth, in your wet little pussy, and in your tight little ass all in the same night."

I shake because I know he's right. I'm so close to caving. Look at what happened tonight. He beat me mercilessly, and I still ached for his touch.

The last shreds of my resolve are fraying away. I'll soon be his.

Kayne unbuckles my wrists from the table and eases me up. My whole body hurts. My butt especially.

"Go inside and lay on your stomach," he says, kissing the shell of my ear gently. I do as I'm told—like the good little slave-in-training I am—and lie down on the plush white carpet in the middle of the room. I close my eyes and try to relax, but I'm still wound so tight. I feel another piece of myself disappear. Each night we spend together, more and more of me goes. Who will I become the longer he keeps me?

Kayne kneels down beside me, setting a bowl and towels on the floor. Watching in my peripheral vision, he dips one of the towels into the bowl and wipes between my legs, then over my back. The water is warm and soothing and smells like lavender. I inhale the scent as he cleans me.

"Baby, this is going to hurt a little bit."

I blast my eyes open to find him holding a small jar. My body and mind lock up as he rubs some balm over my abused bottom. It's so sore I don't think I'm going to be able sit for a week.

"Go to bed," he orders softly when he's done. I do as I'm told. Yet another one of his commands.

I climb onto the bed and rest on my stomach. Kayne re-chains me to the headboard, the padlock clicking over my head. Back on my leash for the night.

He follows me onto the mattress, kneels next to me, and proceeds to rub my back, kissing my shoulders sweetly every so often.

As much as I hate to admit it, his hands feel good. Consoling almost.

I don't understand how he can be so demonic one minute and so angelic the next?

I feel every whip mark over and over as Kayne massages me well into the night. It takes a long time, but he finally eases some my tension. I try to clear my mind and not relive every painful moment of tonight, or any other night since he took me. I concentrate on the dark and Kayne's kneading hands until I'm finally lulled fast asleep. Into the darkness where nothing can hurt me.

"UH OH, SOMEONE WAS A bad girl last night," Jett muses as he looks over my abused skin.

"Do you think you're being funny? It hurts!" I snap

"I bet it does. But it doesn't look so bad. He could have done way worse."

Oh God. I smother my face in the pillow. "It was plenty bad for me!" My words are muffled.

"What happened?"

"He whipped me with a crop!"

"I see that, silly. I mean why?"

"He wanted to spank me, and I talked back."

"That unreasonable motherfucker," Jett scolds facetiously. This has become somewhat of a ritual for me and Jett. Kayne spends the night abusing me, and we talk shit about it the next day. I try not to giggle. It isn't funny. I was brutalized last night! But Jett has become the tiny bit of light in my new dark world.

"How was the orgasm?" He pulls out a small jar balm from the nightstand and rubs some on my bruises.

I stay silent.

"That good, huh?"

I turn my head.

"Imagine what fucking him will be like."

I have. Although I'm not going to admit that to him.

"Is that something you fantasize about? Fucking Kayne?" I ask irritably.

"Don't be ridiculous. I may paint nails and do hair, but my dick is gender specific. Lady love only please."

I laugh. If I didn't, I'd cry.

"What about you? Ever partake in any lady loooove?"

I peek up at him from the gold pillow. "I kissed a girl in high school once."

"And you liked it?" he leers lewdly.

I shrug. "I didn't hate it."

Jett smiles, his eyes sparkling like he's intrigued. "Well, aren't you full of surprises."

"Not really," I disagree.

"Same sex is an acquired taste, sweet thing. The fact that you didn't hate it tells me there's more to your sexual appetite than meets the eye."

"If you say so," I answer, not sure I'm buying his presumption.

"I do." He rubs my ass a little harder and I groan. "You'll come to learn, I'm always right.

KAYNE

I FINISH DRESSING IN A daze.

I fasten my sterling silver cufflinks, adjust my tie, and slip on my suit jacket. I have a meeting in the city, but in no way do I want to leave the mansion. Thoughts of Ellie cloud my mind. The vision of her in her room—alone, chained to the bed, waiting to be played with—teases me. I don't know how long this situation is going to last. It depends on Javier. But every night I spend with her is pulling me deeper into a dark place. The lure of power is seductive. I love controlling her. I love punishing her. I love hearing her cry. It's unlike anything I've ever experienced. The women I've been with in the past have all been willingly submissive. They all knew what to expect and vice versa. But with Ellie, it's more than just dominance. The challenge of her will and fundamental breakdown of her mental faculty is addicting. It's wrong. I know it's wrong, but thrilling just the same. I crave my kitten every night. Like the gravitational pull of a lunar tide. My blood roils from just the mere knowledge I'll be back in her room tonight.

I make my way downstairs and find Javier eating breakfast in the formal dining room. To look at him, you wouldn't think much. He's not a very tall or muscular man. With olive skin and black hair, he comes off like an immigrant worker in his khaki pants and polo shirt. But one look in his eyes tells you all you need to know. He's dangerous: approach with caution.

"Amigo." He smiles balefully. I despise it when he calls me that.

"Javier. Have you heard anything from El Rey about my proposal?" I get right down to business.

"It's under review." He places some scrambled eggs in a warm tortilla, covers it with hot sauce then rolls it up. Ever since he arrived, my kitchen has been inundated with international food staples. If I never see beans and rice again, it will be too soon.

"Do you have any idea when he may respond with a decision?"

Javier shrugs. "When he's ready."

That tells me a lot.

I adjust my shirt collar and check my watch.

"Going somewhere?" he asks a little too interested. It makes me suspicious. But then again, everything Javier says or does makes me suspicious.

"I have a meeting in the city. I'll be back tonight."

"How fun. When the cat's away, the mice will play," he taunts.

I glare at him. "Not too much fun."

Javier just stares back at me. It's no secret our relationship is less than amicable. But we both have something the other one wants. So we play our little pissing game. Tit for tat until one of us ends up on top. And I already know who that's going to be.

I turn to leave.

"¿Cómo está tu puta, Kayne?"

How's your whore, Kayne?

I glance over my shoulder haughtily. "Aún mia."

Still mine.

THE DRIVE INTO THE CITY is tedious. There's traffic through the tunnel and all throughout midtown. I'm dreading this meeting. I tried to blow it off as many times as possible, but Mark is insistent. It's part of the reason I hired him; he gets things done and quickly. But I had hoped to avoid stepping inside Expo until things cooled down. No such luck. The car drops me off in front of the modest-size building with the large hammered metal sign. Mark's little company is doing well for itself.

I take a deep breath and step out onto the sidewalk. It's early May, and the temperature is comfortable. Not so hot you're sweating through your suit; not so cold you need an extra layer.

"I'll call once I'm ready to be picked up," I tell the driver. Usually Jett drives me into the city, but I felt it was safer for Ellie if he stayed behind today, and he agreed. I didn't like that flicker in Javier's eye when I told him I was leaving the house. It's still bothering me. I want to make this meeting quick then get my ass back to Jersey. Mansion is located in an elite country-like suburban community an hour outside the city. It's privately tucked away, inconspicuous to the naked eye, and perfectly situated for my clients all over the metropolitan area and beyond.

I walk into the contemporary-designed building and head toward the elevator. The last time I was here, Ellie was standing right next to me looking a little embarrassed and totally tempting in a tight pencil skirt. What I wouldn't give to live that day over again.

The elevator doors open to a sickly looking Mark. I frown. His skin is pale, his eyes are red, and his clothes are wrinkled. Very unlike the neat as a pin man I've come to know.

"You look awful." I step out of the lift.

"I am awful. I'm a wreck." He doesn't even shake my hand. Instead he pulls out a bottle of Tums and pops two into his mouth. "I haven't slept since Ellie disappeared," he says crunching away.

Oh shit. This is exactly why I wanted to avoid all things Expo.

"Why don't we have some coffee and talk?" I put my hand on his shoulder.

Mark nods. "The conference room is prepared."

I follow Mark down the hall, past numerous employees, to the corner room framed with windows. The energy in the office is different compared to all the other times I've been here. Mark prides himself on having a positive, upbeat work environment. He's always boosting morale and incentivizing his employees. But today, the negative energy is palpable. And I know exactly why that is. It isn't the same without Ellie, and it's affecting everyone. Including me.

Mark plops down in his usual seat at the table as I shut the door behind me. He eats another antacid, leaving the large bottle out on the table.

I decide to pour Mark some tea instead of coffee. I figure it would be easier on a sour stomach or enflamed esophagus or whatever the fuck he has going on.

I place the cup in front of him and proceed to sit across the table.

"Thank you." He lifts the white mug with Expo's rainbow colored logo on it. It's as modern as the sleek building we're sitting in.

"Want to talk about it?" I ask as Mark takes a sip of the steaming tea. I would've at least blown on it first, but by the looks of him, he's not feeling anything but anxiety at the moment.

"It's my fault," he blurts out.

"What?"

"Ellie's disappearance is my fault."

My jaw drops. "Why is it your fault?"

"Because I should have been watching her more closely."

"*Mark*—"

"That beautiful little spitfire is gone. And I'm completely helpless." He puts his head in his hands. This is not good. I knew Ellie being taken would put a strain on her friends and family, but I never imagined Mark would blame himself or fall the fuck apart. I've never really had friends or family who cared about me that much, so maybe I underestimated the impact of her disappearance. She's lucky, and loved, by more people than I realized. I feel a strange twinge in my chest. Jealousy? Envy maybe? Jett is the only person who would give two shits if I ever disappeared. Regardless of the repercussions, Ellie is safer being held captive by me than being tormented at the hands of Javier. I stand by my decision. As deceitful as it is.

"Kayne, you were the last one to see her. What was she like? Was she drunk? Upset? Why did she leave alone?"

As much as I wanted to avoid this conversation, it's clear Mark needs answers. So I will give him *some*.

"Trust me when I tell you, I tried everything in my power to get her to come home with me," I divulge. Although in reality I didn't have to try very hard. I think Ellie would have come home with me even before the alcohol freed her inhibitions. "But Ellie wasn't having it. I think she was playing hard to get," I insinuate.

"She didn't drink that much and seemed fine to leave on her own. I never would have left her side if I thought something might happen to her." It's the exact same thing I told the police when they questioned me. I knew it was going to happen. Luckily for me, the commissioner of New York is a personal friend. You meet a lot of high profile people in my line of work, and sometimes those contacts come in handy. "I offered her a ride several times, but she declined. You know how Ellie is," I lie through my teeth.

"Yes, I do." Mark stares into the light brown liquid. "She's a smart, young girl with a bright future ahead of her. It's breaking my heart to think she'll never have a chance to pursue it."

I sigh. I would never take Ellie's future away from her. If anything, I hope one day to make it brighter. If she'll let me; if she ever speaks to me again after this is all over.

"She's also strong, and I'm sure wherever she is, or whatever she's going through, she'll survive," I try to reassure him.

"I'm trying not to imagine what's she's going through." Mark's eyes water. Damn. I pull out the white handkerchief from my left pocket and hand it to him uncomfortably.

"Thank you." Mark takes it and wipes his eyes. Geez. I'm so bad at the emotions thing. I don't even like my own.

"I wish I could tell you everything is going to be okay. But I'm a realist." And I don't want to look too incriminating. "I can tell you that I care about Ellie just as much as you do. Maybe more." Mark pauses and looks at me for what seems like the first time today. Like he's really seeing me.

"I understand. You two always did have explosive chemistry."

"Explosive?" I widen my eyes. "Was it that obvious?"

"Boyfriend, please." Mark makes a *don't bullshit me* face. "Every time you two were in the same room, I had the bomb squad on speed dial."

I smirk coyly. "Ellie is a bit … incandescent."

"She used to light up this whole office." Mark smiles sadly.

She will again.

"Try not to be so hard on yourself," I tell him.

"That is easier said than done." He twists the handkerchief in his hands.

There's nothing more I can say or do.

After our conversation, and a little bit of work, I bid Mark goodbye. I wish I could've given him more reassurance. Told him I knew Ellie was going to be okay. But my secrets have to stay hidden, because even I can't guarantee the outcome. I can only proceed with what I'm doing, with hope that Ellie will come around and we'll both come out of this alive.

Before I leave, I meander by Ellie's desk. It's filled with papers and sticky notes. Her keyboard has a thin layer of dust and the green plant she keeps on her filing cabinet is wilting. I spy the pictures on her pin board. She's hugging a girl I don't recognize. They look alike so I assume it's her sister. There's another of her with two older people. They must be her parents. She looks like her father. Their pointy noses are the same, and so is the color of their eyes. A deep mossy green. The one of her and Mark I find the most amusing. It's St. Patrick's Day, and they're both wearing *Kiss me I'm Irish* t-shirts, green sparkly top hats, and have a shot glass in each hand. Looks like whiskey. Ellie's cheeks are a little flushed, and she's smiling brightly. If I had to guess, she's a little tipsy. I catch myself grinning as I stare at her. I wonder if I'll ever have the chance to get to know the girl in that picture. I really want to, almost desperately.

Once back outside, I slip into the town car waiting for me on the street. I slide up the privacy screen and try to relax against the leather seat, loosening my tie and stretching my legs. Why didn't I just rent a driver and take my limo? More room!

I shift around uncomfortably, anxious to get home and play with my kitten. I drop my head back, close my eyes, and dream up numerous ways I can make Ellie come. I get hard just thinking about how she tastes on my tongue. I can't wait to see what she feels like on my cock. I wonder if tonight will be the night she finally gives in. I know she's close, so damn close to being mine. The wait is nearly killing me.

I grab myself and stroke, trying to appease the arousal that is now a living, breathing beast ripping my insides apart.

"Driver!" I kick the back of his seat restlessly. "Hurry the fuck up!"

ELLIE

JETT DUBBED ME HIS BRUNETTE Barbie doll.

Once again he did my nails and straightened my hair.

He fed me ice cream for lunch and indulged me in mindless conversation. It was the least boring and least stressful day so far.

I watch the sun set through the large circular window diagonal from my bed. As soon as the first shred of night appears, I know he'll be here.

I wait on my knees; impatiently, nervously.

Tonight I know I'm going to say yes. My mind has finally lost the war. It will be my descent into darkness. I'll finally be his. I try not to think about what that means. All I know is that I need more. My body needs more. It's becoming dependent, like a junkie hooked on drugs, jonesing for the unparalleled pleasure only Kayne can distribute. It's my escape, my avoidance, my diversion to the reality at hand.

The door clicks and my body reacts, adrenaline rippling through me. I stay perfectly still as I listen to him approach. His footsteps sound different tonight. I flick my eyes up at the figure in front of me. It's not Kayne. I snap my head to attention. The adrenaline previously rippling through me has turned into waves of dread. The man rakes over my naked body with cold black eyes and a twisted grin. I spring back, but he snatches my chain before I can get far. He drags me toward him sinisterly until my face is an inch from his.

"Señorita," he growls. I recognize him then. He's the man who showed up at Mark's party.

"Kayne has to do a better job training his slave. If you were mine, your mouth would already be wrapped around my dick." His accent is thick and his tone is menacing. This man is evil.

He unbuttons his pants with one hand. "No!" I push at him, struggling against the tight hold he has on the chain.

He laughs at me. "That word doesn't exist in my world."

He pulls me forward, forcing me to brace myself on the edge of the bed. I swipe at him with one hand spurring him to squeeze the collar until it's choking me. I gasp for air as he brings the head of his penis to my lips.

"No!" I try to turn my head, but his hold is tight and too restrictive. Tears spring. When I try to fight, he chokes me harder. I wheeze and cough desperate for oxygen as tiny stars cloud my vision.

He lets up once I stop squirming, close to passing out.

"Bite me and I'll beat you unconscious." He grabs a fist full of my hair and shoves his cock so far into my mouth I gag.

Oh God, please no!

KAYNE

IT TAKES ME A MINUTE to register what I'm seeing.

Javier has Ellie bent over the edge of the bed by her collar.

"What the fuck!" I roar as he tosses her aside crying and covered in ... *Oh for Christ's sake.*

"Your whore needs work," he sneers.

I see fucking red. The whole room is bleeding crimson.

You can't fucking kill him. Yet. I restrain myself as my heart tries to punch a hole straight through my chest.

"This fucking room is off-limits, and you know it." I step forward with my fists clenched.

"Apparently not." He zips his fly imperiously with that ridiculous smirk I want to smack right off his face.

Javier brushes past me, and it takes every ounce of control I have not to beat him into the floor. As soon as he slams the door, I bolt to Ellie. She looks like she's in shock.

Our eyes meet for a fleeting moment then she loses it. "Unchain me!" she screams, sobbing irrepressibly. She yanks at her collar, then starts erratically wiping Javier's come off her face and out of her hair. *That fucking rat bastard. He's dead.*

I clumsily release the chain from her collar during her fit. As soon as she's free, she darts into the bathroom and turns on the shower. My anger has reached volcanic proportions. I give Ellie a minute, because truthfully I need one myself. Then I follow her into the bathroom.

The muscle I forgot was in my chest cracks for the very first time in my life as I watch her scrub her face furiously under the water, bawling uncontrollably. *My kitten.* The crack fissures so deep it touches my soul.

That tortilla-eating motherfucker did this to make a point. To flex his superiority. To get to me. *Cocksucker.* I want to scream, but I don't want to upset Ellie more than she already is, so I stuff my amplified emotions away and step into the shower with her, clothes and all. Ellie instinctively cowers away from me, still crying. Her face is red from scrubbing and her body hunched in shame. I thank God for the stream of water running down my face. It masks the tears falling from my eyes. This was never supposed to happen. He was never supposed to get to her. I thought if I kept her close, kept her captive, she'd be safe. I was wrong.

I hate being wrong.

It eats me alive.

So does her suffering.

I pull a defiant Ellie into my arms. She fights me tooth and nail, but I'm bigger and stronger, and she knows it. She submits, wilting against me. Her pain is palpable through her wretched sounds. It guts me.

In a fit of sudden rage, she balls her hands into fists and starts pounding on my chest. "You did this to me! You made me a whore!" Then her legs give out and she slumps into my arms.

"He was never supposed to touch you." I hug her tightly. "You only belong to me." I press my lips to her head. She cries some more and I just hold her until the tears subside. It feels like an agonizing eternity. The only thing reminding me we're still alive is the feel of the scalding water and sound of the strong spray.

When Ellie finally looks up at me, it's with dejected green eyes. It liquefies my soul. I drop my lips to hers, kissing her softly, trying to ease the pain, the shock, the after effect. She grabs at my face and kisses me fiercely, as if I'm the only lifeline she has left.

I tighten my arms around her and allow her into my mouth, giving her what she needs; my body and my newly functioning heart.

"I'm sorry, Ellie." I find my balls. "I'm sorry he touched you. I'm sorry I wasn't here to stop him." She blinks up at me naked, defenseless, and so utterly tempting. "I promise no one will ever hurt you again." It's a vow.

"Except you." Her voice is small, but callous none the less.

Burn.

I drop my forehead to hers. "I won't as long as you behave."

"You promise?" She looks up at me with just her clouded eyes.

"Yes."

"I'm trying," she whispers weakly.

"I know. You're a good girl."

She closes her eyes as if surrendering. Giving up. Giving in. "Kayne, can you touch me?"

The question blindsides me.

"Is that what you want, Ellie?" I smooth my hand over her wet hair.

"Yes. Please. Take it all away." She doesn't even hesitate.

I would take every ounce of her suffering if I could.

I lift her face, brushing my thumb across her raw skin. Then I drop a light kiss against her lips. She darts her tongue out, and I know in that instance I have her. A butterfly trapped in my web. My web of lies, and my web of deception. My web of selfishness, because I've always wanted Ellie. And now I finally have her. *She's Mine.*

I turn off the shower without a sound, pull Ellie's listless body out, and then wrap her in a towel. When I lift her up and cradle her in my arms, she looks at me with hollow eyes. It feels like a piece of her spirit is broken, which is the last thing I ever wanted to happen.

In the bedroom I place her on her feet, and then strip the bed, sending the comforter and sheets flying to the floor. She'll get new bedding tomorrow; that set is being burned. I dry her off in silence, skimming over her breasts and stomach, and rubbing between her thighs. Then I dry her hair, soaking up the droplets of water from scalp to tip. When I'm through, she's left naked in front of me wearing only her collar. The thick leather around her neck makes me hard as fuck. It's a symbol, a statement. It tells the world she belongs solely to me.

"Lie down," I order. "On the carpet." She steels herself, breathing heavily, and then walks to the center of the room.

"Look at me." She turns and raises her head. She is so goddamn beautiful it hurts, with those sultry green eyes and light brown hair. "On your back. Spread your legs."

Breathing erratically, she drops to her knees, and then lies on her back. Just like I taught her. My cock throbs. She props her feet up and opens her legs as wide as they can go. I nearly combust in my pants.

"Good girl."

I stalk the seven steps it takes to get to her then unhook my belt, while standing above her. We never take our eyes off each other as I pull my wet shirt over my head and shed my pants. I'm completely naked, same as her.

I kneel down between her legs; her enticing little pussy wide open and on display. I moan deep and guttural in my throat as its soft pink folds call to me. Tease me. Tell me they're finally mine.

I'm going to attempt to be gentle. I don't exactly do gentle. But I can try for Ellie's sake.

"Tell me again that you want me to touch you." I kiss the inside of her thigh.

Ellie closes her eyes and grips the plush rug.

"I want you to touch me." Her voice is raspy from fighting back tears.

"I have wanted you for so long." And now that I have her, I'm going to make sure I bury myself so deep inside her, the only thing she'll feel, taste, smell, breathe, or even think about is me. I know I've said I want her obedience, and her submission, and her body, but what I want most of all is her mind. I want to cloud it, consume it, rule over it. Have her thoughts only be of me. I never knew how deep my affections for Ellie ran until the night of Mark's party. That first small kiss sparked it all. It ignited something between us, something that's been smoldering ever since.

Ellie closes her eyes as I run one finger down her slit, shaking like a leaf as I circle the tip of my finger over her clit. Her body springs to life as I slide it inside her. She gasps, grabbing onto the rug tighter as I push all the way in. I finger her slow and deep, after a while adding a second digit then a third. She moans loudly, her body bowing from the pleasurable intrusion.

I drop my head and suck her clit between my teeth causing her to whimper. I love that sound. I've come to live for that sound.

I work my mouth while simultaneously fucking her with my fingers. I know what she likes. I know what gets her off. She writhes beneath me, flexing her hips, begging for more. For a fleeting second I regret not tying her down. I withdraw my fingers and Ellie groans in protest. I crawl over her, licking my way up her body until we're nose to nose, mouth to mouth. "Tell me you want me to fuck you."

She's panting and flushed, the fear evident in her smoky green eyes. But there's also something more, something dark and desirous.

"I want you to fuck me."

I grab her by the collar and yank, pulling her face to mine. I kiss her hard, forcing her mouth open, giving her no choice but to accept my tongue. I plunge in deeply and swirl it all around, sucking the oxygen right out of the room. Then I shove her back down. My need spiraling.

"Stay still."

I spread her legs wider with my hands and Ellie emits an uncomfortable sound. Then I line the head of my cock up to her entrance and tease her with shallow thrusts. Her pussy tightens, begging for more. I slide into her, taking her all at once. She sighs insufferably as a tear trickles down her cheek. I lean in and lick it off.

I'll swallow every salty emotion she sheds tonight.

Taking her wrists I pin her down, fucking her as slow and as leisurely as I can. As controlled as my body will allow.

"How do I feel?" I ask as I thrust.

"Big," she responds, her fists clenching.

I chuckle not expecting that response.

She starts to shift. "Kayne—"

"Keep those fucking legs open. And no talking. Unless you're asking permission to come." I grit my teeth. The Dom is never far. It's a ramification of this life.

She obeys, crying a little harder. I hold her wrists tighter as I lick her face.

"Cry all you need. It won't be the last time," I tell her as I pump into her harder. Her pussy tight and wet, constricting around me. I nearly see stars.

Ellie's breathing speeds up, becoming erratic and disjointed, as our hips clash together.

"Please, may I come?!" she erupts. Her eyes are screwed shut, her body is tense.

I want to say no, but I'll be nice. Tonight, Ellie needs nice.

"Come, baby. Come as many times as you need."

She lets go as soon as I consent. A flood of warm heat saturates my cock as she clamps down around me. Fuck, Ellie feels better than I could have ever imagined, could have ever conjured in my wildest dreams.

She cries out, struggling against me as her orgasm tears her apart. I watch transfixed as her face strains in ecstasy, her breasts swell, and nipples harden. I suck one into my mouth during the height of her pleasure and another little ripple of arousal washes over me. The sensation makes me crazy. Makes me crave blood.

Her body gives out as soon as her tremors subside.

"Turn over," I order. Ellie immediately rolls onto her stomach. I pull her hips up, forcing her on all fours then slam into her, burying myself to the hilt.

"Oh!" she screams. My desire has me drunk, lustful, and unrepentant. I beat into her, holding on tight, sprinting after my orgasm.

"Who do you belong to, Ellie?"

"You," she strains.

I grab her collar, fucking her harder.

"If I tell you to spread your legs for me, what do you say?

"Yes, Kayne."

"If I tell you to bend over so I can fuck you, what do you say?

"Yes, Kayne."

"What do I want?" I ask as my climax circles like a cyclone.

"My obedience. My submission. My body."

I have all three. I pull out right before I explode and come all over her abused ass. The crop marks still red and fresh. I love it.

I drop back, panting wildly once the oscillating sensations subside and drink Ellie in on all fours.

MINE.

"Lie down," I command. She slides forward onto her stomach, stretching out like a tired little kitten. *My tired little kitten.*

I crawl over her. "Did I hurt you?"

She looks up at me. Her eyes are red and her cheeks are puffy.

"No."

"Are you telling me the truth, or what you think I want to hear?"

She bites her lip. "It hurt a little. You're big."

I hold back a grin. Her response just stroked my ego. Big time.

"I don't ever want you to lie to me, understand? If I ask you a question, tell me the truth."

She nods, pressing her cheek into the plush white rug. I kiss her softly on the corner of her mouth then grab the towel on the floor next to the bed. I wipe my come off her ass then pull her to her feet. She stands like she's supposed to, with her head bowed. Just like I trained her to. It's arousing and odious all at the same time. I draw her face up. "Mine, Ellie."

"Yes, Kayne," she answers, and my insides go berserk. I will never get tired of hearing her say that.

I walk over to the armoire and open the intricately decorated doors with Ellie standing where I left her. I grab what I'm looking for, and then return to the center of the room.

"Look at me."

Ellie lifts her head. I unlock the thick black training collar and remove it from her neck.

"I don't have to wear it anymore?" Her voice pitches.

"No. Not that one." I drop it on the floor.

Her face falls. I lift the new collar to show her. This one is less harsh, more feminine. With rhinestones. It also has a padded inside so it won't rub uncomfortably against her skin. I slide it around her neck and lock it in place. I yank her forward by it and give her a kiss. "I like you collared, baby. I like you naked. I like you mine."

I STAY WITH ELLIE UNTIL she falls asleep.

It seemed wrong to just leave after the night she had. I didn't exactly know what to do with myself once I put her to bed. Should I lie down with her? Sit next to her? Hold her?

Holding her seemed a little too close for comfort. Although, if I had to choose, it would be option number three. But I can't cross that line. For all our sakes. An arm's length is where I have to keep her. Owner/pet. Master/slave. That is as far as the relationship can go.

Sitting in the chair at the table, I watch as she drifts off. The moonlight shining through the wagon wheel window is illuminating her face, highlighting the streaks of tears running down her cheeks. The rhinestones on her new collar reflecting off the light every time she shifts.

Beautiful is too inferior a word to describe Ellie. Inside and out. Even when she's crying, she's the most captivating thing on the face of the Earth. At least to me. I could watch her sleep for hours. Watch her move and laugh and come apart in my arms. She's mine.

Once her breathing levels off and she's sleeping peacefully, I silently slip out of the room.

I thought I had fucked all the murderous rage out of me, but as I walk down the dimly lit hallway, my fury returns.

My legs bring me to the exact place my brain forbids me to go. With extreme force I kick open the door to Javier's room. The lock splinters straight through the wood. That felt good. I walk in to find Javier once again with Spice. He's taken a pathological liking to her. It irks me. She looks too much like Ellie. Same green eyes and brown hair. It heightens the turmoil blistering beneath my skin. I grab the switchblade out of my pocket and pop the knife as I stalk toward Javier. His black eyes widen, and then turn hard. He's not afraid of me. He should be. I slam him up against the wall next to the bed. "Next time you decide to stick your dick where it doesn't belong, I'll cut your nut sack open and watch your balls fall to the floor." I dig the tip of the blade into his crotch. He goes up on his toes. "This is my fucking house. You will respect me and my girls.

"Vivas bajo mi techo, obedeces mis reglas. Comprende?"

You live under my roof, you obey my rules. Understand?

Javier sneers, staring me down. "I obey no one."

This is an all-around dicey situation. One wrong move or one wrong word and I could fuck everything up. All the years of hard work and money spent. All the sacrifices and all the lies, good for nothing.

But at the moment I just don't give a fuck. All I know is if Javier ever lays a hand on Ellie again, the whole compound is going to go up in smoke. "It doesn't look like you have much of a choice at the moment." I twist the knife deeper.

Javier's mouth curves up into a taut deranged smile, despite the compromising position I have him in. "You amuse me, amigo."

"Glad to know I'm good for something."

"You're good for many things," he says cryptically.

"Stay away from what's mine," I warn one last time, then shove myself away him. I cut Spice loose, she's bound and gagged and has been whimpering the whole time. Javier tied her up so tightly to the four poster bed she's suspended over the mattress. Her wrists are rubbed raw from the abrasive rope and there's hot red wax drizzled all over her body. Both of her nipples are completely covered. It looks like the poor girl is bleeding to death. She scrambles up once she's free and rushes out of the room. Fear and relief are both evident in her eyes. She doesn't even bother to remove the ball gag stretching her mouth. My heart lurches. If I hadn't walked in, who knows what else he might have done.

"You cut my fish loose."

"Your gaming privileges have been revoked. No more playtime for you. You've had your fun." The words feel like battery acid burning my tongue. Ellie's horrified face flashes in front of me. It's an image that has been permanently branded into my brain.

"I don't like boundaries, amigo."

"I don't like you," I spit.

I leave Javier's room after that, praying to almighty God I didn't just destroy everything I've worked the last six years for. I don't stop walking until I reach the gym. I lift my hands, not even bothering with gloves, and pound away, seeing Javier's face every time my fist connects with the punching bag.

ELLIE

I WAKE UP ON A bare mattress.

The sheets and comforter are still on the floor and I am back on my leash. My legs hurt, and so does my core. I think this kind of pain is something I'll need to get used to. I handed myself over last night. My obedience, my submission, and my body. I am officially Kayne's. Officially owned.

I huddle into a ball and shiver, but not because I'm cold. Because I'm numb. The image of evil black eyes haunt me. What if Kayne hadn't come in when he did? What if ... I push the crippling, abominable thought away. There's no point in what-ifs. That's what my mother always says. I miss my family terribly. Just the thought of them fragments my pain and loneliness further. I can't imagine what they're going through—not knowing where I am, if I'm dead or alive.

What would they think if they found out I was owned?

I fight back the tears, put my loved ones in a box, and shove it into the darkest depths of my mind. I need to be strong, and missing my family makes me weak. Makes me vulnerable. I have to survive.

I try not to think. I try not to feel. I'm alone, and my existence is abhorrent.

I concentrate solely on something small. The need to pee. I hope Jett comes soon.

I look around my prison cell and idle thoughts take over. Is this where I'll live forever? Will I ever be able to go outside again? Will I always be a dog chained to the bed? A sexual object, to use as he pleases. Before I'm sucked into a rabbit hole of despair, the door opens. I jump to my knees, never knowing if it's Kayne or not. And now that I officially belong to him, I have to act accordingly. A little piece of my hope dies.

"Heel, it's just me." I relax my body and lift my head. Tears streaming down my face.

"Don't cry." Jett embraces me. "It's going to be okay. How do you feel?" he asks as he unlocks the chain from my new collar. There's no fun, lighthearted banter today.

"Numb, abused. Confused."

"I could kill that shithead for laying a finger on you."

"Kayne or the other guy?" I sniff.

Jett's lip twitches. "Nice to know you haven't lost your sense of humor."

"Someone told me I need to be strong." I look up at him drained of life.

He hugs me. "You're rising to the occasion."

"I feel like I'm falling apart."

"You're not alone. You can talk to me about whatever you want. You can cry, you can let it all out."

I take him up on his offer. I melt into Jett and sob, crying every single sickening emotion out. Every one I tried and failed miserably to suppress. Jett just holds me for as long as I need and after what feels like a lifetime's worth of tears, I pull myself together.

"That's a girl." Jett pats me. "Let's get you cleaned up. A hot shower and something sinful for lunch will make you feel better."

"How sinful?" I look up at him with puffy eyes.

He leers. "Something a priest can't even forgive you for."

I smile weakly.

Jett removes my collar. "Sparkly new jewelry," he comments offhandedly.

"It's definitely more comfortable than the other one." I rub my neck.

"Prettier too."

I pee, take a long shower, and eat the most decadent lunch I've ever had in my life; a giant portion of crème Brulee French toast with a side of vanilla ice cream drowned in chocolate syrup. After that, I just stare at myself in the mirror for most of the day. Who is this girl I've become? I still have the same eyes and nose and hair. Except now I'm someone's sex *slll ... pleasure kitten.* I can't even bring myself to use the other term.

"Time to go back on your leash." Jett pops his head into the bathroom, vaporizing my scattered thoughts. "You've been in here all day."

I frown.

"I laid your clothes out. Kayne will be here soon. Wear your hair up, it's a mess." He winks.

With a heavy heart, I pull my long, light brown hair up into a loose bun. It's sort of sexy with tendrils falling down around my face. I wonder briefly if Kayne will like it. *Why do you care!?*

My 'clothes' consist of a pair of black, lace-trimmed boy shorts, knee-high stiletto boots, and my collar. That's it. I don't think I'll ever wear real clothes again. I slip on the underwear and boots, right after Jett secures my new neck jewelry. Then back on my chain I go. "You look sexy enough to eat," Jett comments once I'm perched back on my bed.

"Thank you?"

"You're welcome. We need to work on makeup with you though."

I raise my eyebrows. I never was one for makeup. A little mascara and some blush. I'm even less inclined since I've been here.

"Tomorrow." Jett taps me on the nose. "I'll be back with dinner later."

He closes the door to my prison, leaving me alone to just wait. Minutes tick by. I fiddle with my hands, the chain, and the collar.

I can only so go far. To the edge of the bed is all my leash allows. I shift this way and that, nervously, curious about how tonight will play out. Kayne has full range of me now. What will he do?

I stare mindlessly at my new bedding. I like it, despite the circumstances. It's all shimmery creams and sparkly whites with matching decorative throw pillows. It looks like I'm sitting on a cloud of diamonds. It makes me think of Mark and how he used to call me his magic glitter in high heels. I push the thought away and place him in the box with the rest of my loved ones. I miss him too much. I miss them all too much.

The lock clicks and I bound onto my knees like I'm supposed to. Like a good girl. An obedient girl. An owned girl.

I see Kayne's shoes in front of me as I keep my head down and my hands on my thighs. My heart hammering in my chest. He stands there for what seems like an eternity. My back starts to cramp.

"Hello, kitten, how was your day?" he finally asks.

"Fine, Kayne," I answer like I'm supposed to.

"Look at me." I sweep my head up and look directly into his crystal blue eyes.

"How was your day? Answer honestly."

I frown. "I was lonely. And I feel conflicted." I tear my gaze away from him.

"Honesty, Ellie. I always want honesty. It will get easier. I promise." He runs one finger softly under my chin. "You're beautiful."

I blush, still not looking at him. Does he mean that or does he say it just to play with my mind?

Kayne pulls at my collar bringing me up onto my knees and cups one of my breasts, massaging it gently.

My heart beats wildly. I flashback to last night. My legs still ache from being spread so wide. My lips tender from being kissed so hard. "On a scale of one to ten, how sore are you?" He hooks one finger into my panties and peeks down inside.

"Six," I answer, holding perfectly still.

"I'd prefer four, but six is fuckable."

My pulse races. I remind myself that I handed my body over to him. Freely and willingly. It's his to do with as he pleases. Whatever that may be. Before Kayne has a chance to pounce on me, Jett appears with dinner. He walks through the room with a large platter covered by a silver dome. He places it on the table by the window then leaves without a word. The door clicks behind him and my heart is suddenly in my throat. I stare at Kayne, and he stares back at me. His eyes are roaring with some unnamed desire. My stomach flips.

"Are you hungry?"

Honestly, no. So much for giving him what he wants.

"Yes, Kayne," I answer.

"Good girl." He snaps my underwear.

Kayne unhooks me from the headboard and leads me by my leash to the table. He sits with the chair facing out, his legs spread wide. "Kneel."

I drop in front of him. Then he begins to feed me from his hand. "Open."

I open my mouth and he slips a piece of steak inside. I chew. It's cooked perfectly and tastes delicious. Then he scoops some mashed potatoes onto one finger. I open my mouth again and suck them off. He feeds me like this until almost everything on the plate is gone.

"Enough." His voice is gruff and thick with lust. The bulge in his pants straining against his zipper.

"Lie down." I lie at his feet. Just how I'm supposed to. Minutes tick by, as he gazes at me on the floor, feasting on every naked inch of my body with his mesmerizing eyes.

"Stand," he commands. So I do. He loves to boss me around. Kayne continues to drink me in as I stand before him. My bare breasts on display. The stiletto boots giving me four extra inches of height.

"You are so fucking sexy," he admires darkly. Something inside me twinges. "Pull your underwear down your thighs."

With shaky hands and erratic breaths, I obey. Once my panties are where he wants them, Kayne runs his large hands over my body, feeling my curves, cupping my breasts, squeezing my ass. He moans with satisfaction. Then traces his fingers over my hipbones, down to the middle of my thighs.

When he inserts his thumb into me, I wince and moan all at the same time. He's menacingly quiet as he fingers me, concentrating solely on my face. His stare is burdensome, but I endure it as I let the effect of his ministrations play out on my face. After a few heat-induced minutes, he withdraws his thumb and replaces it with his middle finger. It's only a few seconds before he smears my wetness away from my pussy, and up toward my ass. I gasp. "Shhh." He grabs onto one of my legs with his free hand steadying me. "Remember when I told you I was an ass man?"

"Yes." I tremble.

He slowly sinks his thumb back inside me as his middle finger works its way into my button hole. I tense, remembering how the butt plug felt. Full and intrusive. Kayne's finger is twice as long.

"Relax, Ellie." Kayne tries to pacify me as his finger sinks steadily into my tight little entrance.

The intrusion bites, but every now and again the pain subsides and I'm shocked with a small amount of pleasure. It takes a few slow minutes, but his entire finger finally makes its way deep inside me.

I feel so full as Kayne proceeds to simultaneously fuck my pussy and my ass with his thumb and middle finger. His thrusts are relentless. I start to shake as an orgasm builds so hot inside of me, I fear I might turn to ash.

"Do you like the way I touch you, Ellie?" I want to say no just to be spiteful. But I reply the way I should.

"Yes, Kayne."

"You know I'm going to fuck you here." He pushes hard into my behind. It hurts; heavenly pleasure mixed with hellish pain.

"Yes, Kayne." I'm panting now, my climax is so close.

"Don't you dare come." He works his hand faster, harder. I'm going to crumble.

"Kayne, please," I beg.

"Please, what?"

"Please." I can barely say the words.

"You want to come baby?

"Yes, please." I breathe heavily.

"Say it. Say you want me to fuck you until you come."

I swallow hard. I've never talked like that before.

"Say it, Ellie."

"I want you to fuck me until I come." My voice is a whisper.

"You'll have to do better than that, kitten." He withdraws his fingers, leaving me empty and frustrated. "You need to learn to control your urges. And you're going to have to start talking dirty, baby. I like it." He leans over and sucks my clit. I nearly die.

"What do you say when I tell you to bend over so I can fuck you?"

"Yes, Kayne."

"Good girl. Turn around and grab your ankles." I obey his command like the good little pet I agreed to be. I turn, bend, and grab my ankles. My leg muscles scream. Kayne gets up and moves around the room. In this position, I can't see what he's doing, leaving me raging with anticipation and an overdose of fear. He could have taken me as soon as I bent over, but instead he's shuffling around the room. I tremble from the need and the unknown. When Kayne returns he grabs my hips, and grinds his hard-on firmly against me. I moan. So does he. Then he bends and grabs the chain dangling from my collar. He winds it around my right ankle and locks it in place. Holy shit. Then he attaches another chain to my collar, mirroring his actions on the other ankle. I can't stand up straight. He's literally restrained me bent over. I start to hyperventilate. "Kayne?"

"Shush, Ellie. You look fucking amazing like this." He slaps my ass, and I have no choice but to accept the pain. I'm trapped. I can't lift my head, and every time I try the chains restrict me. I hear him undo his zipper, and see his trousers drop to the floor. My hearts is fluttering like a bird trapped in a cage. "Relax." He rubs my backside gently. Then he slaps me again. My whole being tenses.

"I thought no more punishments." I grit my teeth.

"Only if you behave. And spanking isn't off the table completely." He hits my bare behind hard again. I clench my teeth. I didn't realize there was fine print on our agreement. "Mouth closed, legs open." He rubs the head of his erection against my entrance. "My sexy girl. Who do you belong to?"

"You, Kayne."

"That's right, baby, all mine. No one else's." He slips his cock inside me. Taking my body quickly, inch by combustible inch. In this position he's able to get deeper than he did last night. He fills and stretches me to my breaking point. "Kayne" I whimper, as he completely controls my body.

"How do I feel baby?"

"Big."

He laughs. "Any other description you want to use?" He pumps easily, my muscles tightening around him involuntarily. "I think I feel good. You're squeezing the shit out of me." He digs his fingers into my hips as he starts to move faster.

"Fuck you're so wet, so tight." I'm completely at Kayne's mercy, bent over with my black lacy panties around my thighs, my legs spread wide and my collar chained to my ankles. He tied me up like he owns me, because he does.

He relentlessly slides in and out, hitting my core in the same spot over and over. My orgasm burning brightly within me. "Kayne," I moan insufferably as our hips clash together.

"Ask permission." He slams into me ruthlessly. "Ask me if you can come."

Desperate for the release, I do. "Please, can I come!?"

"I own you, Ellie; don't forget that."

"Yes, Kayne," I answer willingly, trying to keep my orgasm from ripping me to shreds.

"Come, baby. Right fucking now."

And I do. As soon as permission is granted I let go, becoming nothing but sensation, and Kayne's living, breathing sex toy. My climax nearly buckles my knees. But Kayne's tight grip keeps me upright. I suck in air greedily as he pounds away at me, finally finding his own release. He pulls out and ejaculates on my ass, moaning and groaning as he spurts hot come all over my backside. My legs are screaming, my pussy is throbbing, and I'm pretty sure Kayne left fingerprints on my hips.

"Fuck, you're amazing," he sighs, the physical gratification evident in his voice. I guess I should feel flattered, but all I feel like is a dolled-up pretzel, twisted for his pleasure.

After a minute, I feel him wipe himself off me with the cloth napkin from dinner.

How chivalrous.

He then walks around and drops to his knees right in front of me, breathing hard. He lifts my chin with one finger, the chains restricting how far I can look up.

"You're fucking incredible." He's just full of compliments tonight. "I'm going to keep you forever." He kisses me chastely. The word forever rocks my existence. I almost burst into tears. Then he unlocks the chains around my ankles. "Go clean up." I stand up straight, my muscles in agony. I walk into the bathroom and wipe away the arousal dripping down my leg. That's when I catch a glimpse of myself in the mirror. My face is red, my hair is a mess, and both chains are still dangling from my collar. I don't know what to make of myself. Only one word fits. Whore. Kayne's whore.

"Ellie," Kayne summons me.

Fuck.

I clean up quickly then hurry back into the bedroom and stand in front of him.

"Go to bed," he orders. I crawl onto the mattress. Kayne's fully dressed and jingling a set of keys in his hand. The keys that can liberate me.

"How do you feel?" he asks as I kneel in front of him.

"Tired."

"That was only the beginning."

I inhale a steadying breath. "Beginning of what?"

"Your new life." He removes one of the chains from my collar, and then shackles the remaining one back to the headboard. A puppy played with then put back on her leash. He yanks me toward him and kisses me brutally on the mouth. My lips swell he sucks so hard. "Fucking all mine. Stay kneeling until I leave."

I place my hands on my thighs and drop my head. "Such a good girl." He runs his thumb under my jaw. I grind my teeth. I despise that fucking patronizing tone. Kayne silently exits the room. Once I hear the door click, I collapse onto the comforter an exhausted, misused mess.

And weep.

SUNLIGHT FLOODS THE ROOM. I squint as my eyes adjust to the brightness. This time of the morning, when it's quiet and I'm alone, I pretend my prison is a fairy-tale dream. The room is beautiful, open, and airy. The furniture modern but still feminine and the large white rug blanketing the hardwood floor brings a sense of warmth. A princess residing in her castle in the sky. Then I move and my fairy-tale dream turns into a nightmarish reality. I remember I'm trapped, like Rapunzel, chained to the bed. My energy is drained, my limbs hurt, and I feel empty.

And everything that happened last night is going to happen all over again. And again, and again.

I am owned. A pleasure kitten to be touched and prodded and fucked as my owner sees fit. He demonstrated his ownership last night when he chained my collar to my ankles and had his demonic way with me, bent over and helpless. I wish I could get up on my own accord and move around the room. But I'm at the mercy of others, always at the mercy of others in this house. I have a ridiculous fear that one day Jett won't show up and I'll be trapped on this bed forever. My fears are put to rest when the door clicks and Jett appears with breakfast.

"I could have been Kayne," he reminds me. I didn't shoot to my knees when the door opened.

"My legs hurt." And I don't care to obey at the moment.

"That doesn't matter. If he wants you kneeling when he walks into the room, you kneel. Don't cross him. He doesn't like to hurt you."

"Could have fooled me," I say bitterly, rubbing my ass. I still have red marks from when he whipped me.

"Cranky this morning. Last night wasn't satisfying?"

Physically yes. Mentally, no.

This whole situation is utterly fucked-up. No one deserves to live like this. At the mercy of others. Beaten if they don't obey. Treated like an object, a pet, a ... *slave*. I used the word. It's sickening. I can't believe it's become my life.

"I hate him sometimes," I confess, as Jett removes my collar.

"That's fine, just tell me, not him. Release your aggression when you fuck. It's one of the few outlets you have."

I sigh. Sure, sex is a great stress reducer and anxiety reliever. And sex with Kayne can have your blood pressure skyrocketing one minute, and taking a nosedive the next. That's how physically demanding he is. But emotionally? It means nothing. It's empty. I'm empty. When I used to fantasize about Kayne Roberts, his mischievous personality and charismatic smile were always center stage. He was nothing like the tyrant who keeps me captive. Whenever he came into Expo, his demeanor was always professional, but every now and again I would catch a twinkle in his eye or a roguish smirk. I always suspected under that tailored suit was a man with a secret life — someone extreme who liked BASE jumping or race car driving. Never did I surmise his private life entailed an upscale prostitution ring and client list. Or kidnapping and sexual slavery in the first degree.

"Take a shower. Then we're going to do some yoga," Jett says.

"Are you serious?"

"Deadly. Kayne complained you're not limber enough."

"What? Does he tell you what we do in here?" I flush crimson.

"Not graphic details, but I know some things. It's not much different than when we talk."

I think I'm going to die. "It's completely different!"

"How so?" Jett questions.

"It just is!" I spring off the bed and retreat to the bathroom. It's one thing for me to talk about Kayne with Jett, it's a whole other thing for Kayne and Jett to talk about me! Images of my panties around my thighs, my collar chained to my ankles, and a gloating Kayne makes me turn beet red. I can feel the heat actually scorching my skin. I wish there was a door to the bathroom, I'd lock myself in.

I take a quick shower, eat some breakfast, and then am further tortured with downward dog and flying crane. I would never admit this out loud, but I secretly enjoy spending the day with Jett, even if I am naked and mortified half the time. He's funny, easy to be around, and always tries to cheer me up. On some jacked-up level I see him as a friend.

I take another shower — because really what else do I have to do? A nice long hot one that helps ease the tension in my muscles. As I wash my hair I wonder ruefully what compromising position Kayne will put me in tonight. I half dread it, half crave it. Two nights together and my body is already calling out to his.

I dry off, pull my damp hair up into a bun, and walk into my room fully expecting to find clothes laid out for me. Alright, really just a new pair of underwear. But Jett just hooks my collar back on and leads me to the bed.

"Hang out, sweet thing," he says as the padlock clicks.

"Like I have anywhere else to go," I answer snidely, pulling at the chain.

Jett just snickers at me and taps me on the nose. "See you in the morning."

Then he takes his leave, and I am once again a puppy left waiting to be played with. Night has fallen and moonlight is shining brightly through the large wagon wheel window. My owner is late.

When I hear the door click, I pop onto my knees. Kayne's footsteps command the room. "How's my kitten?" He makes quick work of unlocking my leash from the bed.

"A downward dog expert," I reply flatly.

Kayne pauses. "Excuse me?"

"Jett made me to do yoga today."

Kayne's lip twitches. "Did he?"

"Yes, Kayne."

"Good girl." He rubs me under my jaw. He unhooks the chain from the front loop and re-clasps it to the one on the back of my collar. Red flags fly up.

"Go kneel on the floor. Make sure you face the TV." I scramble off the bed and into the middle of the room. I fall to my knees, look down, and rest my hands on my thighs. I'm breathing heavily, and he hasn't even touched me yet. I hear him shed his clothes then click on the television. The familiar sounds of sex fill the room. Only one thing plays on that flat screen—porn.

"Fours, Ellie." I feel him yank on the chain. I lean forward on my hands and knees as Kayne straddles me, the leash pulled so tight in his hand that the collar is forcing me to look up. On the television, two people are heavily engaged in intercourse. A man and a woman going at it on a white leather couch. The camera is at the perfect angle displaying every thrust of the man's large cock into the woman's bare pink pussy. My heartbeat quickens and my core throbs the longer I'm subjected to the erotic display. I've never watched porn before and its effects are startling.

"I hear you breathing, kitten. Like what you see?" Kayne asks lewdly.

I stay silent. I don't want to answer. I don't want to say yes. I don't even know if yes is the right answer. All I know is my body is responding indecently to the visual stimulation.

"Kitten?" Kayne yanks my chain, provoking a response.

"Yes, Kayne." I can barely expel the words.

"Good, kitten," he replies smugly.

I don't know how long we watch, but it's well into the night. Couple after couple partaking in explicit, untamed sex. Kayne just stands over me, holding my leash as my arousal winds tighter and tighter around me.

I'm close to begging when he finally moves, kneeling behind me. I rock lightly, as he massages my backside with a taut grip on my leash. He runs his finger from the top of my ass along my slit and tickles my clit. I'm so over-stimulated, his touch feels like pins and needles. I pant like the pet I am.

"Need me, baby?" He inserts one finger into me and my body electrifies.

"Yes, Kayne." I don't even recognize my own voice.

"Let's see how much." He withdraws, then rolls my clit between his fingers; I nearly convulse. He quickly pulls away.

"Not yet, kitten, not even close." I don't know what he's talking about, but the tone of his voice sends an ominous shiver down my spine.

Kayne grabs my hip with one hand, clamping down as hard as he can. With the other he keeps a tight grip on my leash, the collar straining against my neck.

"Don't take your eyes off that screen." He pumps the head of his cock against my entrance but never fully penetrates me. I'm dying, I need him so bad it feels like I'm going to tear in two. He just rocks lightly, slipping only a quarter of his erection inside me. I try to move my hips to gain more of him, but he holds me steady with his hand and the firm grip he has on my leash, pulling harder every time I move, the collar constricting me.

"Kayne, please." His shallow pumps do nothing but crank my arousal with no offer of relief in sight.

"When I say you're ready." He withdraws completely, just as the woman on the screen climaxes, the man pounding into her relentlessly as he extracts every drop of her desire. I'm about ready to combust.

Then Kayne slams into me without any warning. "Oh!" I cry out, as the collar stops me from jutting forward. The tip of his cock hitting me exactly where I need, in the deepest, most tender part of my body. He thrusts again and again, sending me soaring.

"Kayne, please may I come!" I cry out as my orgasm breaks loose.

"No," he denies me.

"Kayne, please!" I beg as he picks up his rhythm, as if trying to drive me mad.

"I have to come!"

"Don't you dare." He slams so deep inside me that I implode, losing all control.

I feel him everywhere, through every cell and every synapse in my body. The extreme release is heaven sent. Then, right in the middle of my highest peak, he pulls out, deflating the rigorous orgasm that threatened to destroy me.

"No, why!" I collapse, nearly crying.

"Because I didn't give you permission." He yanks on the chain. I want to murder him. I've never felt so high then crash so low in my entire life.

"Lie down," he growls. I drop to my side, my body quivering from the starved arousal still snaking its way through my system. "Bad girl." He spanks me hard. The sensations inside me rattle. He pushes me onto my stomach while the sounds of exaggerated sex still fill the room. His breathing increases from behind me, and I immediately recognize the sound. He's jerking off. A few hellish moments later, he comes on my ass. I feel the spurts and hear his grunts all at the same time. I'm livid as my core throbs, demanding what he just afforded himself.

"Stay." His voice is hard and for some reason it makes me feel ashamed. Why?

"Go to bed," he instructs after he wipes himself off of me. I lift myself up off the floor.

"I don't remember granting you permission to stand," he snaps. He's being so mean!

I glance at him over my shoulder before I sink back down onto all fours. He eyes my every move with a cold expression. I crawl across the room toward the bed. Then climb on it once I reach it. If I had a tail, it'd be between my legs. I kneel on the mattress as Kayne stalks into the table of torture room. My anxiety spikes. God only knows what he's getting out of there. He returns with a pair of handcuffs.

"Lie down."

I lie on my back.

"Put your hands over your head."

I put my hands up, never taking my eyes off him. He cuffs me to the vining iron. "So you can't touch yourself," he informs me.

My eyes water. Cruel bastard. He repositions my leash after that, locking it to the front of my collar then securing it back to the headboard.

Shackled doesn't even begin to describe me.

Kayne gets dressed, shoving his legs into his pants and jerking his brown pinstripe button up over his head.

He then comes to stand over me. "This is a lesson, kitten. I control your pleasure." He circles the tip of his finger around my inflamed clit. I push my hips off the bed and moan insufferably. I need to come so bad, my head is pounding and my body is shaking.

"Kayne, please," I beseech one last time.

"Sorry, Ellie, you have to learn. Would you rather I whip you instead?"

"No." I shake my head vigorously. He did this on purpose just to torment me. Punishment in one form or another.

He leaves me with my suffering and the porn still playing on the TV.

AYNE

I SIT IN THE SHADOWS of my office, monitoring the security feed.

The house is quiet this time of night. Most everyone is asleep, except for Ellie. My frisky little kitten. She's squirming uncomfortably handcuffed to her bed. I know she's achy and miserable, just as she should be. Orgasm control, or denial in this case, is a fundamental technique used to bond dominant and submissive. Or with us, Master and slave. It creates intense arousal and physiological need. Need only I can fulfill.

It's close to sunrise when I catch Spice leaving Javier's room on one of the monitors. She's crying, naked, and has whip marks all over her back. They look above and beyond the normal sexual role play. Son of a bitch is at it again. I stand, about to go to her, when Jett steps onto the feed. I swear, if I didn't know any better, he was waiting outside that door all night. I watch as he gently puts his arm around her and she melts against him, sobbing as they walk off the screen. He has a way with women I will never understand. Each and every one in this house adores him. Me, they respect. But him? It's just different.

I catch Ellie jerking and rubbing her thighs together on screen. She's in agony.

So much for not becoming the one thing I'm fighting against. I may not pour hot wax all over her body, or whip or beat her until she's bleeding, but I am torturing her in my own way.

I run my hands through my hair and groan. Time to go see my kitten. I love what I'm doing to her and I hate it. I know it's wrong even when it feels so right, so good, and is so irresistible.

The sounds of explosive sex and Ellie's heavy breathing circle the darkness as I sneak into her room. The dawn hasn't quite peaked over the horizon, so the only light present is the glare from the television. It doesn't offer much illumination considering the large expanse of the room.

"Please, please, please," Ellie begs once she sees me. "I'll control it. I'll learn to control it."

"Shhh." I pet her head, then shrug off my clothes. It never fails, one look at Ellie chained up wearing my collar, and my arousal roars to life. I don't even need to touch her. I grab the key to the handcuffs off the nightstand and crawl onto the bed, situating myself right between Ellie's welcoming knees. "Don't move," I instruct as I release her hands. She grabs onto the white iron as I remove the handcuffs. "Need me, baby?" I ask while she whimpers feebly.

"Yes," she responds with choppy breaths.

"Say it. Say you need me, Ellie." I hoist her hips up.

"Kayne, I need you." As soon as the sentence leaves her lips I drive my cock into her as deep as it can go.

"Ahh!" Her body twists with ecstasy as she grips the iron, her muscles clamping down around me like a metal trap.

"Shit," I grind out, but don't move as I succumb to the need of her body. Ellie is squirming desperately, but I steady her with a firm hold on her waist. "I want you to touch yourself."

Ellie stills, staring at me like I just told her to jump off a cliff without a parachute.

"Touch myself?"

"Come on, kitten." I encourage her with a tiny thrust. The way she moans you'd think I was fucking her mercilessly. All in good time.

"I've never done that before," she squeaks out.

"Really? Never?" I question her.

She shakes her head.

"Well, there's a first time for everything." I reach for her hand and bring it to my lips. I suck two of her fingers into my mouth, making sure to get them nice and wet, then place them over her swollen clit. Ellie tenses. "Come on, baby, touch yourself. It will turn me on," I encourage her.

"You're already turned on." She sucks in a deep breath. I pinch her ass cheek.

"Oh!"

"Remember who you're talking to, kitten."

"Yes, Kayne."

"Good girl. Now, I want to watch you make yourself come." I rock my hips and Ellie nearly fragments.

It takes several long seconds, but she finally starts to massage herself. Her movements are vapid at first, but after a few minutes, she closes her eyes and begins to explore herself with some enthusiasm. I watch and feel every gesture as her fingers slide easily between her wet folds and around her sensitive clit. She quickly finds a rhythm she likes and her breathing takes off, as does mine. Fuck, she feels amazing. I hold on to Ellie tightly, making sure to subdue her jerky hip movements so that all her pleasure is contained between her legs. She's so close, panting hard while rubbing herself into an orgasm.

"Please may I come?" she nearly cries, her face tight with sexual tension.

"Yes, come, now." I'm close to combusting myself. My heart rate spikes, as she crunches up and makes herself come all over my cock. So fucking good. As soon as Ellie drops down on to the bed, I cover her with my body. She's somewhere far away as she wraps her arms around my neck and her legs around my waist. The sounds of over-the-top sex still constantly streaming from the TV. I begin to rock, pulling all the way out then driving as deep as I can back in. She moans emphatically as I work both our bodies.

Ellie feels like nothing else in this world. Soft, wet, warm, and all fucking mine. I don't think I'll ever get enough.

"Fuck, Ellie, your pussy is so sweet." I thrust my hips as my climax intensifies, Ellie's muscles squeezing all the blood to the head of my erection, making me crazy.

"Open those fucking legs," I nearly snarl. Ellie immediately drops her knees and spreads her thighs. I fasten my arm underneath her back as I piston into her.

I lose all control being with Ellie, feeling her bare skin flush against mine, and her soaking wet pussy engulfing every inch of my rock hard cock. The sensations skyrocket my body and my mind.

It consumes me, changes me.

"Kayne!" She cries my name, and I know just what she needs. The exact same thing I do. To come.

"Ellie, let go. Let go and come with me."

She flutters her eyes open and for a split second just stares. The look is invasive. I feel it permeate all the way to my soul. My rhythm dies down, and I slide in and out painstakingly slow.

"*Ohhhh ...*" Ellie closes her eyes, bows her body, snaps her head back, and comes. Every single inch of me hums as she saturates me with her arousal, and for the first time in my life the euphoric look on a woman's face spurs me to break. I still at the tail end of Ellie's orgasm, my whole existence screeching to a grinding halt as I spill inside her. My entire body is ablaze and Ellie is the cause of the inferno. I drop down on top of her once the ensnaring sensations let go and wrap her in my arms. *What the fuck is happening to me?* She feels so perfect, so right, like she really is meant solely for me. An unnamed emotion suddenly surges within me and I grab her by the collar.

"I want you to understand something." She looks up at me with a penetrating stare. "Every morsel of food you eat, every breath of air you take is because of me. Because I allow it." Her eyes widen. "You live because of me. You live *for* me. Remember that when you fall asleep with my come inside you."

Ellie focuses on me silently. A mountain of power shifting between us.

"Yes, Kayne," she succumbs, and suddenly so do I. I kiss her forehead, her eyes, her cheeks, and her lips for a few elongated minutes, lulling her to relax. She inhales a deep breath with her eyes closed on the brink of falling asleep. I, on the other hand, feel like I can run a marathon. The beast is pacing inside me, like a caged animal demanding to be set free. Once never seems to be enough when it comes to Ellie. I want her all night and every second the shrouded darkness can afford us. I'm wildly tempted to fuck her again, but I don't. Instead, I withdraw from her gingerly just before she dozes off. She winces then frowns, tightening her arms. She's so close to passing out that I wonder if she even realizes she did it. On some absurd level I convince myself she really wants me to stay. *Keep dreaming dickhead.*

I lie wrapped in Ellie's arms a little longer than I should. For the first time in my life, I want to stay tangled in a woman's embrace. In Ellie's embrace. What would it be like to fall asleep next to her? To wake up and have her be there instead of an empty side of the bed. It's such a dangerous curiosity on all accounts, but compulsory all on its own. It spurs me to remove Ellie's arms from my neck and climb off the mattress. I can't get close. I *shouldn't* get close.

I turn off the television then dress quietly; all the while watching my kitten sleep. *What is she doing to me?* She's affecting me in ways I don't understand. Burrowing herself deep within a part of me that I never knew existed.

I grab the door handle with one last glance at Ellie's sleeping form; naked and vulnerable, yet passionate and strong. Everything she is, is everything I'll never be.

With all the will I have, I open the door to leave and run right smack into Jett. It's early morning now, and I know he's come to check on her. He looks at me with questioning eyes as he tries to slip past me into her room.

"Let her sleep," I say authoritatively as I step into the hallway, closing the door behind me. It clicks, locking her inside.

"Is she okay?" Jett asks concerned.

"She's fine." *I think.* Jett gazes at me impassively. I know he wants to check on her. I also know she needs her rest. It's been a long night for everyone.

"How's Spice?" I ask.

Jett responds with a pissed off expression. "She's been better."

"Shit."

"Yeah." He folds his him arms crossly. This living situation sucks for all of us.

I sigh as I settle myself against Ellie's thick wooden door.

"Going to stand there all day?" Jett asks irritably.

I shrug. "Maybe."

Probably.

I'm just not ready to leave her yet.

ELLIE

I'VE TAKEN UP READING, BECAUSE really what else do I have to do when Jett isn't stretching me into next week with yoga or Kayne isn't tying me up and fucking me into oblivion. I'm particularly intrigued — but mostly disturbed — by my current title. Almost all of the dirty adult books on the shelf are mindless sex stories. If you need to get in the mood you read one of those, but this one is different. It's about a girl who was abducted at a young age and sold into sexual slavery to numerous buyers. To say it doesn't strike a chord would be lying. The thought of Kayne selling me never occurred to me until this very moment. It's a terrifying realization. I'm an object, not a person. My rights and identity have been stripped away and my sole purpose for living is to serve another. I haven't forgotten Kayne's assertion *You live because of me. You live for me.* A chill runs down my spine. I want to take the book and chuck it across the room, but I keep my head and continue reading, morbidly engrossed in this girl's horrific story of rape, torture, and forced servitude. She addresses all of her owners as Master. It's creepy. I thank God for small favors that Kayne doesn't make do that.

I read until Jett comes back into the room, close to dusk.

"Evening, sweet thing."

"Hi." I curl my knees up to my chest on the mattress. Not because I'm embarrassed of being naked, but because of the conflicting feelings running rampant inside of me. My mind knows this is all wrong, but my body doesn't care. It's ready for its fix.

Jett takes my book and places it back on the shelf then returns to the bed. He hooks one end of the listless chain back onto my collar and then commands me to drop.

I look at him strangely before I crawl into the position. Completely naked. This is new.

"Good girl." Jett uncoils my leash out from under me.

"No panties?" I ask, my voice elevating.

"Not tonight, Kayne requested you completely naked. And just like this."

I'm on my stomach with my knees pulled up to my chest and my hands over my head. It looks like I'm worshipping a shrine. It reminds me of my first obedience lesson. I shudder.

"When will he be here?" I ask with my face against the sheet.

"I don't know, Ellie, but stay like that until he comes in." I nod slightly.

"See you in the morning, sweet thing."

Jett leaves and it's just me and my thoughts in a compromising position. I'm not alone long. I hear the door click and immediately the room is engulfed with Kayne's dominant presence. My insides quiver.

"Hey, beautiful." He caresses my back and kisses my shoulder. "How was your day?"

"Jett made me do more yoga." I speak into the mattress.

"Good. Limbering you up for me." He spanks me lightly. I tense.

"Apparently."

"I want you as flexible as possible so I can bend you whichever way I want." He drops a soft kiss on the ass cheek he just smacked. In this position, I am overly exposed.

"You look to fucking die for like this."

He massages me in the same place he kissed me. "Ellie, I want to warn you up front. Tonight is going to be intense." He rubs his already erect cock against me.

"How intense?" I can barely utter the words. I'm already sick with anxiety and excited with arousal. I'm turning into a fucking whack job.

"You're not going to be able to walk tomorrow."

"What?" I go to lift my head but Kayne grabs my chain Jett left dangling between my legs, he never secured me to the headboard. My face is pressed firmly to the mattress as Kayne subdues me tight.

"You're mine, Ellie," he reminds me. "I can do to you as I please." I squeeze my eyes shut and swallow the thick fear threatening to choke me. He's going to hurt me.

He yanks my chain. "How do you reply?"

"Yes, Kayne," I say hoarsely.

"Yes, Kayne, please fuck me."

I repeat, "Yes, Kayne, please fuck me." Tears threaten, but I hold them back. I need to be strong, even if I am scared out of my mind.

"Good girl."

I want to slap him. I hope one day I get the chance.

Kayne drops something heavy onto the bed next to me; it bounces slightly on the mattress.

"Bring your hands down Ellie, put them by your sides."

I immediately do what he says. Swiftly, he takes each of my wrists and clamps them down, as something cold and metal runs across the back of my legs.

"Kayne?" I say shaky.

"Shhh." Then he takes my chain and secures it to the rod so I'm tied up tightly. I can't lift my head because of the chain and I can't move my legs or arms because of the cuffs and the bar. I'm scared shitless.

"Relax, Ellie." Kayne starts rubbing my ass that's now sticking high in the air. "You're going to need to trust me. And you're going to need to keep your body loose. The more you squirm and wriggle, the more uncomfortable you'll become."

More uncomfortable? Is that possible?

I can't see Kayne behind me. So I have to rely on my other senses. I feel him brush against me as he takes off his shirt and I hear his zipper lower as he removes his pants. I suddenly feel his tongue against my pussy. I jump trying to snap my head up, but the chain restricts me, acting like a pulley, forcing my knees forward and jutting my ass further into the air. "Told you to hold still."

Kayne begins licking me relentlessly, from the tip of my behind to the bottom of my clit. I'm soaking wet and dizzy with desire within a few short minutes. Then he takes his hands and spreads my ass cheeks as far as they can go, sliding his tongue into my little puckered hole. I shake uncontrollably.

I want to move.

I want more.

I want less.

I want the ache he's commanding quelled. *Now!*

"I'm going to fuck you here, Ellie."

I feel his warm breath brush against me. "I'm going to stretch you with my fingers then bury myself inside you. And that's where I plan to stay. All night." I tremble at his words, terrified of the pain. Recalling how he said I won't be able to walk tomorrow.

"Kayne, please be gentle," I beg in my shackles.

"I won't hurt you, baby. Unless you disobey me, or ask for it."

Like hell I would ever do that.

When Kayne feels he's lubricated me enough, he starts to inch his thumb inside me. The initial intrusion hurts and is so intense, but once he's fully inside, the pain starts to taper.

"Fuck, you're so tight. I can't wait to be inside you." He withdraws his thumb and replaces it with one of his fingers. I'm dying. It hurts, and it doesn't. I like it, and I don't. My body is caught in a feverous mix of pleasure and pain, and it's only the beginning. I don't know if I'm going to survive this night. Just as Kayne slips another finger into me and begins scissoring me open, there's a pounding on the door.

"Kayne!" Jett calls through the wood.

"Jett, the fucking house better be on fire," he growls, continuing his assault.

"There's a situation that needs your immediate attention."

"What kind of situation?" He halts his ministrations but doesn't withdraw his fingers. My body is strung so tight, I could snap at any second.

"A delicate one," Jett relays, and that seems to get Kayne's full attention.

"Motherfucker," he grinds out. "Give me a sec," he barks.

"Hurry up." Jett fumes through the door.

Kayne leans over my subdued face. "I'm sorry, baby, we're going to have to put this on hold for a few minutes." He kisses my cheek, withdraws his fingers then disappears. My body deflates, as I'm left helpless on the bed.

I hear metal sliding across tracks as drawers are opened and closed. My adrenaline spikes. Then I feel Kayne standing behind me once again.

"I really wanted to prime you myself, but this will have to do in my absence. Open." He shoves something hard and metal into my mouth. I know exactly what it is. It's the exact same object he used after he whipped me, except this one is much larger; longer and fatter. My stomach twists. "Ellie, relax." He yanks on the chain attached to the plug and I release it. He then works the extra-large plug into my ass. No inching or easing, just one fluid motion. I groan loudly as it fills me completely. So much more than his fingers did. I'm panting wildly by the time he's through. It fucking hurts. Is this what it's going to feel like when he fucks me? Kayne then tells me to open again. He inserts something hard and rubbery into my mouth. "Suck."

I wrap my lips around the object and do as I'm told. Good little pleasure kitten. He removes it when he's satisfied, then slowly slides it into my pussy. Holy fuck, if I thought I was full before, I'm overflowing now. Then I hear a click and it starts to vibrate gently. The pulse reaches all the way into my womb. My breathing goes from panting to gasping in a nanosecond. He can't leave me like this!?

"You'll be good and ready for me when I get back." Kayne smacks my ass and a simultaneous bolt of pleasure and pain shoots through me. I moan, incapacitated, as the butt plug and vibrator wage war on my body, pushing me to the edge and dangling me there. An orgasm is brewing, but coming nowhere close to where I need to find release. Why did he do this? Why is he torturing me?!

AYNE

I DRESS QUICKLY WITH MY cock as hard as a stone slab and Ellie squirming uncomfortably on the bed.

Whatever the fuck is going on, it better be a red level terror alert. I open the door to find Jett quivering.

"What the fuck?" I ask.

"Just follow me." He hauls ass down the hall. I follow with the same quickness as we fly down one flight of stairs to the second floor and beeline it straight for Javier's room. Crap, this definitely isn't good. Once inside, I see the situation. Spice is flailing all over Javier's bed. She holding her arm, tears pouring down her face.

"That motherfucker dislocated her shoulder," Jett explodes. "I need help popping it back into place."

Son-Of-A-Bitch.

Spice whimpers as Jett and I both climb onto the bed without delay. Me, on Spice's injured side, Jett by her head. She looks up at me in distress. "Okay, baby, we're going to fix it." I talk to her serenely. The last thing I want is her feeling more tension. There's enough radiating off Jett to light up the whole house. "Spice, take a deep breath." I glance up at Jett, his stare is removed, and his face flushed. "Stay with me, brother."

"I'm here," he says, eerily composed. Eerily composed Jett is never a good sign.

"Kayne, please," Spice begs. Her voice is so small. Usually the sound of a woman begging sends me into a state of sexual frenzy. At the moment, it's not eliciting anything sexual from me at all. Unless you count homicidal thoughts as sexually exciting.

"Okay, on the count of three I'm going to pop it back in." I stare into her eyes. The dark green ones that look exactly like Ellie's. My chest aches. This could have easily been her. This and so much worse. I fight to keep my head and concentrate on helping the suffering brunette. "One." I stand up and pull her arm over the edge of the bed. Spice screams. I wait a few seconds for her muscles to relax. I glance at Jett and he nods. "Two." I pull, slow and steady, catching her off guard. She screams again as I roll her arm until I hear her shoulder pop back into place.

As soon as I'm finished, she passes out; I conclude half from stress, half from the pain. Shit. Poor thing. She's been put through the damn wringer ever since Javier stepped foot in this house. I blame myself. Maybe I shouldn't, maybe there's no reason, but nevertheless I do.

"It's okay now, you're okay." Jett kisses her head and caresses her hair. It's a paternal reaction.

"Where is he?" I ask Jett.

"Gone," he replies, not even looking at me. I know he won't drag his attention away from Spice.

"Gone where?" I ask.

"Who cares?" he boils.

"I do, and you better too."

"I heard him say something about wanting a *cerveza*."

"Great, at the local bar, just what we need. A drunk, belligerent abusive Mexican." I run my hands down my face.

Jett lifts Spice off the bed. "I'm taking her to my room. She needs ice. And I'm putting all the other girls on lockdown for the night."

I nod in agreement. "Is there anyone here?"

"One room is occupied. As soon as Spice is comfortable they're getting kicked the fuck out."

"That should be good for business," I comment back handedly.

Jett shoots me a dangerous look.

"I need to get back to Ellie," I pop off, the mere mention of her name should chill him out.

"Fine, go." Jett walks toward the door. I pull on his arm.

"Don't do anything stupid."

He glances down at my hand and then back up at my face. He curls his lip in warning, his aqua eyes ice cold. "If you can handle it, I can handle it."

I know exactly what he means. If I didn't kill Javier after what he did to Ellie, Jett won't kill him for what he did to Spice.

As Jett and I walk the expansive hall in opposite directions, I'm struck with a lifetime's worth of jarring memories. *My lifetime.* It all comes back, the isolation, the fear, and inability to trust. *You're nothing but a paycheck you little fuck. Slam!*

For as long as I can remember, abuse has always been at the forefront of my life. Whether direct or indirect, it affects you all the same.

I start to breathe heavily as the memories swarm like angry bees. I've spent years trying to suppress the hostility, and sometimes uncontrollable rage, if for nothing more than the simplicity of sleeping at night. But with Ellie and Spice and the situation at hand, my past resurfaces like an underwater eruption.

By the time I reach Ellie's door, I'm wound so tight I don't know what I'm capable of.

$\mathcal{E}$LLIE

TEARS START TO WELL IN my eyes long before Kayne returns. The sensations are way too much. I need to move, to satisfy the ache eating away at my insides. If I shift even a fraction of an inch, I feel it everywhere. Between my legs, up my ass, along my spine. I mewl insufferably, needing relief. The tears spill, wetting my face, and all I can do is let them fall. Kayne is the only one who can release me from this prison.

Just when I think my heart is going to explode from the unrelenting stress, Kayne returns.

"Please, please," I beg. "Please let me come. I can't take anymore."

He doesn't say a word, but I can feel the tension rippling off of his body. It scares the living shit out of me.

"You want to come?" His voice is menacing, and I know I'm in for something brutal. He yanks the vibrator out and I nearly fall apart. A second later he slams into me with such force I scream and slide forward on the bed. "Stay fucking still." He pulls me back and begins to pound into me. In a split second, I come apart. Freefalling into oblivion. Then, right in the middle of my orgasm, he ruthlessly rips out the butt plug, sending another crippling wave of ecstasy crashing through my body. I cry uncontrollably, completely destroyed, drained of all energy as I gasp for air on the bed. I'm still seeing stars when he finally comes. He grits his teeth as he stabs into my hips with his fingers and into my pussy with his cock.

Heaven help me.

When it's finally over, I feel like I'm going to break apart. The man can be so vicious.

I start to nod off when Kayne pokes me with his still hard erection. "Sorry, Ellie." He almost sounds remorseful. "I'm not done with you yet." His voice is calmer now. But still dark and thick with desire. "I told you I was going to fuck you here." He pushes the head of his cock against my sore rose bud. "And that's exactly what I intend to do." How is he still hard? I brace myself for the bite. Then feel something cold and slippery against my skin.

"What's that?" I ask, my voice muffled against the mattress.

"Lubrication." He smears it all over me, and then pushes against my entrance again. I groan as he fights his way in inch by agonizing inch, until he's buried deep inside.

Holy fuck! He's triple the size of the industrial butt plug.

"I knew you were going to feel this way," he expels euphorically, completely still. "I used to jerk off to this exact image. Do you know that? After I would leave Mark's office, I would fantasize about what it would be like to tie you down and make you scream." Kayne starts to move in and out in small, controlled thrusts. I feel him everywhere, governing my entire existence. He's infiltrating my body, compelling my mind, and contorting my soul.

Another gargantuan orgasm starts to bloom. My cheeks flush, my muscles clench, my neck strains, and my wrists hurt as he takes his movements from small and controlled to elongated and deep. Every thrust ripping me open, every withdrawal sewing me closed. "All night. I'm going to fuck you like this all night." And there's not a damn thing I can do about it. I'm tied up, at his mercy.

"You're mine, Ellie, and I want to hear you scream."

And I do, over and over, orgasm after orgasm, until our fluids are soaking the bed, my voice is gone, and my body is limp.

ELLIE?" JETT SHAKES ME LIGHTLY. "Ellie, wake up."

I crack open my eyes but don't move my body. It feels like I've been in a car accident. I hurt all over. I groan. Kayne said I wasn't going to be able to walk today. He wasn't kidding.

"Come on, love, it's late. You need to get up."

"How late?" My eyes flutter to the window.

"Five in the evening. You've been asleep all day. Kayne put a punishing on you last night, huh?"

That is definitely one way to put it.

Kayne didn't leave my room until nearly dawn. When he was finished with me, he discarded me like nothing more than an overused rag doll. He chained me back to the headboard, kissed me on the lips and left silently. That was it. I was his sex toy and he used me as such. An object to play with and then toss back on the shelf. Or in my case, the bed. It fucking hurts. I feel empty and used. This life is hard, nothing like the one I dreamed of having.

"Kayne will want to see you soon. Get up."

"I don't think I can walk." My voice is small and hapless.

"Come on, I'll help you." Jett unlocks me and lifts me into his arms. The ache in my back and between my legs is excruciating. I moan miserably.

He carries me into the bathroom. "How about a hot bath?"

I nod.

"Do you think you can stand?"

I nod again. I'm not in a very talkative mood.

Jett places me on my feet and I wince, the contact with the floor vibrates all the way up my body. He turns on the faucet and squeezes some soap into the water. The now familiar scent of eucalyptus fills the room. Jett turns to me once the enormous soaking tub is halfway filled. As soon as he reaches out to me, I crack. I don't even know where it comes from. The emotion wasn't there a second ago, but now tears are falling like an unstoppable rainstorm from my eyes.

"Ellie!?" Jett wraps me in his arms and the embrace hurts. "Are you in that much pain?"

"Yes. No. I don't know. It's just … how am I supposed to survive like this? I feel empty. How am I supposed to live with no emotion? No love? As just someone's pet? To be taken off its leash and played with." I sob inconsolably. "I didn't work my ass off for four years so I could end up like this. As nothing. No one. I was supposed to start school in the fall. Travel. See everything my parents couldn't afford me. And now it's all gone. All my hopes, all my dreams."

"Oh, honey." Jett hugs me tighter and I whimper. "I know this isn't your ideal situation. But there are things going on you know nothing about. Trust Kayne."

"Trust him? He did this to me!"

"What? Gave you several nights of unbelievable pleasure? So you're in a little pain. It will subside."

"No, it's not that." I wipe my eyes. "He's isolated me. Emotionally exiled me."

Jett sighs, as if conflicted. "Get in the tub."

He helps me step in, and I sink into the cathartic hot water. Then Jett crouches beside me. "Let me tell you something about Kayne," he whispers. "When it comes to you, his emotions are more present than you think."

I skeptically look into Jett's aqua eyes. "Are you trying to tell me he cares about me?"

"In his own way. Not everything is always black and white. And some things need to be revealed in their own time."

"What does that mean?" I press.

"It means patience is a virtue and submission is your salvation."

I have no idea what he's talking about. Kayne won't always treat me like an object? That underneath he actually cares? It's hard to believe. He looks at me, treats me, and handles me like I'm nothing but a sexual vessel for his use and abuse. I shift in the tub and my muscles wail.

"How can anyone go that long? He never got soft. What did he do, take Viagra?" I grimace.

Jett whistles pseudo-innocently at my accusation.

I widen my eyes. "He took Viagra?! *Why?*"

Jett shrugs. "He can't get enough of you. You're the first woman I've ever seen him like this with."

"Animalistic?" I snap.

"Infatuated."

"Is that what you call it so you can sleep better at night?"

"Sweet thing, I sleep just fine." Jett kisses me on the head. "Enough talk. Just relax for a while. Okay?"

"Yes, Jett," I sneer submissively.

He rolls his eyes.

KAYNE

I WALK SILENTLY INTO ELLIE'S room and hear her crying. The sound shreds me apart. As her voice carries from the bathroom, I listen to her tell Jett everything she's feeling. She opens up to him, and I'm stung with jealousy. I want her to confide in me. Trust me. *I* own her. Not Jett.

I'm tempted to kick him out and join Ellie in the tub but decide against it. It's clear she needs some space. And some time alone.

When I came to check on her, I wasn't expecting to find her like this. Tears. I hate them and I love them. I know she has to be sore. I wasn't nice last night. I planned to fuck her for hours, but our little interruption sent me over the edge, and I ended up taking my frustrations out on her. It wasn't fair, I know that. But on some sick, sadistic level—it was the best sex of my life. If I'm honest, every time with Ellie is the best sex of my life.

Javier, that walking piece of shit, treating Spice like one of his fucking slaves. I have news for him. *No bueno.* His arrogance is festering under my skin. And someday soon I'm going to return all his little favors.

I lean on the wall outside Ellie's room and wait impatiently while Jett tends to her.

"She's upset," I say, startling him once he finally he exits.

"For fuck's sake, Kayne," he snaps. "Yes, she is. Why are you?"

"I don't like it when she's upset. I like it even less that she confides in you."

"Why do you have a problem with her confiding in me? She needs someone to talk to," he argues.

"She has me. *I* own her."

"How is she supposed to confide in someone who treats her like a whore on a leash?"

I growl. "You know that's not how I see her." Even though I love her on that leash.

"*She* doesn't know that. Treat her like the tin man and you get a steel heart."

"What the fuck does that mean, Riddler?"

Jett bristles. "You know, for a smart guy, you're a dumb dumb sometimes. You want her to confide in you, you want her to trust you. You want her to love you, then show her how you feel. Don't just stick your dick in her and walk out of the room."

I inwardly groan. "You know that's dangerous given the circumstances."

"Well, it's a choice you have to make. She's either your whore or your lover. She can't be both."

Why not?

I pinch the bridge of my nose. This is a sticky situation all the way around. I can't let anyone, even Ellie, know how deep my feelings go. But I don't want her to feel unloved. Or like she's slipping away. Especially from me.

"How should I handle this?" I exhale, banging the back of my head against the wall.

Jett smiles deviously, his aqua eyes gleaming.

"Give me two hours. You and Ellie are going on your first date."

LLIE

JETT REENTERS TO MY ROOM in a rush.

I watch confused as he unlocks my collar and ushers me off the bed. "What's going on?"

"You need to take a shower and get dressed," he says in a hurry, pushing me toward the bathroom.

"But I just spent all day in the tub." Or at least what was left of the day.

"I know." Jett flicks on the water then opens the linen closet and pulls out a bottle. "In you go." He hands me some new soap. "Wash quickly. Hair and everything. I'll be right back."

I do as I'm told. Enjoying the new scent of lemongrass filling the stall. By the time I'm done with the shower, Jett has the folding table opened up and an array of makeup spread out by the sink.

"What's going on?" I ask as he sits me down. I wince. I'm still so sore.

"I'm getting you ready."

"For what?"

"A date." He picks up the comb and a pair of scissors sitting next to me on the table.

"With who?"

"Kayne."

"What?" I look up at him as he begins to part my hair.

"Yup." There's a snip and a chunk of my hair falls to the floor.

"Jett!"

"Trust me, Ellie, I wouldn't let you look anything other than gorgeous."

I suck in a deep breath as he snips away, strands of hair falling all around me. When he's done, he blow dries my hair with the round brush he loves so much. The ends are now falling over my right eye. I try to tuck them behind my ear.

"Don't touch," he scolds playfully. Then he turns his attention to my face, using all the makeup he has spread out on the counter.

"Damn I'm good," he gloats as he lifts my chin and inspects his handiwork. There's a sudden knock at the door and I jump. "Relax, Ellie. That's just dinner." Jett rubs my arms reassuringly. "Stay here."

He leaves the bathroom to answer the door. From where I'm sitting, I can't see into the bedroom, but I can hear everything.

"Perfect, put it on the table," Jett instructs. I lean over to try and see who he's talking to but am only met by a wall.

I hear footsteps then, "Don't we even get to meet her?" a soft, young female voice asks. I freeze.

"Not tonight," Jett responds nicely, but in a hurry. "Now shoo."

There are giggles and then the door closes. Jett walks back into the bathroom with a large smile.

"Who was that?" I inquire, still perched uncomfortably on the table.

"Personnel." He winks. "Come on. Time to get dressed." He helps me stand up with care. I'm slow moving at the moment. The bath and the shower helped relax my back muscles, but my core and behind are still sensitive as hell. Every step reminds me of the brutality from last night.

On the bed are several articles of 'clothing,' sheer white panties, matching thigh highs, garters, and patent leather heels. Jett dresses me quickly, first slipping the satiny low-rise underwear on and then the garters, clipping the thigh highs in place. Finally, he helps me step into the stiletto heels I could use as a weapon, and refastens my collar. He stands back and admires me, but I can tell he thinks something's off. "Ah!" He snaps, and turns for the armoire. After rummaging around it for a few seconds, he returns to me. He holds up a long string of crystals and I look at them curiously. Jett just smirks as he attaches one end to the front loop of my collar, the other end he wraps around my waist and clasps it like a belt. "Body jewelry." He tugs lightly on the strand.

I look down at myself, I feel like I should be modeling for Frederick's of Hollywood.

"Jett?" I ask sadly. "Why are you wasting your time?"

"First, let's get something straight. I never waste my time. Second, sweet thing, I know there is more to you and Kayne than just a Master/slave relationship, and I think it's time we exploit it."

I glare at him cynically. "All I am is a pet to him."

"Do you really believe that?" he questions me.

"Has he given me a reason not to believe it?"

"Maybe that's what tonight is for." Jett raises his eyebrows.

I highly doubt it. I'm sure the minute Kayne tries to touch me, I'm going to erupt into tears. The mere thought of any kind of sexual interaction has me falling apart. And I know any protest will only lead to a punishment. My foreseeable future fucking sucks.

"Come on, kitten." Jett nudges me. "Get up on that bed and be your sexy little self. Once Kayne sees you, he'll be wrapped around your pinky finger in record time."

"You think it's going to be that easy, huh?" I ask as I crawl onto the mattress.

"I know it," Jett confirms as he fixes me to the headboard. "He's halfway there as it is."

Sure he is.

"Wanna know a secret?" He leans into my face. I nod. "You may not believe it, but you hold all the power."

I stare back at him like he's downright nuts.

Jett winks, and then coils the strand of crystals resting between my naked breasts around his index finger. "Kayne is going to love this."

"How do you know?" I inquire.

"Because I know what he likes. I know what all men like."

"A blow job?" I reply dryly.

"Yes, definitely that." Jett laughs. "And a woman who's all their own."

AYNE

TWO HOURS LATER I'VE CHANGED into a new button up shirt and dress pants, per the request of Jett. I have no idea what he has planned, and I have no idea how this night is going to turn out, but a large piece of me hopes well. I want so many things from Ellie that sometimes I wonder if I'm asking too much. Actually, I know I am because I do want her to be both. *My lover, and my pet.*

I arrive back at Ellie's door precisely one hundred and twenty minutes later. When I walk inside her room, I find her exactly where she should be. Perched on her knees, naked and chained to her bed. Her honey brown hair is falling down over her bare chest and now part of her face, too. She cut, what are those things called? Bangs, I think. I stand in front of her and notice something sparkly around her waist. "Look at me, Ellie." I put my finger under her chin and she sweeps her head up. Her eyes are lined with thick dark pencil, her cheeks are pink and so are her lips. Jett played dress-up. Her hair is cut into chunky layers, and she's wearing diamond body jewelry. A thin string of crystals is attached to her collar, which run along her front, between her naked breasts, and belts around her waist. Her panties are a white, see-through material with garters holding up matching pantyhose. White patent leather stilettos finish her unbelievably sexy, temptress look. She's fucking to die for; my cock is banging inside my pants already, begging to be set free.

"You look stunning."

"Thank you, Kayne," she replies in a lackluster tone. Her submission usually turns me on, but tonight I just want Ellie. I want the girl who shared her cupcake with me. Who used to laugh and ramble. *Who used to want me.*

I unlock the chain from her collar, drinking her in a few seconds more. "I'm sorry if I hurt you last night. Are you in pain?" I want to touch her but refrain. I don't want her to think I'm just here for sex. *Treat her like the tin man and you get a steel heart.*

"No, Kayne." Her voice breaks a little bit, and so does my newly functioning heart.

"Get up, Ellie." I draw her off the bed. She eases up with grace, even though I see the agony she's trying to hide on her face. I lead her over to the table hand-in-hand, no chains tonight. Jett put out a spread. There's enough food to keep us locked up for three days. I wonder if that was his intention. I sit in the chair and Ellie kneels on the floor between my legs. She's such a good girl. I let her stay for just a second before I pull her onto my lap. "Sit on me, Ellie."

She blinks curiously but remains silent. *Speak only when you are spoken to.*

"How do you feel? Answer honestly."

She looks up into my eyes with her head still bowed. "I'm hurting."

"I'm sorry. I didn't mean to take it that far."

"What happened last night?" Her voice strains. The sound nearly kills me.

"Just a situation I have no tolerance for."

"So you took your frustration out on me?"

"I did. And I'm sorry."

She looks at me surprised, maybe because my apology is genuine. Maybe because I apologized at all.

"I like it rough, but I didn't mean for my anger to translate." I put my hand on her lower stomach. I know she had to feel it deep in her core when I slammed into her that first time.

"Why are you telling me this? Why do you even care? You made it very clear what I'm here for." There are tears brimming in her eyes.

"I'm telling you because I want you to be able to trust me. To be able to talk to me."

She shakes her head incredulously at me. "How am I supposed to talk to you, when you don't allow me to speak? Or look at you, or touch you?"

"I am trying to figure that out." I grab one of her breasts and start massaging it. I can't be this close without touching her. Her nakedness and her sultriness makes me pine for her, even when she's just an inch away. "But I want to know when you're hurt or upset or lonely. I want you to be able to confide in me. Find comfort with me." I drop a kiss on her shoulder. She smells amazing; whatever soap Jett makes her use is intoxicating.

"How am supposed to be open and submissive at the same time? We can barely have this conversation without you groping me."

"I can't help it. I won't lie. I want you all the fucking time. Even now, I wish we were having this conversation with you riding me. If you weren't in so much pain I'd plant you on my cock."

"Kayne," she admonishes.

"What? I'm only telling the truth. It doesn't feel good when I touch you?" I tease her nipple.

"Yes, Kayne," she answers vacantly. She's made her point.

"Be honest. I'll always want honesty." I tease her nipple a little harder. She stifles a moan.

"Yes. It feels good," she finally confesses.

"Good." I inhale her fresh scent. "Because that's what I want. I want to make you feel as good as you make me feel."

"Then I can't be just your pet on a leash." Her smoky green eyes infiltrate mine.

"I like you on a leash. That's not going to change. I want to dominate you, and I want you submissive."

"Then I don't know how anything's going to change." There's defeat in her voice.

"We'll have a safe word." I think quickly on my feet.

"A what?"

"A safe word." I keep massaging her firmly. "For our emotions. Use it when you feel upset or want to talk. Or just need me to make love to you. Say it. And I'll give you whatever you need." I suck on her collarbone, my cock straining painfully against my zipper. "I'll use it so you know you mean more to me than just sex."

Ellie stays silent while I kiss up her neck and then back down, restraining myself from moving to her breasts even though my mouth is begging to suck on the little pink pebbles her nipples have become.

"Do I?" she whispers softly, the moonlight flooding through the window is giving her smooth skin a silver glow.

"Yes, baby. So much more." I lick her.

"What word?" she asks stretching her neck to give me better access.

"Cupcake." I nip at her skin.

She giggles to herself. "That's perfect." Then sighs into me.

"I thought so." I grope her firmly, more urgently. Shit, my control is completely unraveling.

"Ellie, get on the floor." I can stand it anymore.

"But Kayne—"

"We'll talk more later, I promise. Right now I need you to lie on the floor."

"I don't think I can tonight." She frowns, pleadingly.

"I know. That's why I'm going to fuck your mouth." I grab her face and kiss her ardently on the lips, sucking as much oxygen as I can from her lungs. She's breathing hard, tears dripping down her face.

"Don't think of him, Ellie. Just me. Replace his memory with me."

I won't let fucking Javier get in her head. "I'm going to make him pay for what he did." I trap her face close to mine. "And I'm not going to let him steal what rightfully belongs to me. Now lie on the floor." Maybe I'm being a little harsh. But, tough love and all. It will only make her stronger in the end. I've learned that lesson the hard way, repeatedly.

And I swear, after all this, after everything, I'll make it up to her. *Repeatedly.*

Ellie lies down on the soft rug, bends her knees and draws her hands over her head. I stand, gazing down at her perfect little body dressed only in diamonds, panties, garters, and heels. I discard my clothes in record time, leaving them in a pile on the floor. I kneel between her legs and unhook one garter then the other. Her body goes rigid. "I want you to relax, Ellie. This isn't going to hurt. I promise. I know you're sore." I leave on the thigh highs but remove her clingy underwear, exposing her little pink pussy. It's sticking its tongue out at me, just tempting me to tease it. I lean down and suck on her clit; she bows her body and moans.

I love that reaction. It ignites something inside me. I lick languidly, coaxing her to relax. When she's breathing heavily and her body is loose, I shift, moving around her until I'm kneeling over her head, looking down her elongated body.

"Open your mouth, baby."

She does without hesitation. I lean over and brace myself on the floor with one hand. With the other I skim the head of my erection along her bottom lip. "I want you to suck me, Ellie. And don't stop no matter what I do." She whimpers as I slide my cock into her mouth. "Think of me, Ellie, only me." I lean forward so she can take more of me into her mouth. I support myself above her on my forearms and knees as she begins to suck. Fuck, I already feel it at the base of my tailbone. I grab onto her thighs. "Cupcake." I rasp just before I drop my head between her legs and drag my tongue over her slit. She moans, pulling harder on me as I lick around her clit. I keep her thighs spread as I simultaneously fuck her pussy with my tongue and her mouth with my cock. She's pinned beneath me with her hands still over her head, completely at my mercy, just the way I like her. She starts to rock her hips, no doubt chasing an orgasm. I'm not too far behind her. Her mouth is just as wet and tight as the sweet spot between her knees. Nirvana. Her tongue swirls around me as I pump in and out. Her breath becomes heavy as her muffled moans grow more intense. She tries to squirm, but she trapped. Then in a rush, she comes. The rattling of her body throttles me, and I thrust deeper, sliding all the way in until I touch the back of her throat. The suction and vibrations spur me to crack. My muscles tighten as I come in her mouth, forcing her to swallow every single drop.

My kitten never disappoints.

I make sure to lick Ellie clean before I kiss my way back up her body. She's flushed and panting by the time I get to her face.

"How was that? Did I hurt you?"

"No, Kayne," she answers a little starry eyed.

"Good girl." I grin upside down at her. She smiles back.

I pull Ellie up. "Hungry?"

"Yes, Kayne." Her answer is more playful than serious. I like that tone so much better.

I sit down in the chair and haul Ellie onto my lap. I tug on her little diamond chain with approval. "I think I'll keep this on you."

"Jett said you would like it." She lifts her shoulder to her cheek, half flirty, half shy.

She's never responded to me that way before. It makes my insides flip.

"Jett knows me pretty well," I divulge.

"I'm discovering that."

I feed Ellie a decadent dinner of duck a l'orange. She in turn feeds me back. I've never had a woman feed me before, and Ellie looks like she's enjoying it just as much as I am, giggling when I nip her fingers and moaning when I French kiss food from her mouth.

"Tell me one of your dreams, Ellie."

"I want to see paradise," she answers as I kiss her shoulder. Then her demeanor altogether changes—she withdraws and looks away. Shit.

"Hey." I draw her face back to mine. I know what's made her upset. She thinks she's owned and her freedom is gone. It's the truth. And that's the way it has to stay, for now.

"It's only ever going to be a dream," she says, her voice small and discouraged.

"Don't, Ellie," I respond sterner than I mean to. "Don't ruin tonight," I beseech her.

"Yes, Kayne," she submits.

I shake my head. I don't want to lose playful Ellie. I cup her face firmly, meaningfully. "Cupcake," I whisper against her mouth, right before I claim it.

When I'm done licking, kissing, and sucking her, I lift Ellie into my arms.

"Bed."

She doesn't protest. She looks beat, which is totally my fault. I lay her down, unroll her thigh highs, and remove her shoes. I leave on the diamond jewelry. Then I hook her back on her leash. Every time I see her lying here collared and chained to the bed, it does insane, indescribable things to me. My loins actually throbs.

I crawl next to her and rest my head on her chest, wrapping her tightly in my arms.

"Are you staying?" She sounds surprised. I know why that is. It will be the first time I spend an entire night with her.

"If you don't mind." I nuzzle my face against her soft skin.

"No." She yawns softly, snuggling up to me. Just like she did that night at Mark's party. It felt good then, it feels even better now.

"Sleep," I instruct.

And in no time at all, she is.

ELLIE

I WAKE UP TO KAYNE wrapped snugly around me and sunlight pouring into the room. Morning already.

I try to decipher exactly what happened last night. Did we actually establish an emotional safe word? A word that represents more? I like the idea. I like not feeling empty.

The door clicks and Jett comes to a screeching halt when he realizes what he's walked in on. Or what he thinks he's walked in on. Which is nothing really, but Kayne sleeping soundly on top of me. He backtracks out the door with a smirk on his face.

I lie there silently listening to Kayne breath, inspecting his beautiful features, desperately trying to figure out what makes this complicated man tick. I trace the thick black barbed wire tattoo dripping with blood lightly with the tip of my finger. I've never had the chance to touch him freely before. Kayne stirs ever so slightly, then again. He runs his hand over my body until he reaches one of my breasts.

"Mmmm." He squeezes with his eyes still closed. Then he shifts, digging his erection into my thigh.

"Put your hands over your head."

I do as I'm told. Kayne's eye pop open, the blue a shock of intensity. He smiles wickedly at me, and then wraps my leash around my wrists, somehow securing me to the bed with it. *Boy Scout.* Then he starts licking his way down my body. "How do you feel?" He sucks one of my nipples into his mouth, and the sensation shoots straight to my groin.

"Better." I sigh, completely at his mercy.

"Good. Because I really need to fuck you."

My heartbeat accelerates as he works his way down to my thighs, kissing the inside of each one. I moan, lifting my hips. I want him to lick me. *Oh, did I really just think that?* My body is a lecherous traitor.

He teases me with his tongue, never going near the pulsating spot between my legs.

The most I get is the tickle of his warm breath as he moves from one thigh to the other.

Why does he need to torture me? I find myself begging.

"Kayne, please." I feel empty and exposed, my body pleading to be touched, to be filled. By him. What's happening to me?

"Beg me. Beg me to be inside you."

"Please, Kayne, please," I whimper, as he sucks harder on my skin.

"Please what? Lick you? Fuck you? Beg for what you want, Ellie."

"I don't care! Either! Both! But please just touch me."

God, when did I become so needy? When did this become okay?

Kayne nestles himself between my thighs forcing them further apart. He rests on top of me, pinning me under his body, the head of his cock pushing against my entrance.

"Open wider, Ellie," he orders.

I inch my legs farther apart, as he slowly, mind numbingly, slides inside me. I let out a low moan as he works his hips languidly. Pushing all the way in and withdrawing all the way out. My muscles clench on their own accord, desperate to keep him inside.

"Wider," he commands.

"I can't," I protest.

"Shhhh ... Don't talk back and spread your legs." He shifts one of his thighs so it presses against mine, forcing my already straining legs wider. I pull on my restraints as Kayne pushes the limits of my body. The wider my legs, the deeper he gets. It's trying pain mixed with unbelievable pleasure. It feels like I'm tearing apart.

He grabs me by my collar as he thrusts harder, more erratic.

"Do you like the way I fuck you, Ellie?"

"Yes, Kayne." I barely have any breath to speak, as an orgasm brews deep inside me. It comes on faster with every driving thrust while my wrists start to burn from fighting against the chains. I have no outlet for my restrained body to absorb the sensations, so it all concentrates between my legs, spasming up my center and punching its way into my stomach. This orgasm is going to rock me.

"Kayne, please may I come?" I ask desperately.

"Not yet." He denies me.

"Please!"

"Wait." His chest tightens as he moves inside me. "Now."

With a solid strike of his hips, Kayne kicks me over the edge. I scream, tears pricking my eyes as he exploits the helplessness of my body, reaping every drop of my climax he can. Moments later he grips my collar strenuously as he comes violently inside me.

My small reprieve from physical pain evaporates. Everything is throbbing again; my legs, my arms, my stomach, my vagina.

I struggle to move as Kayne lies sated on top of me, his hand still gripping my collar.

"Where do you think you're trying to go?"

"Nowhere while you're laid out on top of me. I just need to shift." I wince as I shimmy my butt and attempt to close my legs.

Kayne yanks on my collar. "Remember who you're talking to. I'm the only one who says when you can move." His tone isn't threatening, but there is a shroud of reminder that he is still Master and I am still slave. No matter the understanding we came to last night.

Kayne lies on top of me for a while longer, kissing my neck while massaging my shoulders and breasts. I lay perfectly still, my hands still bound, powerless, just the way he likes me.

"Are we ever going to have sex without you tying me up?" I ask.

"Doubtful," he answers, squeezing my breast hard. "Only speak when spoken to," he reminds me harshly. "Vanilla is nice, but kink is king in my world. And now yours, too."

My heart sinks a little. This room, this fifty-by-fifty space, is my domain. Kayne is my ruler, collars and chains my boundaries.

A little while later, after he's finished feeling me up and making me come a second time with his mouth, he releases my bound hands. "Over and drop." He nudges me onto my stomach. I roll over and pull my legs up underneath me, my arms straight over my head. "I want to look at your ass while I get dressed." He kisses my back with my forehead pressed

175

to the mattress. I hear him pull on his pants and zip up his fly. When he finished ogling me, he orders me to my knees. I sit before him naked, sore and chained to the bed. He sighs contently, bringing my face up.

"You're beautiful and sexy and all fucking mine. I vow to keep you safe."

Thoughts of Javier come unwelcome into my mind. I fight back tears. That experience will haunt me forever. Kayne leans in and kisses me, soft and tender, licking the seam of my mouth before he pulls away.

"Cupcake," he says gruffly. Then leaves.

"I NEED TO GET OUT of this room." I splash in the tub. The aromatherapy soap Jett makes me use works wonders. The spa-like scent mixed with the hot bath literally uncurls the tension in my abused muscles.

"And where would you like to go? You're a kept woman, remember?" he snarks from the bedroom.

"These walls and my body never let me forget," I snark back. "I'd just like some fresh air. I've been stuck in here for ... how long have I been here?" I realize I have no concept of time.

"If you want fresh air, we'll open the window," Jett says as he walks into the bathroom, grabs the towel from the rack, and holds it open. Bath time is over.

"It's not the same," I gripe as I pull myself up reluctantly. I could soak all day. "Can't you talk to him for me?" I plead with puppy dog eyes as he wraps me in the towel. "I would ask him myself, but I'm not allowed to address him directly unless he's asking if I like the way he fucks me."

Jett vibrates with laughter. "You're terrible."

"I only speak the truth." I bat my eyelashes. "Please, Jett."

"Those green eyes are lethal," he huffs.

Jett pulls out his phone begrudgingly and adversely types away.

A few moments later his phone pings. He reads the message and snickers as he responds.

"What did he say?" I ask a little too hopeful.

"He said he'll be here to walk you in a little while."

I make a face. I don't like the allusion one bit. But I'm dying to get out of this room. So I'll deal with it. I'm close to scratching at the walls.

Jett dresses me for my outing. A black pair of lace panties with frilly ruffles on the butt, the black stiletto boots Kayne fucked me in, and a sheer black top that reminds me of a sexy beach cover up. The hem barely covers my ass and the plunging neckline barely covers my breasts. *Why even bother?* Complete with blingy body jewelry, my collar, and leash, I'm fit to be walked. Jett pulls my hair up into a messy bun, rims my eyes with black kohl liner and applies several coats of heavy mascara to finish off my dark sexy look. At least, that's what he calls it.

As we emerge from the bathroom, Kayne walks into the room. I drop to my knees immediately, splaying my hands on my bare thighs while keeping my head bowed. Just like I'm supposed to. Kayne growls in approval as he stands above me; menacing, intimidating, domineering. All things Kayne. All things my proprietor.

"I love that you know what I like," he says to Jett, pleased. Something inside me hiccups at his approval. He grabs my leash and commands me to rise. "Let's go, kitten. I'll show you the house."

AYNE

ELLIE LOOKS FUCKING GOOD ENOUGH to eat. When Jett text me asking if he could take her out of her room for a while, I was completely against it at first. I don't want her to know or see too much. For Ellie, the dark is the safest place. But she's been cooped-up in that room for almost three weeks and I knew the request was inevitable. The word *no* when it comes to Ellie is never an option, even if she's unaware of it. I wasn't going to let Jett be the one to take her though. My kitten. My responsibility.

I also wanted to be close in case Javier got any stupid ideas seeing her out of her cage.

I failed her once, I wouldn't do it again. I wanted to kill him right on the spot. I wanted to tear out his fucking throat and watch him bleed the white carpet in Ellie's room red. But that wasn't an option. At least not right then. But soon. Very fucking soon.

I tug Ellie's leash. It's time to go. I lead her out of the room and down the hall. She's walking two steps behind me with her head down, dressed in that fucking little outfit and those boots that drive me absolutely insane. But right now isn't about me. It's about Ellie and keeping her sane. But fuck man, does Jett know what he's doing when it comes to dressing her.

I tow Ellie down the long corridor of doors. I put her in the very last room for a reason. I know she has questions, I know she's remembering what she saw the last time she walked this hall and my threat to string her up and feed her to the wolves. That's all it was too, a threat. I would never have done it. I would never let anyone else touch what's mine.

The main staircase is a sweeping three-level butterfly affair made out of white, pink, and black marble. The decor at the mansion is over-the-top, ostentatious, and impressive. It's supposed to be that way. The clientele who come here are top of the line, prestigious, and expect nothing less than luxury and complete and utter anonymity. I walk Ellie into the west wing and through a long, glass enclosed entryway that leads to the utmost back of the house. Once at the end, I unlock the lavishly decorated doors carved out of wood and push them open.

"Ellie, look up." I jiggle her chain.

She raises her head and gasps. This is my favorite part of the mansion, a botanical garden that holds dozens upon dozens of exotic flowers and wild birds. We enter together and I watch as Ellie's face lights up. I grab her hand and she jumps from the contact. Then she relaxes and gives me a small smile. It twists my heart. I stayed far away from Ellie for a reason. My life, my world, is dangerous. I never wanted to bring her into that. But when the opportunity presented itself, I couldn't resist. Having her here these last few weeks, owning her, a slave to my bed, is my most vivid fantasy come to life. And, being the selfish bastard I am, I'm going to take advantage of every second I have with her. I'm going to push every limit, because when it's over, I'm confident Ellie will never want to see me again.

"It's not exactly paradise, but it comes damn close," I say as we walk farther into the conservatory.

"I love it," she replies as we stroll through a field of orchids sprouting purples, pinks, and whites out of the ground. Then she frowns and I know exactly what's upset her. She still thinks she'll never see paradise. She still thinks her freedom is gone. And for now, it is. I have to let her keep believing that. I squeeze her hand tighter as we make our way deeper into the gardens. Cranes dance by us and cockatoos display their colorful feathers as we come to the waterfall in the middle of the room.

"This is amazing," she breathes as she watches the water trickle down and pour into the clear blue pond below.

After a while of standing hand-in-hand among the peaceful surroundings, I catch Ellie glancing at me out of the corner of her eye.

"Ask me, Ellie."

She turns her head. "I'm just trying to understand. This place, you."

"All you need to know is that I'm an entrepreneur who owns you."

"An entrepreneur who deals in women?" There's a hard edge to her tone. I let it go, this time.

"Not everything is as it seems. You'd do best to remember that. And every woman in this house is here of her own free will."

She glares. "Except me."

Shit, she's got me there. "Except you," I confirm callously. "And that isn't up for discussion."

She huffs with tears in her eyes. Those deep green, hypnotizing eyes. I yank her to me, capturing her in my arms. "Don't make me bend you over and give you something to really cry about."

She sucks in a breath, fighting the urge to unleash her emotions.

"Let's not ruin the moment." I dip my head and whisper in her ear. "Mine, Ellie," I remind her.

She nods, composing herself, but the tears are still evident.

We spend the rest of the afternoon wandering the gardens in silence. I never let go of her hand, and she never tries to pull it away. It sprouts a small seed of hope inside me.

Once we leave, Ellie's relaxed energy shifts as we climb the staircase toward her ivory tower.

Her attention catches when she hears music coming from one of the rooms in the hallway. She really is like a curious cat. I stop, licked with an idea. I drop Ellie's hand and take her leash. Her anxiety spikes as I grab the door handle and turn the knob. She resists, but I yank, pulling her into the room. She flushes cherry red once inside. The room is occupied by two women and a man. One of the women is tied to the bed, arms and legs spread eagle. The man is straddling her head, thrusting his cock in and out of her mouth while the other woman has her face between her legs. Ellie tries to look away, but I grab her chin and force her to watch. Her chest expanding and contracting swiftly as her breathing picks up.

"We shouldn't be in here," she states in a low, uneasy tone.

"Of course we should. And no talking."

I pull her over to the couch against the wall directly across from the bed and command her down to her knees. We both sit facing the threesome with Ellie perched between my legs. It's fucking hot. Besides taking part in it, nothing gets me harder than watching two women go at it. Except maybe if Ellie was one of those women.

We spy together, as the three partake in their sexual acts. I scoot closer to Ellie, slipping my hand under her collar, grabbing it tight, straightening her posture. My erection digs into the middle of her back. She's panting heavily and her skin is heated. I shove my free hand into her shirt and grope her breast as we watch the chained girl writhe frenziedly as she climaxes.

I run my nose along her neck, breathing her in. "Do you like watching?" I ask her. "Do you like seeing two women together?"

Ellie doesn't answer. I know her voice is caught in her throat. The energy in the room is highly erotic and thick with sex. The music evocative. We observe, as the red-haired girl, Sugar, is unchained and the brunette, Cinnamon, takes her place, lying face down on the bed. She's shackled tightly, arms and legs spread wide.

"Have you ever been with a woman, Ellie?"

She shakes her head, as Sugar positions herself underneath Cinnamon's face. I rock my erection against Ellie as Cinnamon begins to lick Sugar. All my girls have pet names; it keeps things ambiguous and fantasy-like. These are two of my best girls, most naughty and adventurous.

Sugar drops her head back and moans as the man slides a condom on and impales Cinnamon from behind. She groans loudly as her tongue works Sugar.

"Would you do that, Ellie? Would you let me watch another woman eat your pussy?" She shivers but doesn't answer. I squeeze her bare breast, her flesh is on fire. "I think you would. I think you like watching, and secretly wish it was you." I slip my hand down into her panties and circle her clit with the tip of my middle finger.

"Will you let me fuck you while you go down on her?" I ask, and Ellie whimpers. I thrust my finger inside her, just as Sugar begins to come, jerking her hips and mewling loudly. "Answer, Ellie." I tug on her collar.

"Yes, Kayne."

"Yes, Kayne what? I can fuck you with another woman?"

"Yes." Her voice is barely recognizable it's so thick with lust.

"Who do you want? If you had to choose. Which girl do you want to fuck?" I ask still working my hand. She's soaking wet.

"The redhead." She strains to answer, her muscles clenching around my finger. There's no way I'm letting her come. Not in front of another man, even if he is balls deep in another woman. I withdraw, leaving Ellie empty and wanton.

She makes a protesting sound. Frustrated is just the way I want her. I drag her out of the room and push her face forward against the wall, pinning her wrists above her head, and grind my throbbing cock into her ass. The thought of Ellie with another woman launches my arousal into outer space.

"Tonight," I promise her.

I PACE ELLIE'S ROOM LIKE a wild animal. She is chained to the bed, naked, and sitting like a good girl. I never dreamed of putting Ellie in a threesome situation, but once the idea presented itself, and she consented, I had to pull the trigger. I arranged with Jett to have Sugar prepared. She was bathed, freshened, and informed of the details. She is not to touch me. Not in front of Ellie. I am merely a spectator. Until I take Ellie. She's the only one I will fuck.

The door clicks open and Sugar appears. She's dressed only in lacy panties, stiletto heels, and a black collar. Perfect.

I send her to stand in the middle of the room, on the white shag rug. Then I go to Ellie. I unchain her from the headboard and lean into her face. "Ellie, I want you to know. I will be the only man who ever touches you. But you can fuck as many women as you want."

Her breath hitches. "Yes, Kayne."

"Tell me this is okay. Tell me the truth."

She peeks up at me through her thickly coated lashes and blushes. "Yes, Kayne."

My dick hardens to almost painful and my insides feel like they're going to overheat. I urge Ellie off the bed and walk her over to Sugar who's standing submissively in the middle of the room. I hook the end of Ellie's chain to Sugar's collar so the two are linked. Arousing does not begin to describe the sight of two collared women linked together for the sole purpose of pleasing you.

"Ellie, Sugar belongs to you tonight. You can touch her, lick her, suck her anywhere you want. Anywhere I tell you to."

"Yes, Kayne," Ellie answers, breathing erratically; Sugar is cool as a cucumber.

I step back and take a seat in the chair at the table under the wagon wheel window. Then I pull my shirt off. It's fucking stifling in here.

I stare at the girls momentarily then speak.

"Ellie, touch her." I don't want to waste a moment. I'm about to burst.

Ellie tentatively reaches up with a shaky hand. Is it wrong her inexperience is turning me on even further?

Ellie runs her hand down Sugar's arm, as if saying hello. Not good enough.

"Ellie, touch her breasts."

Ellie slowly puts her hand on Sugar's left breast and fondles her. My desire spins like a high-speed cylinder.

"Both breasts," I insist. "Tease her nipples, make them hard."

Ellie lifts her other hand, squeezing and kneading both of Sugar's breasts. Rolling her nipples between her thumb and index finger, the exact same way I do to her. My fucking cock has a heartbeat, as I watch my little pleasure kitten feel up another woman. The two girls are a stark contrast. Sugar is tall, red-headed, and buxom, while Ellie is petite in every sense of the word. Salivating for more, I order Ellie, "Suck her tits."

Ellie hesitates.

"Don't make me wait." My tone is authoritative as I bore my lust-filled gaze into her.

Ellie leans in and takes one of Sugar's nipples into her mouth. I nearly combust on the chair. I watch as she swirls her tongue and sucks Sugar with more force than I was expecting. Sugar moans. Still standing with her arms by her side and head lowered, her thick red hair dangling over her face.

"Touch her back, Sugar."

Sugar lifts her hands without delay, sliding her fingers into Ellie's hair as she laves her with her tongue. I unzip my pants and stroke my cock. It can't be ignored any longer as the two women touch each other under my strict advisement. Sugar takes the reins, pulling Ellie's mouth to hers, kissing her softly at first, and then darting her tongue between her lips.

They both brush and caress and fondle each other as they become more comfortable.

"Ellie, how does Sugar feel?"

"Soft," she responds between kisses.

"How does she taste?"

"Sweet."

"How does she smell?"

"Sexy."

I have come to learn Ellie likes monosyllables when she's describing sexual associations. I have also come to learn, I like it.

"Sugar, get on your knees. Lick my kitten."

I can hear Ellie's sharp intake of breath as Sugar drops in front of her, the chain connecting their collars dangling between them.

"Ellie, spread your legs for Sugar." She glances at me with an unsure expression. Her green eyes wild with something penetrative. Something hot, like unsure desire.

"Go on kitten. I'm right here." I stroke myself as she looks at me. As if telling her *I'm all yours. This is what you do to me. Make me fucking rock hard and yearn for you.*

Sugar puts her mouth on Ellie as she looks at me, taking her by sweet surprise.

"Oh!" Her eyes widen, and then shut as her head drops back. She opens her stance and I see Sugar's tongue take charge. Ellie looks blindsided, and it's fucking incredible. I have to stop stroking myself; if I keep it up I'm going to come. And my hand is an unacceptable place to ejaculate when I have two beautiful women right in front of me. One all mine for the fucking.

"Ellie, how does that feel?" I ask as she runs her fingers through Sugars deep red hair.

"So good." She breathes hard, sounding a little disoriented. Her cheeks are flushed and her eyes are fluttering. She's close to the brink.

I almost can't stand it as I heave low breaths.

"Enough." Sugar halts immediately. The power is intoxicating. Commanding two gorgeous women—nothing else compares. "Sugar, stand up."

She complies immediately. Good little robin. That's what Jett calls her.

"Ellie, remove Sugar's underwear," I direct.

With delicate fingers Ellie lowers Sugar's black panties down her long legs, sliding them over her smooth thighs and toned calves.

My arousal roars.

"Sugar, get down on the ground and spread your legs."

She immediately complies, the chain connecting their two collars forcing Ellie down with her. Sugar puts her hands straight over her head and opens her legs wide with Ellie sprawled out on top of her.

"Ellie, pleasure her. Lick her body, suck her cunt."

The room is so thick with sex, I'm suffocating from the sight. She looks at me with wide green eyes.

"Go on." My response is clipped.

With mild trepidation, Ellie assails Sugar, licking down her neck to her breasts, drawing each nipple into her mouth and unleashing her tongue. Sugar moans and wriggles, her reaction to Ellie prompts me to start stroking again as my wildest dream comes to life.

Ellie keeps making her way down, over Sugar's tight stomach until she lands right at the apex of her thighs. She hesitates, and I instinctively order, "Do it, Ellie."

Her mouth makes contact with Sugar's pussy, and I nearly see stars. She licks Sugar with such ferocity she causes the redhead to moan loudly with pleasure. I watch the two of them completely spellbound. When I see Ellie's tongue dart out and swirl over Sugar's clit, my control completely crumbles.

I discard what's left of my pants and drop to the floor, crawling on all fours to get to Ellie.

I kneel behind her, lining myself up at her entrance. I watch entrapped as my little kitten laps up Sugar like she's a bowl of sweet milk. My body is trembling with overpowering need. And the only one who can satisfy it is Ellie; the only way is to bury myself deep inside her. Deep, deep inside her.

I dig my fingers into her hips. "Don't take your mouth off her pussy, no matter how hard I fuck you, understand?"

"Yes, Kayne," Ellie whimpers, and I immediately shove her face back between Sugar's legs. "What did I tell you?"

She mewls in reply.

I slam into her without any sort of warning and she cries out.

My cock thanks me.

I repeat the motion over and over, rearing all the way back and then blasting forward into her. Every strangled, strained sound she makes is muffled as she eats away at Sugar.

"Make her come, Ellie." I mercilessly thrust. "I won't let you come until she does."

Ellie frantically licks Sugar as she writhes and moans, chasing after an orgasm that's just out of reach. Then Ellie does something that nearly makes my head pop off. She begins to finger her. The little extra pressure was all Sugar needed to fall apart. She arches her body in ecstasy as her orgasm seizes her.

"Come," I command.

Fucking Ellie while she makes another woman splinter is my undoing. Trapping her hips, I beat into her with a punishing rhythm until she's screaming my name. It doesn't take long.

My orgasm holds me hostage as I bury myself to the hilt in Ellie over and over, restraining her as the force of each impact bucks her body forward. "Fuck, fuck." I grind out the words as the feel of her tight wet pussy pulsates around me, tearing me to shreds. I come like a man possessed, because that's exactly what I am. A man possessed by a little pleasure kitten who wears my collar and purrs my name.

I collapse on the floor as soon as the sensation dissipates, drawing a wildly panting Ellie close. The three of us lie spent, recuperating from the sexual overload.

I let the girls fall asleep still chained to each other on the shag rug. It's the sexiest thing I've seen in a long time.

I love all that shit. Sex toys, submission, and bondage.

But I love it even more when it's with Ellie. She blows me away. Her strength. Her playfulness. Her willingness. All the things that drew me to her in the first place have manifested tenfold. My little kitten is a force to be reckoned with.

I slip my hand under her collar and feel her soft pulse. The rhythm settles me.

It's quickly become the sole reason for my existence.

ELLIE

I DON'T KNOW WHAT I was thinking when I agreed to have a threesome with Kayne.

All I know is, I was about to tear at the seams as I watched two women and one man have sex while he fingered me.

I stare mindlessly out the window remembering. It's such a beautiful, clear day; the grass and leaves almost seem to gleam.

Who is this person I'm becoming? Every day I seem to inch further and further away from my old life. My old self. I live to please another. Someone who treats me rough, but at the same time is tender. Someone who makes me forget everything, but him.

"What are you doing in here, kitten?" Kayne asks suddenly from behind me. Shit. I immediately drop to my knees. I didn't even hear him come in. It's the middle of the afternoon; he never comes to see me during the day.

"Turn around. Face me," he orders. Dom dickhead is back.

I shift sideways, still kneeling.

"Look up."

I lift my head.

"Answer."

"Just staring out the window."

The room with the table of torture gives me a more panoramic view of the outside with its circular shape and large paned windows. Ironically, I don't feel so trapped when I'm in here.

"I see." He stares at me for a heartbeat, then commands, "Come."

Since I'm still kneeling and he hasn't ordered me to stand. I crawl on all fours, like he trained me to do. Like a cat. Like the pet that I am.

He watches me salaciously as I come to sit by his feet.

"Lie down."

I drop to my side, stretching out my body, resting my head on my arm. I stare up at Kayne, as he stares down. The look on his face is indescribable; there are so many emotions showing. At the forefront arousal and satisfaction. His eyes are wild as he rakes over my naked form.

"I have something for you," he says while still standing over me, the corners of his mouth turned up. He pulls something out of his pocket, a small silver charm. "Get on the table. Kneel in front of me."

I get up and climb onto the table, kneeling submissively on the firm black cushion. Kayne lifts his hand and shows me the trinket. It's a small heart on a clasp that reads 'Kayne's kitten.'

"Now everyone will know exactly who you belong to." He fastens it to my collar. "Me." Holy shit, I'm now tagged, collared, and owned by him.

"Mine." He leans in and kisses me, trapping my face in his hands. He swirls his tongue around roughly, thrusting it in and out of my mouth. "I want to do that to your pussy." He breathes heavily against my lips. Here we go. My body responds without delay, becoming instantly wet. I've lost all control.

"Lie down. Hands by your sides."

On the table?!? The last time we utilized this room, he beat me, then nearly destroyed me with his sexual prowess. And it's about to happen all over again.

I comply, the slave that I am. Kayne restrains both of my wrists in the cuffs with my pulse flying high. Then he moves to the end of the table and grabs one of my ankles. He deftly secures my leg to one of the stirrups with the thick black leather straps—one over my thigh, one around my calf, and one on my ankle. Then he does the same to my other leg. I'm tied down, helpless, and battling for breath.

"Mmm," he expels as he drinks in my incapacitated state. He then rests his hands on the inside of my thighs and pushes, causing the stirrups to click as he spreads me wide. One, two, three, four. My back is arching and my hands are fisting from the torturous stretch. "Ugh," I heave, trying to channel the pain.

"Perfect." Kayne licks his bottom lip as I pant. He loves working me out.

He walks around to my side, never taking that maniacal stare off me. The room is filled with bright sunlight, making me feel more exposed and more on display than ever before; my nakedness and tethered body at the forefront of my insecurity and fear.

"You are so beautiful, Ellie." Kayne rubs my breasts, my shoulders, my arms. He leans down and kisses me, kneading small, firm circles into my biceps. I release a contented moan against his mouth as he lulls me into submission.

He pulls away once I'm relaxed, and then opens one of drawers. I startle my eyes open and track every move he makes, watching with morbid fascination as he pulls out a thin chain with two little clamps on each end. He dangles it front of my face, his expression carnal, hedonistic almost. I look quickly between his luminous eyes on fire with lust, and the tiny torture device he's holding in his hand.

He grins wickedly, then leans over and sucks one of my nipples into his mouth, lashing his tongue against the little pebble as it hardens. I release a heavy breath, then without any warning, he places the clamp on my nipple. It bites, shooting a sharp sensation straight to the apex of my over-stretched legs. *Oh.* Then he does the same thing to the other nipple, vibrating a moan against my breast, just to tease me. The clamp bites down and I groan in protest.

"Fuck, you look so hot." He grabs both my breasts from underneath and squeezes them hard. The clamps pinch at the same time and my eyes roll into the back of my head.

"Oh, God."

"Oh, Kayne," he corrects arrogantly as he massages me, arousal flaring through my entire being. "I'm your maker now."

Not just my maker — my captor, my owner, my ruler.

He's barely touched me and I'm already breathing rapidly and soaked between my thighs. After he's finished rubbing me into restlessness, he picks up the chain connecting the clamps. With an impish gleam, he somehow ties it to the loop on the front of my collar. The chain is pulled so tight, that every time I move my head the clamps nip at my nipples, straining them, elongating them, driving me crazy with pleasure and pain. My heart is beating, my hands are shaking, and my pussy is throbbing.

Kayne jingles my new tag with one finger as I lie confined to the table, unravelling at the seams.

"Mine," he says haughtily.

I just stare up at him with glassy eyes, trying to remain as still as possible. He unbuttons his light blue shirt; the color makes his eyes pop in the sunlight, the brown lightning bolt looking more pronounced. God, for being the devil, his features are divine. Once he's removed his shirt and dropped it on the floor, he leans over me semi-naked and kisses me on the stomach. I try to breathe steadily, but every time he touches me it feels like a volcanic eruption. "Baby, you don't have to ask permission to come." He slowly kisses down my torso until his head is between my widespread legs. Then he licks me lightly, dragging his tongue unhurriedly over my slit. He does this over and over like a lazy lion until I'm vainly wriggling in my restraints. I snap my head back without thinking and the clamps unapologetically jerk my nipples sending a bolt of white hot heat straight to my blistering pussy.

"Oh!" I try not to move, but he's pushing me right to my breaking point, slowly, painstakingly, licking me into an orgasm.

"Kayne, Kayne." I breathe labored. It's a plea, it's an appeal, it's a demand. My insides are wound so tight they're ready to fracture. He just keeps licking though, ignoring my chants, and my body just keeps winding.

Lick, twist, lick, twist.

I'm an elastic band ready to snap.

Then he inserts one finger into my assailable entrance and I combust. My hips buck and I scream. It feels like I am being electrocuted. It looks like I'm being electrocuted. My hands fisted, my body bowed, my head dropped back, my nipples aching and straining as a current of ecstasy speeds through my veins.

I collapse back onto the table when the climax releases me, moaning feebly. My head rolling all over the place like it's barely attached to my body. The nipple clamps still tugging relentlessly.

"Whoa." Kayne chuckles as he wipes his face against my inner thigh.

I'm glad he finds my soul-shredding orgasms so funny. *Asshole.*

He kisses his way back up to my mouth as I come around. I crack open my eyes as he kisses me, to find him staring back at me.

"Hi, kitten." He smiles.

I grunt.

He laughs. "My turn. You ready?"

"No," I say sarcastically.

He yanks on the chain and my nipples yelp. "Excuse me?

"Yes, Kayne," I correct myself.

"Good, kitten." He brushes his lips against mine. "My kitten." He jingles the tag on my collar again, proudly displaying his satisfaction with my new token of ownership.

I watch withdrawn as he positions himself between my legs. The stirrups have my knees high and legs wide. They're starting to ache from being confined and overstretched. Kayne unbuttons his pants and unzips his fly. He doesn't even bother to remove them, only lowering them enough to release his cock.

"Come if you have to come baby." He teases my wet entrance with its head. Then he braces himself on the table, leaning forward, preparing for total body domination. "You have no idea how fucking sexy you look, wearing that tag." He slams into me, and I feel it all the way to my belly button.

"Ah!" I crunch forward and scream out.

"How much it turns me on. You belong to me." He slams into me again and again. The manic desire is clear on his face.

His relentless thrusts combined with the pinching of the clamps catapult me toward another orgasm before I even see it coming. All at once, my muscles are clenching, my neck is straining and my pussy is pulsating as he rams fast and furiously in and out of me; my nipples are in glorious agony as my breasts bounce from the relentless force of his hips' impact.

"I'm going to come!" I cry out.

"Come!" Kayne snaps, as my orgasm unleashes itself, a torrent of arousal drenching us both as my body splits in two. Kayne stills, arching his back as he comes savagely inside of me.

In the daylight, I can see all the cuts of his body, the definition of his chest and strength of his presence. Like a Roman soldier. Suddenly I'm very aware of my unclothed, tethered state. I blush all over. It's not like he hasn't had me in compromising positions before, or even done worse, but the fact that it's the middle of the day and I'm strapped to a table with my nipples clamped makes me feel awkwardly on display.

"Ellie, what's wrong?" Kayne asks, as he pumps his semi-hard cock into me, sighing satedly.

"Nothing." I drop my head to the side then immediately right it, the clamps reminding me who's in control.

"Ellie," Kayne says more firmly, completely nestled inside me.

"I feel a little ... exposed." I chew my lip.

Kayne smiles. Widely. "I like you exposed baby." He withdraws, and then pulls up his pants that are still hanging on his hips. "Exposed and open and only for me." He hoists himself onto the table and crawls up my body like the predator he is, his eyes sparkling with something dark and triumphant. "See, it says it right here." He jingles my tag. "Mine."

"Yes. We've established that numerous times," I quip.

Kayne pulls at the nipple chain playfully and I wince. "Don't sass me," he says still smiling.

"I can't help it, it's reflexive," I answer.

"You know what else is reflexive?" He drops his head and kisses me torridly, his tongue circling and owning my mouth. I moan softly, then strain as he releases my nipples from the clamps. I breathe through the abrasive sensation as the blood runs through my body. Subdued, little sounds escape my throat as he continues to kiss me through the pain.

Pleasure and pain. Pleasure and pain. Definitely two words synonymous with him.

Kayne slips his hand under my collar and strokes my neck lightly with his thumb. My arms are still strapped down and my legs are still buckled to the stirrups. I wonder if he plans to keep me here all day.

"Don't ever feel ashamed or embarrassed with me, Ellie. Your body is perfect. You're perfect." He kisses me tenderly.

"Yes, Kayne," I answer, kissing him back.

"Good, kitten. Cupcake."

I STARE AT MY SHINY new jewelry sitting on the bathroom counter as I soak my sore muscles in a steaming hot tub. A tag for my collar, a delicate white gold heart with the inscription 'Kayne's kitten'. He gave it to me yesterday, right before he strapped me to the table of torture and fucked me senseless with clamped nipples.

I am collared. I am tagged. I am utterly owned by him.

The man is a sexual carnivore. His appetite insatiable. I have bruises on my hips from where he holds me, hickeys on my body from where he bites me, and handprints on my ass from where he spanks me. I look abused. I feel abused. I feel conflicted. My brain keeps telling me this whole thing is wrong. I'm a victim, a pet, a captive. But my body craves Kayne the same way it would crave water in the desert. It has quickly become the slave to him that he wanted, succumbing to all his devious desires and demands.

I take my time getting out of the tub, knowing Jett is in the bedroom ready to torture me with more yoga. It's doing its job and stretching my muscles, which is pleasing Kayne to no end. It also helps loosen my stiff joints the morning after his brutal punishings.

You love it, don't complain. I shove my subconscious into a dark closet.

I get out of the tub, dry myself off, and allow Jett to torment my body further with more downward dog and lord of dance poses. By the time we're finished and he's fed me, it's late in the evening.

I notice thick chains and leather cuffs dangling off one of the stirrups on the table of torture in the other room.

"What are those for?" I ask as he fastens my collar and chains me stark naked back to the bed.

Jett shrugs. "Kayne requested them. He has something planned."

My heart rate takes off. Jett leaves me with my racing thoughts. Always something new, always something kinky. Always something that leaves my body depleted and my soul stirring. Ever since we established cupcake, I've felt different. Yes, he's a domineering prick sometimes. But when he touches me, when he's inside me there's an undeniable connection. The same connection I felt to him before. When we would steal a look or flirt privately in the conference room. The same red hot connection we had that night he took me.

The door clicks and I shoot to my knees. My sitting position. My submission. The heavy steps of Kayne's presence makes my pulse pound and my most private places throb.

He lifts my chin with one finger so I can look him in the eye. The eyes that are crystal blue with a lightning bolt of brown. He tickles my tag with an arrogant smirk.

"Evening, kitten, how was your day?"

"I missed you." The words just roll right out of my mouth. I stiffen and Kayne's jaw drops. His sharp intake of breath is like a vacuum. Then a wide salacious smile spreads across his tantalizing mouth. The mouth that is capable of so many things. My thighs tingle just looking at it.

"I missed you too." He squeezes one of my breasts. "And these." He runs his hand down my torso and cups my pussy. "And this. But," he leans in to kiss me, "I missed this most of all." I moan as his tongue rolls slowly against mine and he pushes his middle finger deep inside of me.

"I hope Jett gave you carbs for dinner, because it's going to be another all-nighter." He breathes against my lips, almost apologetically.

"Come to think of it. He fed me pasta." I sigh as he fingers me slowly. "Did you take another Viagra?"

He halts all movement. "How did you know I took Viagra?"

"Because no human male is capable of lasting as long as you, unless he's medically enhanced. And Jett confirmed my suspicions," I confess coquettishly.

"Did he?"

"We have to talk about something," I say as Kayne stabs me with his finger.

"Well then," he replies cockily, withdrawing his hand leaving me aching. "You want something to gossip about. I'll give you something to gossip about." He pulls me forward by my collar and smacks my ass hard, making me yelp. "No more talking. Lie on your front." His Dom alter ego has sprung to life.

I do as I'm told with a knot in my stomach.

I watch excited, scared, and turned on as hell, as he picks up the chains and cuffs from the table. He stalks back over to me and without delay, secures my ankles and wrists to the bed. I'm spread wide and at his mercy once again. Just as he desires me. Just like he craves me. He then shortens the length of my leash, removing most of the slack. An inch and a half off the mattress is all I can lift my head. My heart rate goes berserk as I hear him shuffling in the drawers under the table of torture. His treasure chest of sex toys.

Oh God.

I feel him drop multiple items onto the bed, and then I hear the sound of clothes being shed. Kayne crawls on top of me, straddling my parted legs.

"Do you know why I take Viagra, Ellie?" he asks.

"No, Kayne." I reply, panting like the pet I am.

"Because having you once or twice is never enough." He shifts, spreading my ass cheeks, then licks my little puckered hole. I clench instinctually. "I hunger to be inside you all the time and the only way to satisfy the beast is to give it what it wants. Hours and hours submerged in your wet pussy and tight little ass."

I hear the pop of a cap and then feel a cold squirt. I try to crane my head to see behind me, but it's a vain attempt. Then I feel something hard and round push on my behind.

"Pussy first," he says, slowly working the large, lubricated butt plug into my tiny rosebud. I moan and groan as it bites and stretches me, Kayne kneading one of my butt cheeks the entire time. When it's finally all the way in, he twists it, causing my entire body to spasm and work against my restraints. *"Oh!"* Afterwards, Kayne props up my pelvis with a medium-size throw pillow, stretching my arms, my legs, my neck and my ass to the max. The silk soft and smooth against my flaming skin

Kayne flutters light kisses over my back as he mounts me.

"You're so fucking sexy. Beautiful, bewitching," he says as he presses the head of his cock against my entrance and enters me slowly, making sure I feel every hard inch of him. He fucks me unhurriedly, keeping a tempered rhythm that rocks the butt plug deep every time he thrusts.

"You're mine, Ellie," he reminds me. "Do you see? I can do whatever I want to you." He starts to pump harder, my insides overflowing with his thick cock and large plug. I lose my mind as the sensations take over, drowning me in a sea of ecstasy.

"I own you. I own your pleasure." He strains as he hits my core square on and my orgasm peaks.

"Oh God, Kayne!" It's the only words I'm capable of at the moment. I need to move, I need to squirm, but he's right, he owns my pleasure. Commands it with his body.

"Kayne, please!" I'm begging now. Always begging. Just like he wants. A slave to him. "Please! Please!"

He pushes deeper, challenging my body as everything south of my navel quakes.

"Please!" I scream, pulling at my restraints.

"I love to hear you beg." His cock swells, punching me exactly where I need. Once, twice, three times and I combust. My climax tearing me open from the inside out. He bucks once more then slams still inside me, groaning animalistically as he comes. I'm left limp as a noodle on the bed with Kayne lying on top of me, both of us breathing like all the oxygen has dissipated in the room. After a few long minutes, he pushes up and kisses me on the cheek. "Round two." My body trembles. Round one just knocked me on my ass. He withdraws, still erect. I know what I'm in for. We've done this before, him taking me all night.

Straddling above me, he bends to grab something.

"Open," he commands with a purple rubber vibrator in front of my mouth. I open and he shoves it in.

"Suck."

I move my head the little it can go and suck on the extremity.

"Good girl," he says in that condescending, domineering tone, as I lubricate the vibrator. Kayne removes the butt plug still inhabiting my ass, and my muscles contract, sighing with relief. Then he pulls the vibrator from my mouth, clicks it on, and inserts it into me.

Oh! It's not quite as big as him, but it still makes me feel full, the vibrations prickling my already sensitive parts.

I hear the pop of a top again and a squeeze. It makes my heart rate jolt. Then he pushes one finger into my ass, all the way to the knuckle. Fuck, round two. I buck and gasp. "Still, Ellie."

I try, but my body involuntarily shakes. Then he slides another finger inside me and starts to scissor me open, as if I haven't been elasticized enough. I shudder as he simultaneously stretches the already sensitive muscle and my core quakes from the hum of the vibrator.

"So fucking ready," Kayne utters as he removes his fingers, and I don't know if he's referring to me or him.

I feel him shift on the bed, quickly positioning himself directly above me. He nips at my shoulder as he pokes his cock into my behind, pushing into me in one smooth, fluid motion. It forces a moan out of me that sounds like a cat in heat. The size of his erection supersedes both his fingers and the plug. My air supply feels thin as I'm filled to capacity once again. The last all-nighter he only fucked me once, then spent the rest of the night balls deep in my butt. Tonight is completely different. Both holes packed, over and over. I don't know if I'll survive.

Would he spare me if I begged him to stop? I'll soon find out, because he wastes no time fucking me, moving in small thrusts at first, then increasingly pushing harder. I feel every jab in my center as his cock bites my ass while at the same time kissing it with pleasure. The vibrator keeping a steady stream of pulsation against my clit and all around my pussy.

I'm dying.

The monumental speed with which my orgasm is building has me petrified. It's too big, too strong, and the only place it has to escape is between my legs. My arms and legs lend no help to the absorption of the impending tremor while I'm restrained like this.

"God, Ellie, your body. It's so good. So perfect. So tight." He thrusts into me, making me wail. "I'm going to fucking come. You're going to make me fucking come," he says through clenched teeth. I can't hold back as both the force of his cock and the vibrator hit my g-spot all at once. "Kayne!" I detonate, my climax ripping me open right down the middle. I break out into a fit of tears. It's the only other outlet my body has for the energy-sucking sensation to escape. I'm mentally removed as Kayne spills inside me, crying into the pillow until the aftershocks of ecstasy taper off.

I have no life left. Two earth-shattering orgasms are all I can take.

I feel Kayne shift, bringing his face to mine and licking up my tears.

"That's exactly the reaction I want every time."

I just lie there panting. I have nothing left in me to respond.

Kayne gives me a few minutes of reprieve, massaging my back, my legs, even my scalp. But a few minutes is all I get, because all too soon I hear the top of the lubricant bottle pop again, and my whole body locks up. What the fuck is he doing now?

I feel him push against my ass, this time with the butt plug. I tremble. No more. "Kayne," I protest. But he ignores me, pushing the plug all the way in.

"*Kayne.*" I strain against my restraints. My rosebud on fire. "Please."

"Shhh, Ellie," he reprimands me. "The only time I want to hear you is when you're moaning in pleasure or screaming my name."

I'm going to be screaming all night. I clench my cuffed fists as he props my pelvis back on the pillow and lines up behind me. I'm on the brink of tears already, my body begging please while howling no all at the same time. My head is spinning without any end in sight.

"All night, Ellie. I'm going to alternate fucking you like this all night," he murmurs in my ear as he buries himself to the hilt. "And I'm not going to stop until my dick is limp and my come runs dry." I draw in a sharp breath as his cock and the butt plug continuously hammer away at me.

Again.

And again.

Putting demands on my body I'm not sure it's capable of withstanding.

"Kayne!"

"I HOPE ONE DAY YOU can forgive me, Ellie." I hear Kayne's voice in the distance. I don't know if it's a dream or reality, but when I flutter my eyes open, I'm in his arms. I shift. No cuffs or chains or collar. For a split second I wonder if it was all a dream. Then I look around the room and realize I'm still confined to my prison in the sky.

"You stayed?" I blink, finding his dazzling blue eyes.

"Mmm hmm." He nuzzles my neck and breathes me in. "How do you feel?"

Crazy conflicted.

"My limbs feel like Jell-O, my wrists are rubbed raw, and there's a pain in my ass." I grimace as I move.

"All a reminder of who owns you." He sucks my earlobe. "You're so soft."

"So are you," I reply as my hips rub against his.

"Don't be a wise ass, I'll spank you." He hugs me tighter.

He's acting weird.

"Why are you still here? Where is my collar?"

"Because I wanted to stay, and on the nightstand," he answers straightforwardly.

"I don't have to wear it anymore?" I stretch in his arms.

Kayne snorts. "Of course you do. How would I find you if you got lost?" He kisses me tenderly. "I just thought after last night, you could use some room."

"You weren't wrong in assuming." I touch the compass tattoo on his chest. I don't know why. I guess just to feel it. I never get to touch him. He moans softly, almost like a purr. Last night was the most intense, excruciating, amazing night of my life. Kayne pushed every physical, emotional, and spiritual limit I have. I didn't think I was going to come out alive.

Someone really needs to steal his bottle of Viagra.

"More," he says. It's a request, not a demand. I touch him tentatively, exploring my newfound freedom. We melt into each other, the same way new lovers would; cuddling, snuggling, stealing soft embraces.

Who is this man? Who is he really? The charismatic businessman or the ruthless Dom? The one who holds me affectionately or brings me to tears? I wish I knew. I wish I could figure him out. Why did he have to take me when I offered myself up willingly?

"Do you remember the first time we met?" he asks, rubbing his nose against my cheek.

"Oh, God. Why are you bringing that up?" I hide my face in the crook of his neck so he can't see the embarrassment.

"Because." Kayne chuckles. "You spilt hot coffee in my lap."

I'll never forget that day. The way he strolled into Expo like he owned it, wearing a light brown power suit and aviator sunglasses. He was intimidating and intriguing, and I was drawn to him unlike anyone or anything else on earth. My body and mind just responded. It was a primitive, carnal response. Then he took his sunglasses off and my inner axis tilted. He looked straight through me with those raw majestic eyes. I forgot who I was and what I was doing. Unfortunately for him, I was pouring coffee at that moment and missed the cup completely. I'd never seen anyone move that fast. Needless to say, I was mortified and Mark almost decapitated me. Kayne was a huge whale to land, and I nearly fucked it all up. Luckily for me, he had a sense of humor.

"You dropped to your knees and told me to take my pants off." Kayne is full-blown laughing now. I'm glad it's such an amusing memory for him. I tried to scrub my brain of it for months.

"I was sort of disappointed you didn't." I lift my head slightly and eye him lasciviously.

"If there wasn't a room full of people, I would have. Then I would have taken yours off too, and laid you out on the conference room table." Kayne threads his fingers into my hair and tugs lightly. He licks my lower lip like he's trying to memorize the taste. "Do you know how many times I fantasized about fucking you on that table?"

"I had no idea you fantasized about me at all." I dart my tongue out to touch his.

"Every time I walked into Expo and sat down for a meeting, I was half listening to Mark, half imagining you kneeling at my feet." He grabs hold of my hair a little harder, taking control of my head. "Imagining you spreading your legs for me and letting me lick you senseless, then driving myself so deep inside you, we'd both forget we were ever two separate people." I moan as he bites my neck and grabs my ass.

"I would have let you." I run my hands up his chest and over his shoulders, digging my nails into his skin in response to the grip he has on my hair.

"Ellie?" Kayne rasps. Sliding his hand along my side. "Can I ask you something?"

"Yes, Kayne," I respond robotically. He spanks my ass lightly. I jolt. Even the littlest bit of pain feels volcanic.

"I said don't be a wise ass."

"I wasn't being a wise ass, I was answering you like you expect me to."

"Not right now. Right now I'm invoking Cupcake."

I crack a smile. "What do you want to know?"

He swipes his thumb across my cheek and I can't help but turn into his touch. "Do you think if the circumstances were different? If we did things the normal way, you could have accepted who I am? My way of life?"

I contemplate his question while searching his eyes. Why does he want to know? What does it matter?

"I'm not sure. What aspects are you talking about?"

Surely not the kidnapping.

"My domineering side. You would have never known about my 'other' business."

I ponder his question some more then shrug. "I don't know how you build a relationship on lies. But you never gave me a chance to find out on my own, so I guess we'll never know." It's an honest answer. He nods, with a small frown.

"How did you end up like this? End up here?" I ask curiously. I have so many questions. There are so many things

I want to know. Kayne rolls on top of me, my body crying out from his weight. He rubs his nose softly against mine, as if conflicted. "That story is for another time. Another lifetime. But I promise one day I'll tell you."

"Why can't you tell me now?"

He shakes his head. "Now's not the time."

"When will be the time?" I question him.

"I'm not sure exactly. But soon. Just try to keep an open mind, and remember things aren't always as they appear. It's all I can say about it."

If I wasn't so emotionally exhausted and physically drained, I'd try to coerce more information out of him. I like him like this, open and affectionate. I like the Dom too. I'm beginning to realize I'm fond of all of Kayne's sides, which I know is a dangerous thing. He kidnapped me; he keeps me on a leash and collared like a puppy. I'm his to control and more and more, I'm acclimating to this lifestyle.

"Okay," I acquiesce.

"Good. Can you get up and take a shower?"

"Jett usually puts me in the bath after one of your punishings."

Kayne shoots me a twisted look. "One of my punishings? Is that how you see sex with me?"

"Sometimes." I shrug demurely.

All the time.

Kayne smiles boldly. "Good. Because no one will ever give it to you as good as me."

On some deep elemental level, I know it's the truth.

Kayne gets up and walks into the bathroom butt naked, and I hear him run the tub. A few minutes later the smell of eucalyptus drifts into the bedroom.

He comes back once the water stops running.

"Can you get up?" He holds out a hand.

I sit up, and every fiber of my being protests, especially the ones between my knees.

Kayne must see the agony on my face, because he scoops me up without a word and carries me into the bathroom. He steps into the tub and submerges both of us into the steaming hot water.

"Ah." It feels like I'm being pelted with stones as the water works to relax my exploited muscles. Kayne leans me against his chest, wrapping me up in his strong arms. I liquefy.

"Who do you belong to, Ellie?" He kisses my temple, the two of us immersed in overflowing bubbles.

"You, Kayne."

KAYNE

ALL I CAN THINK ABOUT is Ellie's ass.

And how she felt in my arms this morning. I pick at my bottom lip mindlessly as I fantasize about her. Her toned body, her sultry green eyes, her sexy smirk, her wet fucking ...

"*Kayne.*" Jett waves his hand in front of my face. "Hello, Kayne. Can you please stop daydreaming?"

I'm trying, but Ellie seems to be all I can think about. She's invaded my life like a force I never saw coming. I want to keep her more than anything. But after all this? After everything I've put her through? A life without her is a fate worse than death. Which is a strong possibility, too, if everything gets fucked up.

"Javier is up to something. We should have heard from El Rey by now. There should be meetings set up. A drop point. Accounts established. None of that has happened. It's been a month." Jett paces in front of my desk.

"It hasn't gone unnoticed," I inform him.

El Rey, *The King*, is one of largest drug kingpins in the world. He is notorious for being a ghost and responsible for over fifty percent of the cocaine and heroin smuggled into the

US. Javier is his right-hand man and our only line to meeting him face to face.

"Well what the fuck should we do? Endeavor is breathing down my neck. They know El Rey is within reach."

"Tell Endeavor to cool their jets. There's nothing we can do but wait. If we make the wrong move our cover will be blown and years of hard work will be worth shit." Jett huffs. He knows I'm right. Situations like these are dangerous and deadly and need to be handled with delicate care.

"How is Spice?" I ask.

"Healing." Jett clenches his fist. He takes looking after the women in the house as a serious task. He dotes over them like prize-winning orchids. They provide an invaluable service of their own free will. They are rare, exquisite creatures, according to him, and seeing one of them hurt nearly sent him on a murderous rampage. Javier seems to have that effect on people.

Jett may look more like a laidback surfer than cold-blooded killer, but he has a dark side just like the rest of us. He wanted to kill Javier. Like, take a rusty kitchen knife and slit his throat. I would have held the spineless worm down while he did it, but we need the Mexican motherfucker alive. "She's recuperating, but she still wants to go."

I groan, annoyed. The girls who work for me come from all walks of life. Some are ex-prostitutes from the slums of the streets looking for a safe environment. Some are from upper class communities, looking to fulfill the piece of them that's missing. Sex fiends with insatiable appetites. No matter where they come from, they're treated all the same. Trained and educated in all sexual aspects to provide my clientele the erotic experience they pay top dollar for.

I don't want to see her go, but I won't force her to stay.

"If she leaves, make sure she's compensated accordingly," I tell him, rocking back in my black leather office chair.

Jett nods with a frown. He doesn't want her to go either.

"I'll have a word with Javier. See if I can grease the wheels." I crack my knuckles irked.

"I think that's smart." He glances at his watch. "I need to check on Ellie."

"Dress her. I want to take her for a walk," I tell him pointedly.

Jett just stares, those fucking aqua eyes probing me.

"What?" I insist.

"You know you can't keep her," he reminds me.

I growl at him. *She's mine.*

"What's going to happen when she finds out the truth?" He treads lightly.

My world will end.

"It will be over." I shrug, trying to play off the inevitable apocalypse.

"Are you going to be able to live with that?" he asks delicately.

"I'll have no other choice," I respond indifferently, while my heart secretly granulates in my chest.

If I'm even alive at all.

I FIND JAVIER EATING IN the grand dining room. Its walls are a light yellow, with an extravagant baroque mural on the recessed ceiling overhead.

"Kayne." He smiles smugly with a mouth full of food.

I sit across the expansive mahogany table from him. I keep my expression cool and my demeanor even colder.

"Javier." I address him.

"Are you here to share a meal with me?" he asks with his thick accent.

"No."

"A woman then?"

"Definitely not," I scowl.

"Then what can I do for you, amigo?"

"You can tell me what the fuck is going on. You have been under my roof for a month. Eaten my food and fucked my women. But made no mention of El Rey."

"That's not a very nice tone for a house guest." He fiddles with the silver knife in his left hand. I track his every movement.

"Have you ever heard the expression constant company is never welcome?" I ask short tempered.

"No. In Mexico, it's mi casa es su casa."

I glare at the complacent bastard.

Six months ago an associate of mine contacted me. A real stand up hell of a guy. He informed me El Rey had caught wind of my tequila empire. He looked into me and liked what he found. An American who exports alcohol out of Mexico and runs an elite brothel. My less than perfect morals intrigued him. He saw an opportunity to do business with me, because what goes better with drugs than alcohol? It's as natural as peanut butter and jelly. That's when I first met Javier. We exchanged correspondences, and as El Rey's right hand, he was responsible for informing me of The King's interests and coordinating the details. They wanted to utilize my exportation of tequila to move drugs into the US. I have plenty of customs agents in my pocket, which El Rey was already aware of. He definitely does his homework. He wouldn't be the man he is if he didn't. Yes couldn't come out of my mouth fast enough.

Three months ago I was invited to Mexico for a sit down with Javier. Me, being an American, had both El Rey and Javier taking extra precautions. You never know who you're dealing with in this business. Friend or foe, ally or enemy. Law enforcement or not. Javier flew me down in a private jet, and then had me amicably escorted by gunpoint to his home. It was the most terrifying car ride of my life. Once there, I realized the true depth of evil I was dealing with. Besides being a main player for one of Mexico's largest drug cartels, he was also a slave trader. He had dozens of girls broken beyond repair. They crawled around his house on all fours like cats and were never permitted to stand. Naked and starved, some were so thin you could see their spine and ribcage. He kept them in tiny metal crates so small they were forced to crouch in a ball. And every night he tortured one of them. For the three days I was there, I heard their screams. And there wasn't one fucking thing I could do about it. I had a mission. That was my focus, as unbearable as it was. The last night the wails were the worst. They were bloodcurdling, echoing through the entire house. The disturbing shrieks still haunt me. I don't think they'll ever stop. I nearly cracked, damning it all to hell. My hero complex flared, but just as I got out of bed to end the madness, the screams stopped. Sometime later I heard digging in the backyard. I peeked out the window to see one of Javier's thugs kicking a body into a shallow grave under the moonlight. He killed her. While I was in his fucking house. No shame, no concern.

I nearly puked at the sight of her bloodied, abused state. After that night, I swore that girl's death wouldn't be in vain. I would destroy Javier, El Rey, and anyone else associated with them.

That time is coming soon. I'm walking a tightrope that keeps getting narrower and narrower, and I just have to keep my balance for a little while longer.

That's why I took Ellie. I knew what Javier was capable of. I flashed back to that moment and saw her lifeless form the moment he said he wanted her.

And as I've said before, like fucking hell I was going to let that happen. If anyone was going to torture her, it was going to be me. So I took her before he had the chance to pursue her. And he would have. Once Javier wants something, he doesn't stop until he gets it.

"What the fuck is going on, Javier? Has there been any word from El Rey? Is he interested or not? I don't have the time or patience to fuck around. I gave him my price and my conditions. They are more than reasonable."

"Yes, he's agreed." He wipes his mouth with the white cloth napkin, and then tosses it on the table. A stupid smile on his face. This prick is always smiling. I wish I knew what was so fucking amusing.

"So what's the hold up?"

"How's your whore, Kayne? Does she miss me?" he diverts.

"She's got nothing to fucking do with this conversation."

"I hear the two of you, you know. I listen at the door while you make her scream. She's very impressive." My blood boils in my veins. That motherfucker is never getting near Ellie again. "What if I wanted her to be part of the deal?" he asks darkly.

"I'd tell you to fuck off," I snarl.

"You'd pass on millions of dollars because of some whore?" He raises his eyebrows intrigued.

"She's mine. I'm prideful, what can I say." I keep my voice firm, desperately suppressing the dread clawing up my throat.

"I'd love to dip my dick and see what's makes her so special." He licks his lips. I want to pull his tongue right out of his mouth and wrap it around his head.

"She a delicacy you'll never indulge in." I glare.

"Again," he taunts me.

"Ever. Again," I threaten. "Talk to your boss. Make the deal. I have everything prepared. If he's not interested, get the fuck out. I don't need his money or your aggravation. I do just fine by myself." I stand up, sending the chair screeching across the hardwood floor.

"Arrogante Americano," Javier spats.

Arrogant American.

"Maybe so, but The King came to me, remember?"

"I didn't forget," he sneers.

"Tiene cuartena y ocho horas," I order directly.

You have forty-eight hours.

Then I stalk out of the room and up the staircase with my heart ricocheting all around my chest. By the time I make it to Ellie's door, I'm a shitstorm of rage, lust, anger, and wrath. I need to bury myself as deep as I can inside of her while she's chained to the bed and fuck her until my murderous thoughts eradicate. She's quickly become the solace in my tumultuous life. With her, I'm the best part of all my sides. All my faces. With her they blend into one cohesive man. She's the glue.

I press my thumb to the fingerprint recognition screen. I had a state-of-the-art lock installed the morning after Javier assaulted her. No way was I going to allow that cocksucker a

217

second chance at picking the lock. He'll have to slice off my fucking fingers before he gets in her room again. I open the door and find Ellie exactly where she should be. Kneeling on the bed, mostly naked, with her tag dangling from her collar. My dick swells to almost painful. She's so beautiful, so perfect. All mine. I don't say a word as I stomp over to her.

I push her onto her back, possess her mouth, and drag her legs apart. I grind the missile my cock has become against her, and she moans. But it's not in pleasure, it's an anguished sound. She's in pain, and it's because of me. It's all because of me. She would never be in this dangerous predicament if it wasn't for *me*. It takes everything I have to beat back the beast and pull my lips away from hers. They're swollen and red from my forceful kiss. She's looking up at me curiously. Always curious, always lively, always playful. That's Ellie. Intense and bewitching. I've been drawn to her since the moment we met. Somewhere deep down I have always felt something proprietary when it came to her.

I run my fingers along her face, soaking in her beauty. Her acute green eyes rimmed in black, her high cheek bones dusted in pink, her full mouth stained a dark blush.

"I would kill for you." I speak the words that can never be taken back. I speak the truth.

She sucks in a breath, her breasts swell, and her eyes widen. I kiss her again, darting my tongue between her lips. I don't want a response. I just want her to know in a roundabout way how I feel.

After a few minutes of indulging myself in Ellie's mouth, I pull away.

"Are you ready for your walk?" I skim her neck with my teeth softly, wanting nothing more than to rip her panties off and live inside her.

"Are you?" she pants.

"Wrong answer, Ellie." I tweak her nipple, and she jolts.

"Yes, Kayne," she corrects herself immediately.

"Good girl."

I reluctantly remove myself from her and my cock curses me. But she's already in pain, and I'm not in the mood to punish her body more than I already have.

I unlock her chain from the headboard and urge her up. Once on her feet, I begin to lead her out of the room, but her leash jerks in my hand. I turn to find her standing there, gazing up at me through her lashes.

"Come on, kitten." I jingle her leash.

She takes two steps forward then drops to her knees.

She looks up at me with her hands on her thighs and lust in her eyes. She's asking something. Permission?

I pet her head. "Is there something you'd like, Ellie?

"Yes, Kayne." She licks her bottom lip seductively. My already throbbing cock is now kicking. My little kitten wants to play.

"Go ahead then." I press my pelvis forward.

She lifts her hands to my belt and unbuckles it. She then unclasps the waist of my slacks and lowers my zipper. She hooks her fingers into my underwear and drags both my boxer briefs and pants down, springing me free directly in front of her face. Does she know how much I need this? Need her?

Ellie darts her tongue out, licking the tip of my erection. It feels like an electrical shock through my system.

I slide my hands into her light brown hair. Jett left it down, and it's sexy as hell. Just like Ellie. She works my cock into her mouth. Sliding it in and out, taking it a little deeper each time. I groan freely, loving the feel of the way she takes me. Possesses me. Of her initiating the blow job in general. My grip tightens in her hair as she swallows all of me, the head of my pulsating erection touching the back of her throat. I try to stay still and let her suck me to an orgasm, but it feels too damn good, too damn tempting. I hold her head and thrust into her mouth. She absorbs each jab, never moving; the goddess that she is on her knees. My orgasm moves quick, snaking its way down my spine and tingling my tailbone. I come so fucking hard I roar like a wild animal. Ellie swallows every drop of my release, sucking me until I run dry.

I can barely stand as the remnants of my climax vaporizes. Ellie just stays on her knees with her head bowed, waiting for my direction. I run my hands through her hair reverently.

"You little minx." She looks up with blazing green eyes. I scratch her under her chin.

She smirks impishly.

I barely recognize the woman in front of me. She's a seductress. A temptress.

And I realize now, she's not the only one who's owned in this room.

JAVIER'S FORTY-EIGHT HOURS ARE almost up. I can't wait to throw that Mexican piece of shit out with the trash. There are going to be some very unhappy people if this deal doesn't go through. A lot of wasted hours and money spent, but that's the nature of this fucked-up business. Everyone is a snake. Everyone is out for blood.

There's a knock on my office door. I look up with just my eyes. "Come in."

Javier appears in front of me. I'm shocked he actually used his manners. He saunters haughtily into the room and takes a seat in the wing-back chair across from my desk.

"Coming to say goodbye?" I ask snidely.

"Quite the contrary. El Rey will be arriving in two days. The arrangements will be made prior, all accounts approved. He will stay for one night for a face-to-face meeting. Then I will stay behind to make sure the shipments arrive effortlessly."

"I have full faith in the company I use," I tell him arrogantly.

"I'm sure you do, but what's the saying, better safe than sorry. Don't you agree, amigo?"

"Let's get something straight." I lean forward menacingly. "I am not your amigo. We do business. I tolerate you in my house. That's it." I tap the pencil I'm holding against the desk repeatedly. Riled, agitated, and on the brink of committing a homicide.

"Yo comprende," he responds with dark eyes.

"Good. Now get out," I bite.

Javier stands but moves slowly. "I'd like to throw a party. El Rey hasn't stepped foot on American soil in over a decade. Let's make his one and only night a memorable one."

"You want to throw him a party?" I raise my eyebrows. Javier nods.

"Okay." I smirk deviously. "I'll throw him a party he'll never forget."

"Excellente." Javier smiles wily, then walks out of the room.

I snap the pencil in two, wishing it was his neck.

ELLIE

SOMETHING RAPTUROUS TOOK HOLD WHEN Kayne professed that he'd kill for me. He meant every syllable. I could feel the verity vibrate through my bones. Then, insanely, I dropped to my knees, and for the first time since the night he took me, I craved to please him. To sate him. I don't know when things changed, or how they changed, but making Kayne fall apart had my adrenaline pumping and my pussy throbbing. For a split second I contemplated lying on my back and splaying my legs so he could have me, but when he grinded himself against me moments before, I knew my body couldn't handle another punishing. My mouth was the next best thing, and it seemed to work just fine. I was especially proud of myself when his eyes rolled into the back of his head.

My time with Kayne has been enlightening, to say the least. It's blossomed a desire inside me that I never dreamed existed. He pushes all my limits, all my boundaries, all the confines of my mind. He's making me into someone new. Someone strong and sexual and barely recognizable. Someone who's learning she loves to serve him.

Presently, Kayne is feeding me dinner. I'm on my knees between his legs, taking pieces of beef bourguignon straight from his hand. It's sweet and tangy and sinfully delectable.

"Ellie?"

"Mmmm hmmm?" I suck his fingers into my mouth a little further than necessary. His breathing accelerates.

"Behave," he chastises with just the slightest hint of menace. I quake with need.

"Yes, Kayne," I purr.

His eyes dilate as he zeroes in on my lips and then my naked chest. He didn't touch me last night. He gave my body some reprieve, but I fear whatever he has planned tonight will make up for the lost time.

"Tomorrow night I'm throwing a party. A very special guest is arriving," he says. "You need to be on your best behavior. Can you be a good kitten for me?" He feeds me another piece of meat. I nod while I chew.

"Yes, Kayne," I say after I swallow.

"Good girl. I want to show you off. I want everyone to see what's mine. And be green with envy." He jingles the tag on my collar, and then glides his thumb and middle finger down my delicate diamond body jewelry until he reaches the middle of my breasts. He touches one nipple so softly I barely feel it, and yet it still somehow manages to make me tingle between my thighs.

"This is going to be a party unlike any you've ever been to. It may be a little shocking. I want to warn you now. You know the business I run."

I blink at him inquisitively as heat creeps over my skin. I know exactly the type of business he runs. I've seen it, I've experienced it. I fucked one of his employees because of it.

"Yes, Kayne."

"And no one will touch you but me. Regardless of what they perceive." His tone is resolute.

"Yes, Kayne." My voice wavers.

"Mine, Ellie. Only mine." He yanks my collar, bringing my lips to meet his. The kiss is gentle. Emotion filled. It floods me with confusion. What's happening here?

"You have been such a good girl." He gropes me. "But I'm dying to spank you." He palms my ass and my heart rate accelerates.

"Yes, Kayne," I respond immediately, remembering what happened last time he told me he wanted to spank me.

"I told you that lesson would stick," he says haughtily.

He definitely remembers, too.

Kayne pulls me to my feet by my new leash. A thick chain with delicate pink ribbon threaded through the links. My legs are wobbly. My body hasn't fully recovered from the other night, and I'm not particularly inclined to pain. It's moments like these that bring blaring clarity to my situation. I can't say no. There is no, *no*. Or stop. No amount of begging will change his mind. He's only given me the choice once, with Sugar.

"On the bed. Get on all fours. Facing the headboard."

I immediately do as I'm told. I walk over robotically with my heart jack-hammering in my chest, crawl onto the mattress, and position myself on my hands and knees.

I watch as Kayne picks up the shackled cuffs lying on the table of torture, and then another chain from one of the drawers. I try to breathe steadily, but my body instinctively reacts to what's on the horizon. Kayne walks over to the bed and places the items next to me. He kisses my back, starting from the middle of my shoulder blades, down my spine until he reaches my tailbone. Then he sheds his clothes, shrugging his collared shirt off first, then his pants. Naked, he's a god — tall, toned, the standard of excellence.

"Get up and grab the top of the headboard." He kisses my neck, right above my studded collar.

I scurry up the gargantuan bed and reach as high as I can, my fingers not quite making it to the top. Kayne crawls up behind me and presses his hard body flush against mine, pinning me against the vining iron. He loops the cuffs through an opening then secures both of my wrists. If it weren't for the pillows, I would be dangling by just my arms. Then he fastens the end of my leash to a high curve forcing me to look up. I'm panting now, in yet another unyielding position.

"Mmmm," he moans as he takes advantage of my overstretched body. Touching me wherever he wants. Massaging my breasts, my ass, my thighs, my clit, jutting my hips out a little farther after he's finished copping his feel.

"Ready?" he growls primitively in my ear and I hear the clink of the other chain. I panic. I don't want the pain. At least not that much.

"Kayne, please don't." My voice strains from the pool of tears welling in my eyes. "Please don't hurt me." I tremble in my restraints as I await the first blow. But nothing comes. Except soft kisses across my skin.

"Shhhh, Ellie. I'll never hurt you again." I feel him fasten the other chain to the back loop of my collar, a second leash. "Unless you make me." He says it flippantly, but there is still an undercurrent of menace in his voice. A warning. A message: don't fuck with me.

He massages me gently, lulling me into submission, then tightens his grip on the chain. The collar strains in two directions and I can no longer move my head.

"Fuck, you look so hot like this."

I whimper as he rubs his cock against me, then lands the first blow. A sharp smack right to my ass cheek that stings like a son of a bitch. My body tenses all over. He hits me again and I grit my teeth, absorbing the pain, unable to move. He rubs my heated skin, tempering the sting.

He hits the same spot again—the fleshiest part of my buttocks—and I cry out.

Oh, God what did I ever do to deserve this?

"You're doing so good baby," he coos, licking my neck. "Let's see if you're wet." Kayne slips his finger between my legs and slides it through my folds. "Fuck, Ellie. You're soaked." He withdraws his finger and lines the head of his cock right at my entrance. I brace myself, for what I don't know. Another hit? For him to take me hard and fast, like he usually does?

He rocks against me, entering me slow and controlled, the movement foreign to me. "God. Ellie you feel so fucking right." His voice is thick with lust as he pushes himself all the way in. A drawn out moan escapes my lips. He's so big for my little body. Every time, stretching me wide, and filling me to the point of almost bursting. I'm helpless under his strict command; my wrists tethered over my head, my body dangling, my neck strained. He fucks me leisurely, sliding all the way out, then driving his cock directly back in. I'm losing my mind, the pace is perfect. It's sending me to another planet. Then he whacks me again and I jolt back to the here and now. My relaxed muscles clench hard causing him to groan.

"One more baby. Then that will be five. You've been such a good little kitten, it spared you from ten." The last hit is the hardest of all. I scream his name in protest.

He drops the leash—it smacks my backside—and grips my hips with both hands. Digging his fingers into my flesh, he still continues to move slowly. Like he's savoring me. He never savors. He always just takes. Takes from my body, takes from my mind. This is different. The way he touches me, the way he moves.

"You have no idea how much you mean to me, Ellie. How much I want to keep you." He removes one of his hands and begins to rub my clit, circling it lightly. Mind-bendingly good.

"Kaaaayne," I moan, as everything aches; my arms, my ass, my pussy.

"Do you like that, Ellie?"

"Yes, Kayne."

"Tell me the truth."

My brain is on autopilot as he twists all of my senses. "I love it. I don't ever want you to stop."

My orgasm is arresting me, the same way my wrists are tied. It's coming on strong, full force. But I need more of him to explode.

"I don't ever want to stop."

"Please, please," I whimper.

"Please what?" He presses harder against my clit with his finger.

"You know." I'm shaking, unable to push myself over the edge.

"Say the words," he demands. "I want you to tell me to fuck you."

I'm so desperate to come, I'd say just about anything to him right now.

"Fuck me, Kayne. Please fuck me, make me come," I nearly sob.

"Anything for you." He sucks on my neck right above my collar as he begins to pound into me, feeding my body exactly what it needs. Exactly want it's starved for, even though it's fed every night. My climax pressurizes then explodes, unleashing a hailstorm of ecstasy. I come unashamed, while screaming his name.

"Fuck, give it to me," he grinds out, thrusting harder. "Give it all to me. I want every fucking ounce."

He wrings me out. My body going slack in my restraints as he ruptures, stilling forcefully, buried deep inside me. He drops his head against my back and breathes heavily, as he recovers from the euphoric high.

After he comes around, Kayne hoists me up, so I'm straddling his thighs. It takes the pressure off my arms and neck. He massages my shoulders while dusting soft kisses across my fevered skin.

"You are so sexy. I can't tear my hands or my lips or my eyes off you. You're my most prized possession," he growls in my ear. "I meant it when I said I would kill for you, Ellie. I'd do anything for you."

A rash of goose bumps erupts all over my body. I feel safe. I feel wanted. I feel desired. In this new life, my goals and ambitions are vapor. And as much as that saddens me, my existence has morphed into something else entirely. I secretly enjoy the things he says, and the way he makes me feel. I believe him when he tells me I'm important. It gives me a sense of purpose to please another. To please him.

"Tired baby?" he asks as he continues to rub me down.

"Yes, Kayne." I'm physically depleted and emotionally spent. Every interaction with Kayne drains me completely.

He removes the second chain, unbinds my hands, and hooks my leash back in its usual spot. My arms and back feel stretched, sore. He forces me to lie down on the cool satin, all while watching my naked movements with his mesmerizing eyes. I feel like they're peeling away every layer of my existence. I want to know what he's thinking. Why he's looking at me like this might be last time he ever sees me.

"Sleep baby." He kisses my forehead lightly and moves off the bed.

"Aren't you staying?" I ask timidly.

"Not tonight." He slips on his pants. "A lot of things are going to change very fast. I have to make sure everything is ready.

"Changes?" I ask, my voice small.

Kayne chastises me with a harsh facial expression. "Shhhh. No more talking. No questions." Then his eyes soften as he runs a finger lovingly along my jawline. So mercurial. "Sleep, Ellie."

"Yes, Kayne," I reply forlornly.

I don't want him to leave.

KAYNE

TWELVE HOURS.

The countdown has begun. Tonight is what I have lived the last six years for. El Rey will be on American soil. He will be in my home. The deal will be made. Shit will implode. My mission will be complete. And I have no idea where it will leave me and Ellie in the aftermath. My stomach actually rolls thinking about what we have coming to an end. Whatever that may be. Having her in my life on a daily basis has made a mundane existence shine with brilliance. She invaded my heart like a sneak attack and now she's a permanent fixture.

"Everything is set." Jett has been rambling for the last half hour and I don't think I've heard one word he's said. "Kayne." He snaps his fingers in front of my face. "Are you listening? This is the most important night of our lives. Let's not fuck it up, okay?"

I curl my lip at him. If he were anyone else I would snap his skinny ass like the twig he is.

"Do they hurt?" I ask randomly.

"Does what hurt?" he asks lost.

"Your balls. Do they hurt being strangled in those fucking pants all day?"

"Hate on my style all you want." He grabs his junk. "My shit shoots just fine."

"Good to know. Because if it didn't I'd have to hire a new trainer."

"You won't need one after tonight." He smiles coyly.

I involuntarily grimace. Jett's eyes soften.

"Don't fucking look at me like that," I snap.

"Like what?" His eyes widen. Like he doesn't know.

"Like you feel sorry for me or something."

"False accusation. You're an asshole scumbag who doesn't deserve an ounce of pity."

Man, ain't that the truth. I glance at the security feed. The mansion is quiet. No one is around. All the girls are preparing, Ellie is sleeping, and Javier is lurking.

It's the calm before the storm.

"Since we're on the subject," Jett probes. "Are you going to be able to handle whatever happens after the shit goes down?"

Probably not.

"I'll have to, won't I?" I look over at him. He's dressed in a light blue V-neck shirt and tight white pants. His normal attire.

"She may forgive you." Jett slips that in there.

"Would you forgive me?" I counter.

"Well, that's not a fair question, is it? No one knows you better than me. And knowing what I do, I would say hell no. And tell you to fucking die."

I glare at him. "Is this supposed to be a pep talk? Because it sucks. "

"Ellie doesn't know all your dark corners. She may take pity on you." He paces in front of my desk. "After a shitload of spoiling and groveling on your part of course. Are you man enough to handle that? You prideful jackass?"

"I don't know. Maybe. Probably. If it means I get to keep her." I cross my arms and brood.

"We both knew this life wasn't going to last forever."

"Yes we did," I sigh.

"Maybe she'll forgive you." He reiterates.

"Maybe pigs will fly and your dick will breathe in those pants."

"Hater."

"Dream on. Speaking of Ellie—"

"Already covered." Jett raises his hand to halt my sentence. "Your jaw is going to drop."

"Oh really?" I cock an eyebrow.

"Yup. It's your last night together. Thought I'd make it special."

"Well aren't you just my fairy fucking godfather in heinously ugly skinny jeans."

"You're just jealous you can't pull them off."

"Insanely." I roll my eyes. "Go see to my kitten. Make sure she's happy." I dismiss him.

"I think the only time she's happy is when she's with you," he says over his shoulder as he walks out the door.

I really fucking hope that's true.

ELLIE

JETT HAS SPENT THE LAST two hours primping me. I have never been dolled-up this much in my life. He has straightened my hair and pinned half of it back. Smoked my eyes out with purple shadow and black eye liner. Put on false eyelashes and stained my lips a bright pink. Presently he is slipping me into some sheer intricate lingerie number that's nude-colored, floor length, and has a plunging neckline. There's a butterfly pattern on the front made out of white lace that barely covers my breasts and wraps around my ribcage. With a skimpy thong to match, I think it's the most clothing I've worn since I've been here.

Jett crosses his arms and stares at me, admiring his handy work.

"Bellemiso." He makes that gesture where he kisses the tips of his fingers.

I eye him entertained. "You are a very odd individual."

"I know. One of a kind."

"How did you come to be this way? If you were gay, I'd understand."

Jett smiles his oh-so-pretty smile while running a hand through his blond hair. "One day I'll tell you the whole story. But the cliff notes version? I grew up around a lot of women."

"Sisters?" I ask.

He laughs like it's some kind of private joke. "No, not exactly, but my mom did take in a lot of strays. Me and a house full of females, I learned a few things."

"Like how they think and what they like?"

"Yes, that, among other *things.*" He emphasizes the word things.

"What things?" I probe.

He clams up.

As close as I feel to Jett, I know very little about him. Besides his favorite color being blue, his favorite ice cream mint chocolate chip, and his weapon of choice, wax.

"Jett, since I've been here, you have bathed me, dressed me, and groomed me. Made me laugh and consoled me. It's sort of unfair. You know more than most about me, and I know nothing about you."

"You know that I care about you," he counters.

"Jett." I put my hands on my hips and glare playfully at him.

"Those eyes are killer." He sighs as his resolve crumbles. "My mother was a Madame, Ellie."

"What?" I respond bemused.

"Yup. I grew up in a very affluent whore house. While other boys were playing football in high school, I was learning the family trade."

I'm rendered speechless.

"It's how Mansion came to be," he informs me.

"Mansion?" I question.

"Yes, that is what we call the business. I train all the women who work for us."

"Train? Like how Kayne trained me?"

"Yes. Very much like that."

"And they just let you?" The concept is foreign to me.

"Yes, Ellie. Some women crave to be controlled. It's a lifestyle that isn't always understood. But in this house it's done in a safe environment with likeminded people. Happy you asked now?"

"I guess," I reply blankly, trying to digest this new information.

"Not what you were expecting to hear?" he asks casually, as he fiddles with my hair.

"No," I divulge truthfully.

"It never is." He laughs. "I'll tell you more about my upbringing and Mansion one day. But for now," he claps his hands like it's back to business, "we need to get going. Kayne is going to flip. Like lose his shit completely when he sees you."

"You think?" I bite my lip, glancing down at my ... outfit? No, ensemble.

"I know," he says confidently. "I've known Kayne a long time. And I know what he likes."

I frown, now knowing what I do about Jett, Mansion, and Kayne, I suddenly feel a little inadequate. "Has he been with many women?"

Jett's mouth falls open. "Umm?"

"That many, huh?" I respond insecurely.

"No, not exactly. It's just this lifestyle allows for an open tap of unadulterated pleasure. He's never hurt for company."

"Then why did he take me?" That is the question I feel I will never find out the answer to. Jett rests his hands on my arms. "You're going to know soon enough, sweet thing. And it's something Kayne has to explain."

"I don't like the way that sounds, Jett."

"And you shouldn't."

I swallow hard, a sudden upshot of fear grabbing me. "He keeps telling me things are going to change. Is he going to sell me?"

Jett's pretty aqua eyes bulge. "Where did you get a ridiculous idea like that?"

I shrug. "I'm a slave. Slaves get sold."

Jett shakes his blond head. "No more erotic suspense novels for you. And I can say with absolute certainty he would never sell you. But he is afraid he won't be able to keep you."

"I don't understand."

"You don't have to. All will be revealed in time. "Jett walks over to my bed and picks up my collar. "Final accessories." He fastens it around my neck then goes to the armoire and opens one side of the double doors. He returns with rhinestone wrist cuffs attached to several strings of thick crystals. One string he fastens to the D-ring on the front of my collar, then he clamps each of my wrists. I'm a dolled-up pet. A kitten on an ultra-extravagant leash.

"Perfect. It's time, sweet thing."

"Time for what?"

"You're unveiling. This party is important. Be on your best behavior. Listen to Kayne. Stay by his side no matter what."

"He has me on a leash, where do you think I'm going to go?"

Jett snickers. "I've become quite fond of you, little one. And that snarky mouth."

"It's all I have left. My snark."

Jett looks at me with a melancholy expression. His acute eyes sad. They remind me of a puppy in the pound. I wish I understood what he was feeling. I want to ask, but I think I've exhausted my allotment of questions for the day. I'm meant to live in the dark. And Jett and Kayne are experts at keeping me there.

Jett leads me toward the door by my shiny new jewelry.

"Where are we going?" I ask curiously. Kayne is the only one who takes me for walks.

"Kayne's room."

"Why?"

"Because you're his birthday surprise."

"It's his birthday? Is that what the party is for?"

"Not really. He'll probably decapitate me for telling you. But I don't give a fuck." He looks back and winks at me. I follow Jett through the dark hallway with the deep purple carpet and hand-blown chandeliers toward the sweeping staircase. I can hear music playing faintly from the first floor as we walk down one flight of stairs to the second level.

"Wait till you see this party. It's my best yet. Going to be a real *bang*."

Something in my gut jolts from way he says *bang*. I don't like it one bit.

We stop at a huge wooden door where two very large men are exiting.

"Everything set up?" Jett asks them.

"Done," the tall blond responds. He reminds me of Thor with his brawn and long wavy hair.

"Excellent."

Jett ushers me inside Kayne's room and it strikes me as strange being here. The only environment I know him in is my room and our walks around the mansion. I observe my surroundings, noting it's very much a man's space. Understated, with dark cherry furniture and glossy wood floors. Against the back wall is an impressive canopy bed with maroon bedding. Very majestic, very commanding, very magisterial. Just like my owner. What I find most peculiar is the giant birdcage in the middle of the room.

"We have to hurry. Kayne takes a long shower, but I don't want to run the risk of him walking out and ruining the surprise."

"What surprise?"

"Why you, of course." Jett leads me inside the enormous cage with shackles hanging in the center. He removes one pair of cuffs from my wrists and replaces them with another. My heart races as I dangle dead center in the middle of the cage.

I feel like a virgin sacrifice.

"These cages are decorations for the party. I thought it would be a fun birthday present for Kayne to have his own captive angel. That's the theme." He smiles. The irony of his statement is not lost on me.

"I'm already his captive," I remind him dryly.

"True. But I think deep down, you like it. You like serving him. And obeying him. And being dominated by him."

I don't respond. Partly because I don't want to admit he's right, and partly because I think my affections go way deeper than like.

"You look entrancing, sweet thing." He pulls a red ribbon out of his pocket and ties it in a bow around my chest. He then pulls a thin chain out of his other pocket. He's like a walking vending machine tonight. He takes the delicate cord and weaves it through my fingers suspended above my head.

"What's that?" I look up.

"Kayne will know." He smirks devilishly, and right then I know I'm in trouble.

"My work here is done. I'll see you at the party, gorgeous girl. Behave." He taps my nose playfully with his index finger.

"I don't know how much trouble I can get in just hanging around." I pull on the restraints. If it wasn't for my heels, I'd be stretched and struggling on my toes.

"Well, just in case you get any ideas." He winks, closing the cage door. Then leaves the room. All I can do is wait. Now that it's just me, I can hear the hushed sound of the shower running. I jingle the chain around my fingers trying to figure out what it is. But all I see is silver metal. The wait for Kayne becomes suspenseful. I wonder what he'll think of Jett's present? What he'll think when he finds me in his room. He's never brought me here. Never even suggested it. So I wonder idly if he'll feel like I'm encroaching on his personal space. I'd rather like to avoid him taking out his displeasure with Jett on my behind. I tell myself he won't do that. Please don't. Please don't. I hear the shower turn off, and I tense in my chains. I drop my head submissively as I wait for Kayne to find me.

"Well, what do we have here?" I hear his voice and look up through my eyelashes. He's walking toward me slowly. The hunter stalking his prey. His eyes are wide and there's a mischievous grin on his face. "A sexy little kitten in a cage, just for me?"

"Jett said I was your birthday surprise."

"My birthday? He spilled the beans?"

"Yes, Kayne."

"Look at me, kitten."

I raise my head. He's standing in front of me in just a towel and tempting smile.

"This may be the best birthday present I ever received."

My cheeks heat. He looks like a hungry cat about to devour a helpless canary.

"Watch me get dressed." My eyes follow him as he moves through his room, pulling out clothes from his dresser and closet. He lays everything on the bed, and then discards his towel. He's standing in front of me stark naked, moving gradually so I get a good look at every inch of his hard sculpted body and the tattoos on his chest, arm, and side. He's freakin' drool worthy. I'll never deny it.

"Like what you see, kitten?" Kayne asks flirtatiously.

"Yes, Kayne," I reply with a raspy voice. Just looking at him has my mouth dry and body responding.

"Good." He smiles, then proceeds to get dressed. This feels so intimate. Watching him in the privacy of his room. Seeing him in a completely different light than I've ever seen him before. Once he's dressed in a plain white dress shirt and white pants, he joins me in the cage; his shirt partially unbuttoned.

I stare up silently, while he stares down.

"I guess I should unwrap you now." Kayne tugs lightly on the ribbon and the bow falls apart.

He drinks me in from head to toe, scanning his luminous eyes over my face, my chest, my torso, my legs, licking his lips as he goes. It's all at once nerve-racking, stimulating, and sexy as hell.

"I need to give Jett a raise," he tells me as he leans in and kisses me. There's no warning or asking of permission as his tongue invades my mouth. Jabbing and rolling, he asserts his dominance. His control. Reminding me I'm his. Like I could ever forget.

When we break apart I can barely breathe, my lungs working double time to suck in oxygen.

He runs his hands over my body, taking advantage of my powerless state.

"God, you're beautiful," he moans as he squeezes my breasts, fondling both of them at the same time. Kayne rests his head against mine, inhaling deeply like he's memorizing my scent. "Everything is going to change tonight, kitten." I look up into his majestic eyes. The brown lightning bolt more pronounced, ominous almost.

"You keep saying that, but what do you mean?"

"It means all will be revealed," he sighs forlornly.

"What will be revealed?" I urge.

"You'll see. Then it will all make sense."

"Is something going to happen to us?" I ask warily.

"Maybe."

"What?" I press, needing to know.

"I'm not sure. Possibly everything."

"I'm scared," I admit abruptly.

"Of what?"

"The unknown."

Kayne runs his thumb across my cheek. It's such a consoling caress.

"Do you trust me, Ellie?"

I pause, drinking in the earnest expression on his handsome face. Do I?

"Yes. I trust you," I tell him truthfully. When did everything between us shift? I don't really know. What I do know, and what I can say with certainty is, when I look at Kayne, there's more than just lust or need or want in his eyes. There's devotion and admiration.

"Good. Because I'll never let anything bad happen to you. I'll never let anyone hurt you again," he says pained. "I don't want to lose you, Ellie. Ever."

"I don't want to lose you either," I reply, unable to stop the words even if I wanted to. I am truly owned by him.

"You won't. Even if you push me away," he assures me resolutely. He then kisses me, causing my body to sway in the restraints. I tighten my fists and stiffen my limbs in an attempt to not lose my footing. The little chain Jett wrapped around my fingers clinks, spurring Kayne to glance up. He reaches for it, unraveling it from my hand.

"Fucking, Jett." He plays with the shiny string.

"What is it? Another present for you?"

"It's more a present for us." His blue eyes flash with venturesome lust as he dangles the strand in front of my face. It's long with a tiny clamp on the end.

"What's that for?" I ask cautiously.

"I can't wait to show you. Open your legs."

I do as I'm told. Kayne threads one end of the chain through the loop on my collar, the other end he slips into my dainty panties, then, using his fingers, spreads my folds wide. There's a sudden bite of pain as he pinches my clit with the clamp. "Oh God!" I gasp. Then he pulls on the chain and my knees go weak as a bolt of stinging ecstasy spirals through me.

"So you behave." He kisses my cheek lightly.

A ravenous urge builds within me as he repeatedly yanks on the chain commanding the clamp.

"Kayne, please."

"Please what, baby? Stop or go on?" he taunts me.

"I don't know." I drop my head back as my body depletes of energy. The sensations are much too much.

"You have no idea how sexy you look," Kayne breathes against my neck. "You have no idea what your body does to me." He grabs my ass and grinds his erection against my aching clit. I groan as the clamp pokes and prods at me, making me dizzy with desire. "You have no idea what I would do to keep you." He nips at my skin.

"Fuck, Ellie," he says tortured, grabbing my face in his hands. "I ... I ..." He searches my eyes, desperate and afraid.

Afraid of what, I can't begin to imagine. "... I want to watch you come." He cops out.

Reaching down, he slides my thong over to the side, and then inserts one finger into my throbbing core.

I moan uncontrollably as he strikes the right spot over and over.

"Shit, you're wet baby."

"You're going to make me come." I pull on the restraints as my body seizes, the clamp working the sensations double time. I buck in the shackles with my climax just out of reach.

"Kayne, please!" My voice is hoarse and my body is trembling.

"Not yet, kitten." He slows his rhythm, and I nearly combust into tears.

"Why?" I plead.

"Because I want you to remember who controls your pleasure. No matter where you go or who you're with. You'll always be mine." He leans into my neck, and I realize too late that he has the chain to the clit clamp between his teeth. Before I know what's happening, he slips another finger inside me and jerks his head. The dual sensations cause me to spark, splintering my existence into a thousand tiny pieces as Kayne commands my pleasure. His words echo like the threat they are. And the promise. My body gives way as every muscle strains, leaving me demolished in the restraints. My arms feel like they are going to dislocate, but I can't bring myself to stand. I'm destroyed once again. My mind, my body, my soul, my heart. They all feel like they're bleeding.

"Remember my words, Ellie." He hoists me up.

"Yes, Kayne," I reply, like I'm doped up on something. Like I'm doped up on him.

"My kitten." He smoothes his hand over my hair. "Recuperate and I'll clean you up."

He leaves me hanging, literally, and disappears into the bathroom. Kayne returns with two folded hand towels and a small bowl of water. He drops to his knees in front of me and removes my lacy thong. With the first towel, he wipes between my legs. With the second, he dips it into the bowl and proceeds to wash me. The water is warm and fragrant with something I can't place. It feels incredible as he moves up the inside of one thigh and down the other. His touch is so skilled and wonderfully tender. When he's through, he pats me dry; remaining on his knees he gazes up at me with an idolizing expression. The moment is surreal and also oppressive. The weight of his stare is almost too much to endure, but no matter how hard I try, I can't bring myself to turn away.

"Can I ask one thing of you?" Kayne places his hands gently on my hips.

"What?"

"Forgive me." He drops his head. "Forgive me for every wrong I have ever done to you."

The request sidelines me. Forgive him? Forgive him for kidnapping me? Forgive him for forcing me into sexual slavery? For beating me and humiliating me? For not protecting me and letting some scumbag accost me?

Forgive him for penetrating my heart, because even after everything, I want to remain his?

"I forgive you," I say delicately.

He heaves a sigh of relief. Then places a soft chaste kiss right below my belly button. It feels almost reverent. This man is so complicated and intriguing and frustrating and exciting. One minute he's an ice cold Dom, the next his affection could warm Antarctica. I'll never understand.

Kayne suddenly drops, his entire body falling to the floor at my feet. He places a light kiss on my ankle, then on the inside of my calf, my thigh, my stomach, both of my breasts, my neck then finally my mouth. He kisses me firmly, but affectionately, like he's trying to communicate something.

"You own me as much as I own you," he sighs against my lips. His eyes closed, his voice woeful. There are a million conflicting emotions spiraling through me. I should hate him, but I don't. I should want to run, but I won't.

"Kayne ..."

"Shhhh, baby. No more talking. There's been enough said."

And before I can make any leeway, he puts me right back in my place.

AYNE

I FINISH GETTING DRESSED WITH my kitten watching me in her cage. She's tethered, clamped, and collared. I don't think anything is hotter. I button my shirt and slide my belt through the loops. Dressed solely in white, per Jett's request.

Tonight everything changes.

My life as I've known it for the last six years.

I never take my eyes off Ellie. As much as I want to stick a plug in her ass and fuck her delirious in that cage, I'm refraining.

I almost told her everything.

I almost told her I love her.

I almost told her she was free.

I don't know how I'm going to handle it if she walks away.

If?

When.

She says she's forgiven me. But I know once the curtain falls, the past will be our biggest obstacle. The truth will derail everything, and I'm dreading that unavoidable moment.

My phone beeps and I check the message.

Jett: Go time. It's been a pleasure serving with you.

I chew the inside of my cheek. Sentimental motherfucker.

"Time to go, kitten." I turn to Ellie with the most sorrow I have ever felt in my life. I keep my expression stoic, but the emotion reaches all the way from the tips of my fingers to the bottom of my soles.

I unclasp Ellie from her binds and rub her wrists. Then kiss her lightly on the lips. She's regarding me quizzically. I know I'm acting all kinds of weird, but I feel like a short-circuiting television. Cutting in and out between protection, duty, obligation, and love.

"Best behavior tonight, kitten." I buckle each of her crystal wrist cuffs. Then I grab both her leash and the newly added chain dangling through her collar's ring and yank lightly. She groans as the clamp tugs on her clit. My dick stirs. The clamp will keep her in line and aroused until I'm ready for her. "Head down, walk behind me, and only speak when spoken to."

"Yes, Kayne," she pants, and it revs my sex drive like a turbo engine. I will never get tired of hearing Ellie say those words. I will dream about them when I'm asleep and long to hear them when I'm awake.

I lead Ellie out of my room, loving the fact she was in my space. I fantasized about her sleeping in my bed, with a secret hope she'd become a permanent fixture one day. I have a foreboding feeling though, 'permanent' will never be an option with Ellie.

As we approach the staircase, the distinct sound of dance music floats up around us. Jett went balls to the wall for this party. Go big or go home, right?

We're going for a sonic boom.

Ellie and I walk down the extravagant stairs; the foyer already filled with people dressed solely in white. As we descend, I scan the crowd. Many people I recognize — most on my client list — and many I don't. I hope everyone has fun while they can, because it all ends tonight. I walk Ellie through the foyer and into the great room. I feel all eyes on me and my tempting little kitten. I have never owned a slave before, willing or otherwise. I like control, I like to fuck, and this lifestyle affords me that, with no strings attached. I never had to worry about conventional Dominant/submissive roles.

I was never interested in being responsible for someone else, until I experienced what it was like to break down another human being and truly be in control of them. To literally rule their life. Watching Ellie crawl on the floor and lay at my feet while she wore my collar was a rush unlike any I've ever known before, and probably unlike any I'll ever know again. For the first time, I not only wanted to take care of another person, I wanted them to take care of me. I want *her* to take care of me. That's probably the most terrifying admission of my pathetic existence. I've never depended on anyone; I was never given the chance. Ellie opened up a part of me I didn't even know was there. I want to keep her my kitten forever. Not an option, I know. Doesn't mean a man can't dream.

I shake hands with a few associates in passing as I stride into the room with Ellie in tow. It's dark, with black lights illuminating the walls and everyone's white attire. Even Ellie's dainty white lace glows. It looks like she's wearing only a skimpy bikini. I travel deeper into the room, snaking my way through the crowd with a tight grip on Ellie's leash. She's a fraction of a centimeter behind me, but I feel her everywhere; brushing up against my body, highlighting my heart, sweeping over my soul. She makes it hard to concentrate.

Everything looks as it should. People drinking, dancing, and partaking in immoral self-indulgence. Women, half naked on chains, are being felt up by anyone their Master will allow, while lewd acts are being performed on the white wing-back chairs and tufted flatbed couches. If Ellie is in shock, her outward appearance isn't showing it.

We make our way to the very back of the room where there's a roped-off section. This, right here, is what makes Mansion's parties legendary. We dubbed it the playroom. An open space set up with tables, crosses, and swings. Basically everything your average kinky fucker could desire. What makes the playroom so special is that it comes complete with women, ready and willing. Take your pick of apparatus and have at it with the girl who's already there or one of your own choosing. I told you, my girls provide an invaluable service. The medieval stocks are always a favorite. At least that's what our clients tell us. Women confined, with their hands and head trapped between wooden boards, bent over, accessible for the taking.

The playroom serves a dual purpose; entertainment for those who want to watch and entertainment for those who want to partake. We feed all appetites here.

I pull Ellie in front of me and rest my hands on her hips. "Look, kitten," I murmur in her ear.

She looks up and directly in front of us is one of my girls—Pepper —strapped to a table, exactly like the one in Ellie's room. Her hands are tied above her head and her legs are secured to the stirrups, spread wide.

"Do you remember that day, kitten? When I strapped you to the table in your room?" I ask seductively. "I fucked you right after I gave you this." I run my nose against her neck and tickle her tag. "You came so hard. You like being mine."

"I could never forget," she responds, breathing strenuously. I can feel her heartbeat knock against my chest, as clear as *Seven Nation Army's* bass pumping through the room.

We observe Pepper lying on the table like a lamb waiting for the slaughter. She doesn't lie there long. Soon she's taken; her indefensible state an open invitation to anyone who wants her.

"Watch, kitten." I hold Ellie's face, as Pepper is fucked by a dark-haired man dressed solely in white.

"Do you wish that was us? Do you want me to tie you down and satisfy your ache?" I tug at the delicate chain attached to the clit clamp. She drops her head back against me and groans.

"Answer me." I jerk a little harder, my erection digging into her back.

"Yes, Kayne!" Her body stiffens and I release the chain.

"Soon, baby. But not yet. I want you frustrated." She moans like she's already there.

"You're mean," she murmurs with her head rolling all over my shoulder.

"I know." I kiss her cheek.

I force Ellie to watch Pepper come. It's a spectacle of a scene. Screaming and writhing and deep penetration. Either that guy's really good, or she really needs a promotion. Whichever, it is a good show.

Ellie is nearly falling apart in my arms by the time they're done. Rubbing herself against my erect cock with panting little breaths.

"You like to watch, kitten," I remark smugly. "I approve. Do you want me to take you in there and fuck you? Maybe pin you to the cross or secure you to the stock?"

She leans her head back and looks me in the eyes. Her eyelashes are huge tonight. "No."

"Why not?" I challenge, dipping my face closer just so I can inhale her scent. She smells like lemons.

"Because I don't want to share you with the public."

Okay. Time out. I wasn't expecting that answer.

I tighten my arms around her. My spirit flying high. "I don't want to share you either. Unless it's with Sugar," I leer.

Ellie chuckles. "Only behind closed doors." She flutters her long eyelashes. I nearly fragment. My frisky little kitten.

I grab her boob. "We have to go." I can be frisky too. I turn her around and give her a quick kiss on the lips, then snatch up her leash. I need to get back to prowling the floor and stop getting distracted by my sultry little pleasure kitten, with her gorgeous eyes, tempting mouth, and smokin' hot body.

All in good time, baby. All in good time.

I spot Jett a few minutes later. Just the person I am looking for. He's standing next to one of the many cages scattered all over the room containing captive angels. Girls dressed in barely there lingerie and huge white wings, dancing provocatively. It sort of reminds me of a Victoria's Secret runway show. As I get closer, I realize it's Sugar in the cage. It doesn't surprise me. She's his favorite girl.

"He's here," Jett informs me as I stand casually beside him.

I spy the room and spot Javier standing next to an older, light skinned man with silver hair.

"El Rey is American?" I've never seen a picture of him. He prides himself on being a ghost. The simple fact he's here is exceedingly rare. And it's a rarity that needs to be exploited.

"Half. Actually," Jett informs me. "The genes must run strong on his father's side."

"Clearly. What time is it?" I ask as the music thumps and strobe lights flicker on the ceiling.

Jett glances at his watch as I continue to survey the room. "Nine fifteen. Eleven thirty-seven is execution."

"Got it." I squeeze my grip on Ellie's leash and glance back at her. She's pressed against me, her cheeks are flushed and her eyes are down. The clamp and our little peep show must be weighing on her. Two and a half hours, kitten. Two and a half hours left. I look back at Jett and zero in on Javier and El Rey walking our way. Here we go. As the two men approach, I look both of them in the eye.

"Senor Roberts," El Rey addresses me, shaking my hand. He's a tall, well-groomed man with viciousness in his dark brown eyes. "I thank you for welcoming me and celebrating me in your home."

"Mi placer. Es un gesto para expresar mi entusiasmo para las actividades futuras."

My pleasure. It's a gesture to express my enthusiasm for future endeavors. I respond in his native tongue to show respect.

Piece of shit.

He smiles brightly. "Yes, I look forward to it. Javier has confirmed everything is in place and the first transaction should happen next week. I'm very pleased."

I glance at Javier. He hasn't taken his evil stare off Ellie since he reached us. It makes me want to stab his soulless black eyes right out of his head.

I feel the tension rippling off of her. She recognizes him, and she's scared.

"As am I," I respond evenly, even though a reel of murderous images are playing through my mind.

He nods with approval, and the deal is done. Funny how such a simple exchange can fortify a multimillion dollar business partnership. A very illegal, dangerous, clandestine agreement.

I smile insincerely. "Now that the formalities are out of the way. Please enjoy. Indulge. Jett went above and beyond for the guest of honor."

"Yes, I'm interested to see where this night goes. White attire?" He looks at Jett.

Jett shrugs, holding on to one of the bars of Sugar's cage. "All I can say is be prepared for a bang."

El Rey cocks an eyebrow. Javier glares. I keep smiling. Javier then turns his attention to Ellie. She's been perfect this whole time. If I wasn't holding on to her leash for dear life, she'd be a figment of my imagination.

"How's your whore, Kayne?" he asks, and Ellie stiffens.

I want to slit his throat open and remove his vocal cords with tweezers.

"Still mine," I growl.

El Rey glances behind me, and then very lightly tugs on her chain drawing her out from behind my back. I hear her expel a little gasp, the clamp continuously doing its job. Which pleases me and pisses me off all at the same time. I'm the only one who's supposed to pull her strings.

"She's quite stunning." El Rey drinks her in with a greedy stare. Ellie stands perfectly still, with her head down and hands cuffed in rhinestones by her side. "Look up, my dear."

She doesn't move. He frowns. "Not trained?"

"She's trained. This is her first outing." I jingle her chain, knowing she feels it right between her legs. "Look up, kitten."

Ellie sweeps her head up, breathing hard. Her eyes are glassy and her cheeks are bright red.

"Exquisite." He regards her, stepping closer. "Is she for sale?"

"No," I immediately reply.

"Borrow, then?"

"No."

"No price at all?" he questions.

El Rey could pay, I have no doubt. But Ellie is invaluable.

"No. This one is mine." I glare at Javier. *Got that Mexican scum of the earth?*

"I don't blame you for keeping her all to yourself." He runs his thumb down her chest and over the delicate chain attached to the clamp. Then he tugs and Ellie nearly falls over. I need to count to a thousand so I don't flip my shit on the spot and go on a shooting spree. But this is part of my cover. Having him believe I'm as big of a douchebag as he is.

"We have plenty of pets to play with," Jett chimes in, gaining both Javier and El Rey's attention.

"Yes. I'd hate to miss out on the festivities." El Rey steps away from Ellie, but Javier lingers a second longer. Then he squeezes her breast. Ellie whimpers and retreats behind me. I will cut his hand off for that.

"Your whore still needs work," he sneers.

I glare at him, throwing daggers with my eyes. Soon motherfucker. Soon.

Jett leads Javier and El Rey toward the back of the room, and I know exactly where he's taking them. The playroom. Mansion's VIP area for public sex and women for the gorging. That should keep them occupied for the rest of the night.

I wait until the three of them are out of sight, then turn to Ellie. She's shaking. I take her face in my hands and force her to look at me. "You did so good." I kiss her lips as a tear escapes down her cheek. I lick it off.

"How about we relax and have a little fun?"

"Fun?" she repeats curiously. She probably thinks I want to fuck, given the environment and porno being projected on the wall. But I have something else in mind.

"Mmmm hmmm." I grab her hands and start to sway my hips to Flo Rida's *Wild Ones* pumping through the room. People are dancing all around us, and I think it's time we join in. Ellie smiles brightly as we begin to move. I swear it's the most genuine smile she's donned since the night of Mark's party. The night everything went so terribly wrong. I pledge after this is all over, I'll keep that expression on her face for the rest of her life. I will do anything to keep her safe, keep her smiling, keep her mine. I'll walk over jagged glass, run through a blazing fire, crawl on my hands and knees through the desert, wear a collar and lie at her feet.

Anything.

Cannons suddenly blast, pelting everyone in the room with liquid color. There's Jett's bang. They ring in succession, one after the other, turning a sea of white into waves of splotchy color. My shirt, my pants, my face, even my hair, is splattered with a vibrant rainbow. The same with Ellie. We kiss passionately and laugh foolhardily as we smear color all over each other while dancing to the music. In my entire life, I have never been so happy. This single moment will live infinitely.

I grab her ass and grind my hips against her. She moans in agony. The clamp is torturing her.

"Uncomfortable baby?" I murmur in her ear.

"Yes," she pants, and I'm sure if she could sweat through her tongue she would.

"Need me to take care of you?" I rest my cheek against hers and trap her face with my hand.

"Yes, Kayne." It's a desperate plea.

That's all I have to hear.

I drag my multihued kitten off the dance floor and through the first door I see, making sure to lock it behind us. We're in one of the mansion's zillion bathrooms. I think this is the first time I've ever been in this one. It's decorated in several different shades of blue.

"Bend over," I order.

Without delay she braces herself on the speckled cobalt vanity right between the double sinks. My cock throbs. There's nothing more tantalizing than Ellie wide open and prime for the taking. I lift the long sheer material of her lingerie up her back and then glance at her in the mirror. There's paint all over her face and in her hair, across her chest and down her stomach. It looks like we've been rolling around in colorful mud. I grind my erection against her ass and she lets out an injured moan.

"Need me baby?" I taunt her.

"Yes," she heaves.

I slowly unbuckle my belt and unzip my fly, all the while watching Ellie watch me. She looks like a starved animal, and the son of a bitch in me loves it.

I press the head of my cock against her entrance and she juts her hips back begging for it. "Stay," I order, and she stops moving.

I reach over her shoulder and grab the thin chain attached to the clamp, drawing it behind her. Then I tie it to the loop on the back of her collar, making sure there's no slack. She's breathing savagely with wild eyes.

This is going to be intense.

I lace my hands behind my head and stand steadily with my legs spread apart. Ellie watching me idly through the mirror.

"Go on, kitten. Move. Take your pleasure. I want to watch you make yourself come."

She stares at me silently. I've never given her control before and by the look on her face, she has no idea what to do with it.

"Fuck me, Ellie." I nudge my hips infinitesimally.

She trembles, steeling herself on her hands. And after an elongated beat, she impales herself onto my cock and cries out, her head snapping back as her body ingests all of me. She's soaking wet and fucking on fire.

I watch, entrapped, as she begins moving urgently, pumping her pussy hard against me. I don't budge, even though the need to grab her hips and pound into her is suffocating me. She doesn't last long, a few heated seconds, before the orgasm eating her alive grabs hold. Ellie claws at the blue granite as she screams through her soul-sucking climax, the physical exertion visible on her pretty face as she saturates me with her arousal. My little kitten, in the throes of ecstasy— nothing is more powerful or stimulating.

My cock twitches and my heart hammers as the urge to fuck her senseless takes over.

She collapses forward after the tremors pass. Damn, that clamp is no joke.

I lean over her and kiss her behind the ear.

"My turn."

"Kayne," she cries, with her cheek pressed against the cool stone. Soft sobs wracking her body. "Cupcake."

Instantly, everything inside me feels like it's freefalling. All at once I withdraw from Ellie, spin her around, and plop her on the counter in front of me. I wrap her legs around my waist and slide back into her delicately. She shudders. She's still sensitive and hot as a fever.

"What happened, Ellie?" I hold her face in my hands, dropping soft kisses on her cheeks, her nose, her eyes, anywhere and everywhere I can get my lips. She looks up at me with a harrowing expression.

"I just need to touch you." The anguish in her voice rocks me. It's the first time she's ever invoked cupcake, and I know exactly what she needs.

Me.

A connection.

Sometimes I forget Ellie isn't accustomed to this life. She endures everything I throw at her, no matter how taxing. Her strength seduces me, constantly spurring me to push both our limits.

I rip my shirt open, sending the buttons flying everywhere. She places her hands on my chest, her right one landing directly on top of the intricate compass tattooed on my pec. She explores my body, touching my face, my arms, and my stomach all while I'm nestled snugly inside of her.

"I'm yours, Ellie. Every single inch." I want to assure her. I want her to know she can have me if she wants.

She eyes my torso, brushing her fingertips over words inscribed on my ribs. *It takes a certain kind of darkness for the stars to shine.*

"What does it mean?" she asks.

I swipe my thumb across her cheek. "It's a reminder that sometimes you have to do bad things for good reasons."

Ellie creases her brow as I feather soft kisses against her lips. "I hope one day you'll be able to understand."

"Understand what?" she asks a little dazed.

"Me." I shift inside her and she sucks in a sharp breath.

"Take it off," she pleads, rocking her hips. I instantly remove the clamp and she winces, breathing through the pain as blood rushes to her clit.

"Better?"

"Yes." She looks worn out, but the lust in her eyes is evident. She's not sated yet.

"What do you need?" I ask, dotting kisses on her lips.

"You." She tightens her legs and wraps her arms around my neck.

I'm hers for the taking, the devouring, the destroying.

I lean forward, with Ellie latched onto me for dear life, and brace myself with one hand on the countertop, aligning us at the perfect angle. I thrust slowly, in and out, savoring her soft sighs and indulging in her pleasured moans. God, she feels good. Tight, wet, warm, euphoric.

"You're perfect." I punch deep inside her. "Perfectly made, just for me."

She groans, sliding her hands into my hair. Her muscles contracting, squeezing me tight, driving the orgasm I'm fighting to control right up the fucking wall.

"Make me forget," she pleads, undulating against me. "Make me forget everything but you."

I grab her ass and slam into her. What my kitten wants, she gets.

"Oh, God yes!" She lifts her legs higher, giving me deeper access. I slam into her again, and again and again until she's flooding with desire.

"More," she demands, so more I give. Striking my hips over and over, our skin slapping together as her starving little pussy eats up every inch of my cock it can.

Wet, hot, branding arousal, that's what she damns me with. Because I know no one will ever make me feel the things she does. No one will ever wield my emotions or satisfy the beast that hungers only for her. I need to keep her.

The relentless pounding and asphyxiating contractions of Ellie's core causes my orgasm to spark at my tailbone. There's no controlling it as it ignites up my spine.

"I'm going to fucking come," I warn her.

"So am I!" she cries out, a rush of warm heat drenching my cock, spurring my orgasm to catch fire all over my body. We freefall together. A symphony of untamed, feral sounds echo around the room, bounce off the walls, and ricochet straight through my soul.

Holy fuck.

Did she feel it? Our connection, our link. *You're mine.*

With ragged breaths I open my eyes and hold her tight. "Will you stay with me, Ellie?" I ask in desperation. "Would you wear my collar not because I forced you to, but because you wanted to?"

She pops her eyes open, her gaze the darkest I have ever seen, like I'm staring straight into an evergreen forest.

She searches my face with confliction on her own. I never find out her answer because someone starts pounding on the door.

"Fuck off!" I snarl, still staring right at Ellie. I need to know, *will you stay?*

"Amigo," Javier's voice penetrates through the door like a buzz-saw. Ellie stiffens in my arms.

"You're safe," I whisper.

She nods silently, with wide frightened eyes.

"Que?" I answer.

"Your presence is requested." I don't like his slimy tone one bit.

Fucker.

"Coming," I snap, withdrawing from Ellie, beyond irritated. I was hoping to still be in the bathroom when the shit went down. I glance at my watch, ten after eleven.

We put ourselves back together in a hurry. We're still covered in color and now smell like sex. The scent I've come to live for.

I grab Ellie's leash once she's done cleaning herself up, kiss her on the lips, and then wind the chain around my hand. "Behave. I'm right here; I won't let anything happen to you." I kiss her again. I never want to stop.

"Amigo!" Javier pounds on the door wildly. Yup. Definitely cutting off that motherfucker's hands.

"Fuck you!" I bark, and then look over my shoulder at Ellie. "It will be over very soon." I try to reassure her as I grab the door knob and turn.

She nods, panicked and confused. I think her ability to speak is gone.

I swing open the door to Javier, two of his thugs, and three semi-automatic weapons pointed right at me.

"That was quite an earful," Javier says lewdly with that evil smirk.

"WHAT THE FUCK IS THIS?" I spit.

"Armed escort. Move." Javier motions with the pistol in his hand.

With no other option at the moment, I do as he says; walking down the hall surrounded by muscle and machine guns. I keep Ellie close. This shit isn't good.

We're forced into my study at the front of the house. It's away from the party and very secluded.

"I think El Rey would have something to say about you treating your host like his." I sneer.

"I'm sure he will." Javier smiles brightly. A moment later The King is strong-armed into the room at gunpoint.

Definitely not good.

"What's the meaning of this?!?" he demands outraged, looking between me and Javier.

"Hostile takeover." Javier lifts his gun and shoots El Rey right in the head. Ellie screams as The King's body falls to the floor and bleeds out all over the hardwood. I stare Javier down as Ellie quickly crumbles.

"Shut your bitch up!" He motions with the gun. "I'd shoot her too, but I have plans for you both."

I try to calm a trembling, pleading Ellie down, but she's in shock. It's no wonder, she's been traumatized over and over ever since she stepped foot in this house.

"Shhhh. Ellie. Calm." I yank on her chain, trying to command her. I'd rather wrap her in my arms and console her, but the moment calls for dictative actions. She looks at me with the most distressed eyes I have ever seen on a living human being.

"Kneel," I order, my voice firm, cold, and calculating. Nothing like the man she was with moments ago. I'd much rather be that man, but he has flaws and feelings. And those two things can get you killed.

"Do it," I hiss through my teeth and spank her so hard my hand stings. She drops to my feet so fast her knees slam against the floor.

If we survive this, the penance I will pay.

"I'll teach her better." Javier snatches her leash out of my hand and drags her across the room. I bolt forward but am met with several guns shoved into my chest.

"Not yours anymore," he heckles with a grip so tight on Ellie's collar he's restricting her airway. She's gasping and clawing at the leather begging for oxygen.

I'm quaking with rage from the inside out. I am going to kill him. Fuck cutting off his hands, I'm just going to put my fist through his chest and rip out his heart. I watch helplessly as he ties the leash to a thick gold sconce high on the wall.

"Kneel," he orders her.

Ellie doesn't move quickly enough and he shoves her down, the collar nearly hanging her. "Move and I'll rape you in front of everyone with that letter opener on the desk." My steel-plated letter opener that looks like a mini sword. Ellie kneels with barely enough chain to reach the ground. That cocksucker has turned her collar into a noose. She stares at me with pleading eyes as she slowly starts to suffocate.

I weigh my options. There aren't many. I have no gun, I'm outnumbered, and I don't want to go all Rambo and end up getting her killed.

As I formulate a strategy, Javier drops another bomb. He pulls something out of his pocket and throws it at my feet.

"Recognize that?"

I stare down, studying the scrap of something on the floor. I nudge it with my toe and then realize what it is. My head snaps up. "Where is he?"

"Gone," Javier sings. Terrorizing me.

All rational thought evaporates. That scrap on the floor in front of me is skin. Jett's nautical star tattooed on his left arm, Javier sliced it off. In a moment of unbridled rage, I go after him.

He lifts his gun without hesitation and shoots me in the shoulder; pain rings through my whole body as I grab my arm and fall to my knees. Son of a bitch.

Javier stands over me and presses the barrel of the gun to my forehead.

"What's yours is now mine, amigo."

He presses harder and I steady myself with my heartbeat echoing in my ears and my blood whooshing through my veins like white water rapids. I glance at Ellie fighting for her life and fearing for mine. Then I look at the clock on the wall and erupt in a fit of laughter.

Javier looks at me like I've lost my mind. Maybe I have.

Eleven thirty-seven.

"Jett's death won't be in vain." I glare at him manically. *"BANG."*

Moments later, a dozen men dressed in black and armed for war flood the room. They break through the bay windows and kick down the door. When shots ring out, I hurl myself at Ellie, shielding her with my body. I yank on the chain, pulling the sconce right out of the wall. The gunfire lasts only a few seconds, but I'm sure it feels like years to her.

When the commotion ceases, I lift my head with Ellie trembling uncontrollably in my arms.

"It's okay. It's over now." I smooth her hair and kiss her head repeatedly while she latches onto me like it's the end of the world.

I'm sure for her it is.

I glance around. Javier, El Rey, and all their thugs lay dead on the floor. The room is destroyed, bullet holes in all my books, the walls, and my desk. The cherry wood looks like it's been chewed on by wild animals.

"Can you stand?" I ask Ellie delicately.

She looks up at me, drained of life.

I lift her to her feet and secure her in my arms. I'm never letting go. "It's okay. It's over. It's all over."

"Agent Rivers."

I stand at attention at the call of my name. "Commander."

Ellie looks at me funny. *Yeah, kitten, we have a lot to talk about.*

"You alright?"

I nod. "Affirmative, sir."

"Nice work." He puts his hand out. Commander Adams is the A-typical Army commando. Short buzz cut, thick mustache, and no nonsense. He's one of the best people I know. Next to Jett.

My heart sinks. I hug Ellie tighter with the arm I still have around her. She's the only thing grounding me at the moment. The only thing holding me together. I try not to think of Jett and the terrible end he faced. Images upon horrific images infiltrate my mind.

"Thank you, sir." My response is strained.

"Debrief at 0800. The house will be wiped."

"Sir," I answer mechanically.

Ellie watches our exchange. I know she thinks she's in the twilight zone.

One of the Special Forces soldiers wraps her in a blanket as I converse with Commander Adams. Then he tries to remove her collar. I want to growl, but I don't. *Mine.* When he finds he can't because of the padlock, he disappears. Good riddance.

"Get that wound taken care of, Rivers. See you in the AM."

I nod compliantly.

"Sir?"

"Yes, Solider?"

"Did the team I requested deploy?"

"An hour ago."

I nod again. I sent a fleet to diffuse and disband Javier's slave operation. The team was instructed to evacuate the estate and then burn the house to the ground. I vowed I wouldn't let that girl's death be in vain and I always stand by my word. Now I'm freeing them all.

Commander Adams gives Ellie a once-over, then cocks an eyebrow at me. He leaves without another word after that. Ask me no questions, and I'll tell you no lies. That's how this operation works. Execute the mission. End of story.

"Please tell me what's going on before I fall to pieces." Ellie finally speaks once we're alone.

"I'll tell you everything, but I want to get you out of here first." I put my arm around her to lead her out of the room, but she backs away.

"No, Kayne, now. Here. Tell me." There are so many emotions laced in her voice. She's scared, confused, upset, and rightfully so. I've kept her captive for a month, told her nothing about anything, and then just dropped it all in her lap.

A room full of dead people is not exactly where I wanted to have this conversation, but Ellie seems adamant and my time as her proprietor is over. I owe her answers, and it's time to fess up. Heaven help me.

"What's going on is it's over. Everything."

"What's over?"

"My mission."

"Mission?" she repeats, trying to understand.

"Ellie." I drop my forehead to hers. Where do I start? I guess from the beginning. "I spent my entire life in and out of foster homes, and to say my upbringing was rough is putting it mildly. When I was eighteen, I joined the Army. It was either enlist or live on the street." Ellie frowns, her eyes compassionate but hard at the same time. "I scored particularly high on certain parts of the aptitude test and was recruited for a pilot program called Black Dawn. It's where I met Jett."

"Jett was in the Army?" Ellie interrupts.

"Hard to picture, I know." My lip quirks solemnly. Every inch of me hurts, inside and out. And the mere mention of Jett's name magnifies the pain twenty-fold.

"Mutual friends," she muses.

"Excuse me?" I question trying to understand her statement.

Ellie's eyes water. "He said the two of you met through mutual friends. I understand now. Sorry, go on." She wipes a stray tear away from her cheek. I want to lick it off of her finger, but I don't. Instead I continue.

"We were trained for three years in covert ops."

"What, like spy school?" She tightens the blanket around her.

"That's one way to put it. After the training was complete, they let us out into the world. Leaving us to our own devices." She looks at me puzzled. Explaining this is harder than I initially thought. "They gave us free license to break the law, with hopes of aligning and infiltrating ourselves with drug dealers, arms traders, terrorists. Really anyone who is a threat to national security." Ellie looks around the room at the covered bodies and blood oozing all over the floor.

"So that makes you what exactly?"

"An undercover special ops agent for a covert operation called Endeavor. For six years I have lived and worked under the alias Kayne Roberts. I have assumed the identity of an entrepreneur, liquor distributor, and proprietor of an elite sex club called Mansion," I spew. It feels like an act of confession. "It was a cover. A government trap used to lure the enemy. And it lured one of most notorious drug lords on Earth. That was my mission, bring down the bad guy."

"So Kayne Roberts isn't your real name?" she asks.

"No, Kayne Roberts doesn't exist. Kayne Rivers does."

I can see the wheels grinding as she digests this information. I'm no one she's ever known me to be. Not since day one.

"Is Jett really dead?" Her voice cracks, it's like she's coming out of a coma.

"Yes." I put my hands on her arms, heartsick. Death is a harsh reality in this business. Jett and I both know that. We willingly chose this life, fully aware of the consequences. It still doesn't make losing my best friend, my brother, any easier. I take a cleansing breath—my shoulder is fucking killing me—as I grab onto Ellie. She has no idea she's my support. My rock. My everything. And I have to tell her.

More tears spill out of her eyes.

"No need to cry, sweet thing. Those fuckers had it coming."

I whip my head over to find a ghost standing next to us. I don't think I've ever been so elated in my life.

"Jett!" Ellie throws herself at him before I can move. Apparently I'm not the only elated one.

"Easy, killer." He winces as he catches her in his arms. He looks like shit, all bloodied and bruised.

"You're alive," she weeps.

"Barely." He smiles weakly, his left eye swollen shut. "It's going to take more than three goons and a paring knife to take me down." He lifts up his sleeve and shows me his arm. There's a thick white bandage around his bicep. "That was unpleasant."

"So was this." I point to my bleeding shoulder. "The fucking thing went straight through."

"I'm glad you're alright." He grins, dried blood caked on his mouth.

"You too."

Jett looks uneasily between me and Ellie. He knows we need our time. And it's now. "Well, I just wanted to find you and let you know I was alive before you started planning a funeral." He smiles at me with sad eyes.

"The night's not over yet. A funeral might not be taken out of the equation." I glance down at Ellie.

She frowns.

That moment the solider chooses to return.

"Ma'am." He holds up bolt cutters. Motherfucker. Then he snaps Ellie's collar in two. The leather falls to the floor, landing right at my feet. It feels like a bomb just went off. Ellie looks up at me with wide eyes as she grabs her neck.

"Am I free?"

269

Jett takes that as his cue to leave.

"I'll just be over there." He backs up, thumbing in the direction of the door.

Traitor. I shoot him a death glare.

"You've always been free," I reluctantly admit, snapping the delicate strings of crystals off her wrist cuffs.

"I don't understand." Her voice wavers.

"I did it to protect you," I blurt out. Cause really how do you tell someone that you kidnapped them and turned them into your sex slave so some other pervert didn't get to them first?

"Protect me from what?" Ellie spits.

"Not what, who. Javier, he wanted you. The night of Mark's party, he wanted to take you. So I took you first." I start to ramble. "I did it to protect you. You saw how he is. What he was capable of. I couldn't let him get near you."

"He did get near me." She starts to tremble.

"It was a drop in the bucket compared to what he could have done."

I see the storm brewing in her eyes. "It wasn't a drop in the bucket to me. Why didn't you just tell me? Why put me through all ... *that?* All those *things?*" The agony in her voice destroys me. I know she's recounting every second of the last month. Everything I forced her to do, the brutal fuckings, the spankings, the chains, the collars, the beatings, the humiliation.

"I couldn't. I had to make you believe. I had to make everyone believe." I take a step forward and she takes a step back. It guts me.

"Ellie, I'm sorry. I'm sorry for lying to you, I'm sorry for hurting you, I'm sorry for falling in love with you."

The words that have been stinging the tip of my tongue finally spill out. She looks at me dejectedly. I fly into a panic.

"Ellie, please." I feel her slipping away. "I love you. Forgive me."

She shakes her head, recoiling. "Get away from me," she hisses, taking another step back. I take another step forward.

"Ellie, stay." It comes out more like a command than the desperate plea I meant it to be.

She glares at me, disgusted.

"Ellie, *please* stay with me," I beg. The tables have finally been turned. Tears pour out of her eyes as she looks anywhere but at me.

"Jett!" she suddenly calls out frantically. I watch, helplessly, as she flies across the room and into Jett's welcoming arms. She sobs against his chest as he wraps her in an embrace. My jealousy flares.

I have never wanted to hurt Jett so badly before, but at the moment I want to break every bone in his upper body just so he can't lift his arms. I'm the one who's supposed to be hugging her, consoling her. Loving her. *Mine.*

All I can do is watch numbly as Jett leads a broken Ellie out of the room. He throws me a sympathetic look over his shoulder just before they disappear.

My existence has just been eradicated. Everything is gone; my life, my soul, my beating heart. My eyes water as I stare into the void. I blink rapidly as something trickles down my cheek. I wipe my face. Tears. I lick my hand, they taste just like hers.

ELLIE

IT FEELS LIKE I JUST woke up from a hundred-year dream.

The air is cool, but my skin is on fire. It's the first time I've been outside in I don't know how long. The sky is clear and dotted with thousands of stars and the moon is a thin crescent above our heads. Jett is talking to me, but I can't decipher a word he's saying. My thoughts are just a mess.

"Ellie!" I hear Kayne's distraught voice echo behind me as Jett tries to usher me into the back seat of a blacked-out SUV. "Ellie, wait, please, just listen to me!" When I feel him grab my arm, something inside me snaps.

"Get your hands off me!" I screech, batting him away. "I don't want to hear anything you have to say! I hate you, you asshole!" I start throwing punches. Kayne deflects my fists with his forearms in an attempt to shield himself from my physical explosion. I do manage to get one good shot in. My open hand connects with his face; the loud slap rings out and my palm stings just before Jett encircles his arm around my waist and tosses me into the back of the Suburban. I breathe erratically as I crash against the leather seat.

"Jett, get out of my way." Kayne tries to climb in after me, but Jett blocks him with his body.

"Kayne, back the fuck up." He shoves him hard and Kayne is forced to take a step back. Jett uses the split-second separation to hop into the car and slam the door. "Drive!" he barks at the man behind the wheel. Less than a moment later we peel out, tires screeching as we pull away from the house. I glance back to see Kayne's shrinking figure crouched on the driveway with his hands laced behind his head.

Ellie, I'm sorry. I'm sorry for lying to you, I'm sorry for hurting you, I'm sorry for falling in love with you. I take one look at Jett and unstoppable tears start to fall. He pulls me into his arms as I begin to sob. For God's sake, it feels like I have been crying for an eternity. It's a wonder my body doesn't just give out from dehydration.

As we drive, my life comes into sharp clarity. Like a fog has lifted. *You've always been free.* I cry harder and I don't understand why. I'm free, but I have the heaviest feeling of loss crushing my chest. It's almost suffocating me.

"Shhhh, Ellie." Jett comforts me. "Everything is okay. You're okay."

"I'm far from okay, Jett!" I explode. "I was just held captive for I don't know how long and forced to do unspeakable things with a man I once worshiped. I feel betrayed. I feel humiliated. I feel …" *Alone.*

"He did it to protect you." Jett defends Kayne.

"There had to be another way!" I demand, my emotions overflowing everywhere. There's no containing them.

"There wasn't. It was a split-second decision and we ran with it. Kayne couldn't allow you to be tortured at the hands of a monster. It was the only way to keep you safe. We both agreed."

"You both agreed to what? *Him* becoming the monster?!" I shout. The man driving the car never turns his head to look at us. He just steers the car, keeping his attention on the road. I'm grateful for his disinterest. Or his feign of disinterest. I'm sure I look and sound like a raving lunatic right now.

Jett scowls at me. Like he has any right. "Let me paint you a picture, Ellie. Say Kayne did tell you exactly who he was and exactly what was going on. And Javier came into your room that night and found you munching on popcorn and watching a movie instead of chained to the bed. Do you know what he would have done?"

I shake my head slowly.

"He would have tortured you until you talked. Until you divulged every one of Kayne's secrets. Do you think you could have handled him yanking out your teeth one by one? Or carving you up one tiny slice at a time? Because that's the kind of fucking animal he was."

I swallow hard, my throat sore from trying not to cry, my eyes wet with residual tears. "And after he finished with you, he would have gone after everyone else in the house. There was more than just your life at stake. So yes, we mutually agreed it was the best way. It wasn't premeditated. If you belonged to Kayne, theoretically Javier should have stayed away."

"Well he didn't stay away!" I wipe away the tears that are now escaping down my cheeks, reliving the aggressive, inhumane way he orally raped me.

"Evil is unpredictable. But he got what he deserved. Javier's death will ripple through the trafficking community. Countless lives will be saved."

"At what expense?" My voice is an agonizing whisper.

"Ellie, the world is at war, and sometimes innocent bystanders get caught in the crossfire. What happened to you was unfortunate, but you can't tell me you honestly believe Kayne is a monster."

"I don't know what to believe."

"Yes, you do. Believe what's in your heart. Over the last month I watched the two of you fall in love and now he's falling apart because you left him."

"He doesn't love me," I reply desolately. He can't. None of it was real.

"No, you're right. He doesn't love you. His feelings run so much deeper than that. He's obsessed with you. He always has been. Since the moment he met you, you're all he's ever wanted," Jett informs me directly. "And for Kayne to feel that way is huge. Beyond Mt. Kilimanjaro huge."

I shake my head furiously. "No." I don't want to believe it. I want to believe Kayne is a monster who doesn't deserve me. *No matter where you go or who you're with. You'll always be mine.*

"Javier wanted you." Jett clutches my arms and shakes me. "He would have stopped at nothing to get you, and once that happened, Kayne wouldn't have been able to intervene. Javier would have killed you. Do you understand? It was the only way." Jett's phone rings in his pocket and we both pause. He pulls it out and glances at the screen then looks up at me; his aqua eyes illuminating from the oncoming headlights on the opposite side of the road. "Kayne."

"Don't!" I frantically smack the cell phone out of his hand before he can answer it.

"Ellie!?" Jett chastises me.

"I don't want you to talk to him!" I don't even want to hear a susurration of his voice.

"I never want to see him again."

The End

Book 1

Thank you for purchasing Owned! Do you want more Ellie and Kayne? Be on the lookout for **Claimed** coming soon!

Add it to your TBR on Goodreads.
Did you enjoy Owned? You can let me know by using the hashtag #ILikeYouCollaredBaby!

#Facebook #Twitter #Instagram

Make sure to check out the first chapter of Slade by Victoria Ashley after the acknowledgements.

PLAYLIST

Out of The Black- Royal Blood

Wild Ones- Flo Rida

Control- Puddle of Mudd

Sing- Ed Sheeran

Seven Nation Army- White Stripes

What You Wanted- One Republic

Stay With Me- Sam Smith

ABOUT THE AUTHOR

M. NEVER RESIDES IN NEW York City. When she's not researching ways to tie up her characters in compromising positions, you can usually find her at the gym kicking the crap out of a punching bag, or eating at some new trendy restaurant. She has a dependence on sushi and a fetish for boots. Fall is her favorite season. She is surrounded by family and friends she wouldn't trade for the world and is a little in love with her readers. The more the merrier. So make sure to say hi!

ACKNOWLEDGEMENTS

I NEVER SET OUT TO write a dark romance. In fact, when these characters first came to me, I rejected them. I wasn't interested in exploring that side of my psyche. But Ellie and Kayne were relentless, screaming to be heard and drowning out all of the other characters in my head until I finally said fuck it, opened up my notes app and began typing away. I wrote close to twenty thousand words that weekend, and soon this dark erotic romance I never wanted to write took over my life. It would have never been possible without the help of some amazing people.

My beta readers, Heather Davenport, Candy Royer and Ashley Grimes, you suffered through a horrific first draft and still loved every word. Your feedback was vital in bringing this book to the next level.

Glenda Sue Smith, for giving me the courage to actually put the words on the page.

My editor, Jenny Sims, thank you for all the extra suggestions and being available for every one of my neurotic moments.

To Christine and Nichole at Perfectly Publishable, you ladies rock and thank you for making the inside of this novel as pretty as the out!

My fantabulous cover designer Marisa Shor at Cover Me, Darling. Cupcakes!! I heart you hard core lady. You never disappoint.

Holly Malgieri at Holly's Red Hot Reviews, thank you for coordinating yet another blog tour, blitz, shout out, cover reveal, and putting up with my multiple projects at one time! You're a rock star!

My personal assistant, Zee Hayat, thank you picking up my slack!! What did I ever do without you?!

A special thanks to Naughty and Nice Book Blog, Summer's Book Blog, Panty Dropping Book Blog, Six Chicks and Their Love of Books, Confessions of a One-Click Addict, AJ's Bootylicious Book Reviews.

AND OF COURSE THE READERS!

To my family who supports me every day, even when I'm working on a secret project I never want to talk about. Without you, I'm nothing.

Last but not least, this book is dedicated to the victims of sexual abuse and human trafficking. You are true survivors, inspirations and fighters. "What lies behind you and what lies in front of you, pales in comparison to what lies inside of you." - Ralph Waldo Emerson

Slade by Victoria Ashley

Chapter One Excerpt

Slade

It's dark.

I love it with the lights off. She insisted on teasing me this way. My arms are tied behind me, my naked body bound to a chair. Goose bumps prickle my flesh as she softly blows on my hard cock, almost breaking my willpower. Her lips are so close, yet not close enough. I insist on teasing *her* this way.

"Na ah, not yet, baby."

She tilts her head up, her blond hair cascading over her shoulders as her eyes lock with mine. They're intense, desperate. She's silently begging me with her eyes, asking me to let her touch me already. I'm used to this. She needs to learn that when you're in my house we play by my rules. "Slade," she whimpers. "Come on already."

"Look down, baby." She tilts her head back down and runs her tongue over her lips as she eagerly looks at my cock; no doubt imagining what it tastes like in her mouth. "That's it. Don't move."

I lift my hips, bringing the tip of my head to brush her lips. "You want me in your mouth?"

She nods her head and lets out a sound between a moan and a growl. Damn, it's such a turn on.

"How bad do you want it? I want to fucking hear it?"

Her nails dig into my thighs as she growls in aggravation. "More than anything. I want it so just give it to me, dammit. You already know how bad I want it."

A deep laugh rumbles in my throat as she scratches her nails down my legs in an attempt to hurt me. What she doesn't realize is that I welcome the pain. I get off on it.

"Is that all you got, pussycat?" I tease. "If you want my cock, you're going to have to do better than that."

She looks angry now; determined. Standing up, she points a finger in my chest. "You're the one tied up. This is supposed to be my game. Why do *you* have to torture me and make me wait?"

Biting my bottom lip, I nod for her to move closer to me. When she gets close to my face, I slide my tongue out and run it over her lips, causing her to tremble as I taste her. "Show. Me. How. Much. You. Want. Me."

Straddling me, she screams and slaps me hard across the face before yanking my head back by my hair. If I could get any harder, I would.

Fuck me.

"Now, that's what I'm talking about." I press my stiff cock against her ass, showing her just how turned on I am. Then I look her in the eye. "Show me what you can do with your mouth. First impression is always the most important."

A mischievous smile spreads across her face as she slithers her way off my lap and down between my legs. Gripping my thighs in her hands, she runs her tongue over the tip of my dick before suctioning it into her mouth. It hits the back of her throat, causing her to gag. She doesn't care; completely uninhibited. She just shoves it deeper.

Fuck yeah.

I moan as she swirls her tongue around my shaft while sucking at the same time. It feels fucking fantastic. "I told you it's worth the wait, baby. Just wait until I get inside you. It feels better than it tastes."

She pulls back and licks her lips. "Then why don't you show me. My pussy has never been so wet." She stands up and bends over in front of me, exposing her wet lips. I can see the moisture glistening from here; beckoning to suck me inside. She smiles as she runs her fingers over the folds as if she's teasing me; testing me. "You like that?" she asks seductively, tantalizing me. "You want this tight little pussy all for yourself, you greedy little bastard?"

I nod, playing into her little game. She seems to think she's in charge.

"Well, come and get it." She inserts her fingers into her mouth and sucks them clean, before shoving them into her entrance, fucking me with her eyes. Her ass moves up and down in perfect rhythm as she purrs. "I'm waiting." She shoves her fingers deeper. "I want to see those muscles flexing as you ram into me. I want you to . . ."

Well you won't be waiting for long.

Breaking free from my restraints, I stand up, grab her hips and flip her around before slamming her back up against the wall. "What were you saying, baby?" I growl into her ear. I grip both of her ass cheeks and lift her as she wraps her legs around my waist, squeezing. "I'm not sure you can handle what I have to offer." I grip her face in my hand before leaning in and biting her bottom lip, roughly tugging. "You're finally about to get what you've wanted. I just hope you don't have shit to do for the next few days because this might get a little rough. Last time to make your escape, because once I start there's no stopping until you're screaming my name loud; so loud it fucking hurts my ears." I search her eyes waiting to see if she's changed her mind; nothing but raw heat and lust. She still wants it. She's brave. No girl walks into my bed and walks out unscathed. So, she'll get it. I lift an eyebrow. "Okay, then."

I take wide strides across the room to my king-sized bed and toss her atop the mattress. Before she can blink, I am between her thighs, spreading them wide for me. I run my tongue up her smooth flesh, stopping at intersection of her thighs and clean shaven pussy. "You ready for me to make you come without even touching you?"

I begin blowing my cool breath across her swollen, wet pussy. She thrusts her hips up; no doubt her hungry little pussy wanting more and just as I'm about to show her my skills, there's a knock at the damn door.

Bad fucking timing.

Gritting my teeth, I shake my head and look toward the door. "Give me a sec." I step down from the bed and motion for Lex to cover up. When she's done, I call for Cale to come in. "Okay, man."

The door opens right as I'm reaching for my pack of cigarettes and switching the light on. My dick is still standing at full alert, but I could care less. This shit head interrupted my night. If he doesn't like seeing my dick hard, then he should have known better than to come up to my room in the middle of the night.

Stepping into my room, Cale takes notice of my hard on and quickly reaches for the nearest item of clothing and tosses it on my dick. I look down to see a shirt hanging from it. I shake it off. "A little warning next time, mother fucker. I'm tired of witnessing that shit."

Lighting my cigarette, I laugh and take a drag. "Jealous, prick?"

Ignoring me, he walks past me when he sets eyes on Lex. She's been coming to the club for a while now and she's sexy as hell. All of the guys have been trying to get with her, but she's wanted nothing but my cock this whole time. He raises his eyebrows and slides onto the foot of my bed. "Damn, Lex. You get sexier every time I see you."

Gripping the sheet tighter against her body, Lex growls and kicks Cale off the bed. "Go fuck off, Cale. I don't want your dick."

Jumping up with a quickness, Cale reaches for my jeans and tosses them to me. "I don't want to fuck you, Lex. I want to pleasure you. This dick is special." He nods toward me. "Unlike Slade's."

"Fuck you, Cale. What the hell do you want?"

He turns to me after smirking at Lex. "The club just called. We gotta go."

"It's not my night to work, man. Isn't Hemy working?" I take a long drag of my cigarette, letting the harsh smoke fill my lungs as I close my eyes. I really need to release this tension. I will fuck her in front of him if I have to. It wouldn't be the first time I've fucked in front of an audience. "I'm a little busy right now." I dangle Lex's thong from my finger. "If you can't tell."

Not getting where I'm going with this, Cale pulls out his phone and starts typing something in it. "We need to go now. There's a bachelorette party and the chicks asked for us specifically. You know what that means. Plus, Hemy is getting eaten alive right now."

Oh shit. I didn't think it was possible, but my cock just got even harder.

"Well, then I guess we better get started." I put out the cigarette, push past Cale and slide under the sheet. I reach for the condom on the nightstand and rip the wrapper open with my teeth. "This is going to have to be a quick one," I mumble before spitting the wrapper out and rolling the condom over my erection.

Lex looks at me questionably and nods to Cale. "You're going to have sex with me while he watches?"

I smirk as I flip her over and shove her head down into the mattress. "If he doesn't get out of my room, then yes, I'm going to fuck you while he watches." I peek over my shoulder at Cale and he lifts an eyebrow, his interest now peaked. "You've got three seconds and the counting started two seconds ago."

Pointing to Lex, he starts walking backwards while chewing his bottom lip. "As much as I'd love to watch you get fucked, I'm out. This dude gets too wild and I'll probably hurt myself just watching." Picking my wallet up from my dresser, he tosses it at my head, but misses. "Hurry your ass up. I'm changing my shit right now and then we need to go."

Lex moans from below me as I grip her hips, pull her to me and slide inside her. She's extra wet for me, making it easy to give her a good quick fuck. "You're so fucking wet. You were craving this cock weren't you?"

"Dude," Cale complains from a distance; although, I can still feel his eyes watching us.

"Your three seconds were up." I thrust my hips, gripping her hair in both my hands. "Mmm . . . fuck." *Damn that feels good.* "I'll be out in a minute."

"Leave, Cale!" Lex moans while gripping the sheet. "Oh shit! You feel even better than what I've been told. So thick and oh shit . . . it's so deep."

"Damn, that's hot."

"Out!" Lex screams.

"I'm out. I'm out." Cale backs his way out, shutting the door behind him. The truth is, if it weren't for Lex kicking him out, I could've cared less if he stayed and watched. I'm not ashamed.

Knowing I don't have a lot of time, I need to get this chick off fast. That's my rules and I don't have many. She gets off, then I get off. There is no stopping in between for me. Once I start, this is a done deal.

I can feel her wetness thickening. "You've gotten wetter. You like him watching, huh?" I yank her head back and run my tongue over her neck before whispering, "I would've let him stay; let him watch me as I fuck your wet pussy. Does that turn you on?"

Before she can say anything else, I push her head back down into the mattress and slam into her while rubbing my thumb over her swollen clit.

Her hands grip the sheets as she screams out and bites down on her arm, trying to silence her orgasm.

Slapping her ass, I ball my fist in her hair and gently pull it back so her back is pressed against my chest. "Don't hold it back. I want to fucking hear it. Got it?" She shakes her head so I thrust into her as deep as I can go. "Show me how it feels."

Screaming, she reaches back and grabs my hair, yanking it to the side. This makes me fuck her even harder. "Oh yes! Oh God! Slade, don't stop."

Reaching around, I grab her breast in one hand squeezing roughly and bite into her shoulder, rubbing my finger of the opposite hand faster over her slick clit. Her body starts to tremble beneath me as she clamps down hard on my cock. "Oh, shit. Stop, I can't take it. It feels so good, Slade."

I grip her hips and brush my lips over her ear. "You want me to stop?" I pull out slowly, teasing her. "You don't want this cock filling your pussy?" I shove it back in, causing her head to bang into the wall. "Huh, do you want me to stop?"

She shakes her head. "No, don't stop. Shit, don't stop!"

"That's what I thought." I push her completely flat on her stomach, holding my body weight with one arm as I grip the back of her neck and fuck her with all my strength. I want her to remember this because it's the only time she'll be getting my cock and we both know it. It's how I work.

She's squirming below me, shaking as if she's in the middle of another orgasm. "Slade! Oh shit!"

A few thrusts later and I'm ready to blow my load. Pulling out, I bite her ass and stroke my cock as I come.

The relief gives me a high; a fucking drug that I can't get enough of. Nothing else makes me feel this way. Actually, nothing else makes me feel. This is it for me.

My own personal hell.

Made in the USA
San Bernardino, CA
13 November 2014